Cold Brew Corpse

Also available by Tara Lush

Coffee Lover's Mysteries
Grounds for Murder

Cold

Brew

Corpse

A COFFEE LOVER'S MYSTERY

Tara Lush

CROOKED
LANE

NEW YORK

Published in the United States by Crooked Lane Books, an imprint of The Quick Brown Fox & Company LLC.

Crooked Lane Books and its logo are trademarks of The Quick Brown Fox & Company LLC.

Library of Congress Catalog-in-Publication data available upon request.

ISBN (hardcover): 978-1-64385-788-6
ISBN (ebook): 978-1-64385-789-3

Cover design by Brandon Dorman

Printed in the United States.

www.crookedlanebooks.com

Crooked Lane Books
34 West 27th St., 10th Floor
New York, NY 10001

First Edition: December 2021

10 9 8 7 6 5 4 3 2 1

To Marco, my love.

Chapter One

I t was a killer night for a date on Devil's Beach.

I peered out my kitchen window at the backyard. The thermometer tacked to the wooden bird feeder under a palm tree read ninety-five degrees. Late summer in Florida felt like wrassling an alligator in an oven nestled inside a steam room.

My date had mentioned something about grilling at his house, so we'd likely be outside for at least part of the evening. I had to be mindful of comfort. Or, rather, discomfort: underboob sweat, hair frizz, chafing. You know. The usual, for a Floridian.

"Heels or flip-flops?" I murmured to Stanley, my Shih Tzu puppy. He was perched on the bed and stared up at me with mocha-colored eyes as I slipped a foot into one closed-toe shoe, all Cinderella-like.

I studied my legs. The black, four-inch Louboutin stilettos from my previous life in Miami looked smokin' hot with my little silk slip dress, which was also black, of course. The shoes screamed sophistication and sex, and I was sorely lacking in the former and wouldn't be engaging in the latter this evening.

Not because I didn't want to, mind you. My date—Noah Garcia, the police chief here in Devil's Beach—was everything I wanted in a man. Handsome, kind, a little geeky around the edges. He read books and shared my love of science fiction TV shows. He was also a crusader for justice. In his previous job, he'd been an internal affairs investigator at a big-city department, taking down corrupt cops.

In his first three months here on sleepy Devil's Beach, Noah had revamped the department's use of force procedures. He'd quietly woven himself into the unusual fabric of our community, probably because he had a wry sense of humor, a gentle temperament, and the sexiest eyes on the planet. Okay, that last part was strictly my opinion—and that of every other woman on the island under the age of eighty-five.

His only downside was that he didn't share my love of coffee. Odd, because he was Cuban American, and they were the ones who brought the best *cafecito* to Florida's shores. To his credit, he'd said he'd try to enjoy the life-giving elixir, just for me. It meant a lot, considering I ran Perkatory, the island's most popular café.

But I'd been divorced only a year. Not only was tonight my first date since the breakup, it was the first night since my early twenties that I'd be going out with a man other than my ex-husband.

The pressure was on, like a stovetop espresso maker about to blow.

No, the stilettos would send the wrong message. Save those for the second date. Possibly even the third or fourth. Slow was my new middle name with men. I'd hopped into bed with the man who would later become my ex back in Miami, and look how that turned out.

Plus, the thought of my feet being encased in unforgiving leather in this humidity made me irritable.

2

Cold Brew Corpse

"Guess it'll be the formal flip-flops, Stanley." It was Florida, after all, where everyone owned not just the cheap rubber variety but flip-flops appropriate for special occasions too.

I pulled off the stilettos and sheathed them back in their chamois storage bag. I reached in the closet for a silver sequined pair of sandals, shoving my feet between the toe thongs. Cute. My dark hair, which had been in a bun all day, was loose and curly. For once, it fell in beachy waves and not an unruly mass of frizz.

Stanley let out a sharp bark, then launched his compact body off the bed and tore out of the room. Aha. Dad must be here to pick up the dog. I didn't like leaving either of them alone for hours on end.

Sure enough, a few moments later there was a knock, then the rattling of the doorknob.

"Coming," I called out. Stanley pranced on his golden paws, his toenails clicking on the hardwood floor. Next to me, Dad was his favorite human, with Noah a close third.

I flung open the door to find Dad holding a bottle of wine in each hand.

"Lana, you don't need to keep the lock bolted like that. We're on island time here. How soon you've forgotten our laid-back ways." He pushed past me, striding into the house and stopping in the middle of the living room. "Your mother and I didn't lock the doors. We lived here for twenty-five years and never had a problem."

"I'm aware of that, since I was here for eighteen of those years with you. I feel safer when things are locked up tight. Old Miami habits die hard."

Dad set the two bottles on the glass coffee table. He sank onto my overstuffed olive-green sofa, and Stanley flung himself into Dad's lap. A vigorous face-licking commenced.

3

I rested my hands on my hips and motioned with my nose at the wine. "Planning on drinking with the dog tonight?"

"Heck no. I'm not imbibing this month. It's sober September. I'm trying an experiment. No substances. Stanley, down. Don't stick your tongue in my mouth."

"Sober September? That's a new one." Dad had a medical marijuana card.

"This wine's for you. I didn't think you'd have time to buy a decent bottle to bring to Noah's tonight."

"Thanks. I'd planned on picking one up." It had been a busy Saturday, and my father's considerate gesture allowed me to relax a little.

"Noah mentioned once that he enjoyed a good Merlot. And I know you like your Chardonnay. I was at that fancy new wine store, chatting with the owner. Did you know she came all the way from Minneapolis to open her shop here?"

"Oh yeah? Hang on, I need to grab something in the bathroom. Keep talking."

And talk he did. By the time I plucked my makeup bag off the counter and returned to the living room, he'd detailed the background of the store owner and her favorite grape varietal (Cabernet Sauvignon). He even knew the owner's husband's profession (coral reef researcher) and his favorite wine (Pinot). I had to laugh. Dad was such a gossipy extrovert, it was difficult not to marvel at his natural charm. He was the kind of guy everyone loved. People felt compelled to tell him things.

"She sounds nice," I murmured absent-mindedly, opening a pressed-powder compact and dabbing some on my shiny nose. I angled my body toward a window for better light.

Dad gently picked up Stanley and moved him to a tropical-print pillow while wiping dog slobber off his silver beard. He leaned forward, grabbing the trophy I'd won a few hours earlier at the Sunshine State Barista Championship.

"That was some coffee making today, Lana. You and Erica were incredible. I was so nervous for you both. What a showdown." He brought the prize close to his face and studied the inscription on the bottom.

I smiled as I held the compact in one hand and wielded a lip gloss wand in the other. Erica was a barista at Perkatory, and we'd been a team, pulling espressos like a well-oiled java machine. "I was more shocked than anyone that we won. There was some serious competition."

"Munchkin, I'm happy that you're happy. And thrilled you've done so well with Perkatory. It was touch and go a few months ago. I didn't think you or the coffeehouse would make it." Dad set the trophy down and leaned back, then made an exaggerated *oof* sound when Stanley jumped on his stomach with his front paws.

I snapped the compact shut. "Let's not jinx anything by celebrating our good fortune yet. I'm hoping today's win will bring us more business, and then we can hire another barista."

"Bring *you* more business. It's your café." Dad's tone was reproachful.

"You still work there. You own the building. It's ours. I'm back in action."

"Single and ready to mingle." I loved when Dad chuckled. It was infectious. "Oh! That reminds me." He stretched out his long legs and dug into the pocket of his cargo pants. "I have your phone."

"Goodness, I almost forgot. Thanks." I put the compact away and stuffed the makeup bag in my oversized purse.

He set the cell on the table, next to the wine bottles. "Er, I think something happened to the battery. I took a bunch of videos of you at the coffee competition; then it went dead."

I scooped it up and pressed the side button. Usually my phone was like a security blanket and I kept it nearby at all times. But the competition's rules prohibited us from carrying phones while making drinks—they didn't want contestants looking up recipes on the internet—and so I'd handed mine to Dad hours ago. In the rush of winning and the whirlwind of getting ready for the date, I'd forgotten all about it.

"You figured out how to take videos? Awesome." I stabbed at the power button. Nothing.

"Yeah, I sat next to someone from the Chamber of Commerce during the competition, and she showed me how. I took a bunch of 'em for you."

"Cool. Can't wait to see." When the phone refused to come to life, I let out a strangled groan. "I don't have time now, so I'll charge it in the car. Not like I'll be using it tonight."

I slipped it into my purse, checking my face once again in a mirror by the door.

"About that. Dear, will you need me to take Stanley all night?" Dad cleared his throat, signaling his discomfort with the conversation. "Should I expect you in the morning?"

I rolled my eyes. "I'm not planning on sleeping over. This is our first date. I'll be by to pick up Stanley. Or since you live so close to Noah's condo, maybe I'll crash at your place."

"You know where the key is." Dad stood and hoisted the puppy in his arms. "Okay, Stan. Let's pack snacks and make tracks. We've got big plans tonight, little buddy. I'm going to whip up some vegan jalapeño poppers."

"Be sure to wear gloves with those peppers. And please don't feed Stanley too many dog treats. See how chubby he is?"

I scratched Stanley's golden fur. Although I was an animal lover, I hadn't been in the market to adopt a pet. But when a barista at my coffee shop turned up dead a few weeks ago, I couldn't send his puppy to the animal shelter, so Stanley became mine.

"Bye, pupperoni. Only kisses. No biting." Being only six months old, Stanley was in a feisty phase. His little needlelike teeth had worked to my advantage recently, when his eagerness to nip at ankles had thwarted my barista's murderer—who also who tried to kill me.

"He'll grow out of that nipping thing. It's a phase."

"I hope so. We've got puppy kindergarten coming up this week. Don't we, small dude?"

He wagged his golden tail in response. He was possibly the cutest thing I'd seen since my Hello Kitty erasers in fourth grade.

I kissed the top of his head. Then I pressed my mouth to Dad's cheek, right above his silver beard. "Have a good night, you two."

For a second I paused, studying Dad and Stanley. A moment of pure joy crashed into me like a wave. I'd been back on Devil's Beach for only a few months. At first I'd worried it was the wrong decision to come home. In the beginning, I'd missed my old city life something fierce. Now? Seeing Dad with his goofy grin and being able to hang with him any day of the week was a gift.

I'd made the best choice.

"Want to do a quick Reiki healing to center your energy?" Dad looked at me hopefully. He'd been into New Age woo ever since Mom had her stroke and died. It used to annoy me, but now I thought it hilarious. Most of the time, anyway.

"I'm good, thanks. I'm fine. Was thinking about how great it is to see you so often." I smiled. Today he wasn't wearing his usual ponytail, and his silver hair was almost to his shoulders. "Your hair's getting awfully long."

"Meant to ask you. I was considering getting it cut like Steve Winwood in his 'Higher Love' video. What do you think?"

I scrunched my eyes shut, and an image of a man with a fluffy mullet came to mind. "Did someone forget to tell me that the eighties are back?"

He chuckled. "Listen, we're off. Try to relax and have a good time with Noah. Remember: he's not the dastardly Miles Ross. Allow yourself to be open to all possibilities, my dear. Don't be so closed off."

I snorted, thinking of my philandering, slippery ex-husband, known to millions around the country as the Miami correspondent for a popular TV network.

Dad squeezed my arm and said good-bye, then toted Stanley out of the house. I hurried from room to room, shoving the wine bottles into a paper bag branded with my coffee shop's name and logo.

My gaze swept around my comfy living room. I'd decorated it in bold tropical green and coral hues, gently used teak accent pieces, and a few haphazardly placed rattan chairs. This was my happy place. What would Noah's condo look like? Organized and spotless, I guessed.

I grabbed the bag of wine and bounded out, double locking my doors. I didn't care what Dad claimed about the safety of Devil's Beach.

Halfway to Noah's, I realized I'd forgotten the mango pie I'd made early this morning. It was my best yet, one that didn't require baking or more than five ingredients. Usually I'm a store-bought kind of girl, but I'd wanted to impress Noah and needed an outlet for my precompetition anxiety. So I'd gotten up at five to assemble the pie.

I glanced at the clock. Driving home would take only a few minutes but would put me at risk of being late. Something told me Noah was a punctual person. Perhaps it was his always-crisp clothes, or how his desk was free of stray papers and empty coffee cups.

I had the wine, so maybe we'd skip dessert. Or perhaps dessert would be something else entirely. The thought made me flush, and I tuned my radio to a local station that played nothing but seventies and eighties music to tone down the lusty thoughts in my mind. I tried to blast the air conditioner, but it emitted only a cool wheeze. Someday I'd have the money and time to fix it. Or get a new car.

Fleetwood Mac's "Go Your Own Way" came on. I sang at the top of my lungs as I drove a few miles over the speed limit, soaring past the majestic royal palms that lined Beach Drive, past the shop selling three-for-twenty T-shirts for tourists, past the Dirty Dolphin bar. It was a locally infamous place where throngs of people crowded the outdoor patio, sipping frozen piña coladas from tall, neon-pink plastic glasses.

I gave a little wave as I drove by the marina where my friend and barista, Erica, lived on a sailboat. Then I rounded a corner and arrived at one of the most secluded and stunning strips of sand on the island. It had been named one of the best beaches in the United States three years in a row by Stephen Leatherman—aka "Dr. Beach"—a coastal scientist and famous author.

Dad's home was up ahead. He lived by himself in a bungalow. He and Mom had built the little tropical oasis right before she died. I cruised by his house but didn't spot his Prius. Hmm. He and Stanley had probably stopped somewhere to chat.

After his property came five behemoth McMansions, then Noah's building. He lived in a newer, expensive condo, the only one on the island with a concierge. That level of security was a bit fancy for Devil's Beach residents. I pulled into the parking lot.

As far as I could tell, the place was fairly devoid of humans. There were only two cars in the lot, and I parked in one of five vacant visitor spaces. Why would Noah want to live here, in this ten-story, half-empty building? There were nicer, hipper condos downtown in the renovated historic brick buildings, places within walking distance of funky restaurants, the police station, and my café.

This was the opposite of historic or funky. It was the only glass-and-concrete structure on Devil's Beach, and I remembered how Dad had called me in Miami about five years ago, telling me all about the pitched battles between the zoning board and the developer.

It was the type of place that catered to rich folks with second homes. While well-off, Noah didn't seem exceedingly wealthy. He'd probably chosen the location for its quiet and security. Since he'd previously lived in Tampa, I suspected he'd sold a home there for a tidy sum.

He lived on the eighth floor, and I imagined it had a stunning view of the Gulf of Mexico from the balcony. There was only one walkable attraction here: the beach, with its fine sugar sand.

I reached for a mint in my purse and checked my hair, making sure the beachy waves were intact. They were. Score one for the salt-spray product.

As I walked to the main door, my silver flip-flops twinkled against the black asphalt of the parking lot. I spied a hint of the glittering turquoise pool and sandstone deck overlooking the beach and the Gulf of Mexico. Curious, I rounded the building to get a peek, thinking I might find Noah at one of the poolside grills. He wasn't there. The grills, which were next to a tiki hut on the far end of the deck, were empty.

Admittedly, the place was stunning, and for a split second I imagined lounging with him on the pristine white chaises. We'd mix our own artisan cocktails and on weekends come here to swim and watch the sunset together. Yes. That was how our life would unfold. We'd have friends over, and I'd make a giant spread of snacks. Stanley would join us, and he'd be so well behaved that he wouldn't pee on people's towels.

First things first. Namely, a first date. And maybe a second, if I was lucky. Chuckling under my breath at my absurdity, I made my way back to the front entrance. The main doors were on a motion sensor, and they slid open.

Subzero air hit my face and practically froze the sweat off my skin. Goodness, it felt amazing.

A woman in her twenties sat at the concierge desk. She was reading a hardback book—a thriller I had on my nightstand, in fact—and peered up over hip, black-rimmed glasses. She seemed familiar to me, and I vaguely recalled her coming into Perkatory.

"Welcome to Gulf View Condos." Her voice bounced around the tasteful yet bland taupe-and-cream lobby. "How can I help you? Are you here to visit a resident?"

"I am." I smiled wide. "I'm Lana Lewis, and I'm here for Noah Garcia. He lives in unit eight-oh-one, and he's expecting me."

The woman blinked, then shut her book. I stepped closer to the counter. She slid her glasses off and placed them so they aligned perfectly with the top edge of the novel.

"Hi, Lana. I'm Rebecca. Chief Garcia mentioned you'd be coming by. He wanted me to give you this." She turned and picked up a piece of white paper, folded in half. "You're the owner of Perkatory, right?"

I nodded. She mentioned something about how she loved our cold brew coffee.

After murmuring a thanks, I reached for the paper and unfolded it, scanning the six lines of handwritten text in one sweep while my heart sank.

My first date with Chief Noah Garcia, something I'd desired since the day I'd met him three months ago, was officially canceled.

Chapter Two

Cupcake—

I managed a smile despite the disappointment gripping my stomach. Noah had started using that nickname a few weeks ago, possibly because I occasionally made cupcakes and sold them at the café. From any other man, I'd hate it. From him, it was terribly endearing.

His handwriting was blocky and precise, exactly as I'd imagined. The words were in jet-black ink.

Right as I was about to prep the grill, my dispatcher called. An urgent situation requires my attention, and I had to head to the scene.

Urgent situation was underlined twice. Huh. I wondered what was going on. Devil's Beach was normally sleepy. Crime operated at two speeds: drunk tourist and drunk local.

I tried texting and calling you several times but you didn't answer, so I left a note instead. I apologize for postponing our date like this. Call me. xo, Noah

Blergh. How depressing. I sighed, then glanced at the woman behind the concierge desk. "Thanks," I murmured, unable to hide the sadness in my voice.

"He seemed pretty gutted that he had to leave. I think he was looking forward to tonight."

When Rebecca saw the surprised expression on my face, she added, "Yeah, he told me a few days ago you were coming over. I even teased him about it. That man hasn't had a date since he moved here. At least not one that I've seen, and I work here five nights a week. He'd put on a brand-new shirt and everything. Very handsome."

A new shirt? *Aww.* My openmouthed shock turned to a smile. "Well. That's interesting. Thanks. And uh, I appreciate you giving me the note. I'll give him a call."

As soon as I charged my stupid phone.

I waved good-bye to Rebecca and returned to my Honda. Crap. My cell charger wasn't in here. Where was it? Had I brought it to Perkatory? Sometimes I cleaned my car and stuffed everything into one of my many duffel bags, then toted those somewhere else, leaving them at work, or at the house, or at Dad's. It was a shell game of junk. Yeah, it was probably in the second-floor office at the coffee shop, now that I recalled.

I could go home, but I was all done up. I needed to be out and near people, not in my living room, wallowing in disappointment.

Hauling butt out of the condo parking lot, I sped back to downtown Devil's Beach and Perkatory. I parked in my reserved space in the alley and walked around to the front.

It was so hot that a bar of chocolate would be drinkable if left outside. By the time I reached the entrance, a sheen of sweat covered my face. I spied something happening at the business next door to Perkatory. There was a uniformed police officer holding a roll of yellow crime scene tape. Well, that was an interesting sight.

Instead of going into my coffee shop, I walked a few more paces toward the cop. My family owned this building. It was a four-story brick behemoth that spanned the entire block. Many decades ago, it had been a hotel and pit stop for people sailing from Tampa to Havana.

Now the top floors were empty, and there were three businesses on the bottom floor—Perkatory, a souvenir shop named Beach Boss, and Dante's Inferno, the hot-yoga place.

The cop was next to the studio door.

"Hey there," I called out in a friendly tone.

The officer raised his head as I approached with a smile. I was familiar with most of the beat cops from the local police force because they usually stopped by Perkatory for their daily dose of java. This one must have been new, because I didn't recognize him. It being Devil's Beach, there weren't that many officers, because there wasn't much happening here.

"Can I help you?" He was about my age—thirty—with short, blond hair and blue eyes. He had that hard, flinty stare that some officers have. Distrustful of the world. I'd learned to steer clear of those kinds of cops during my time as a crime reporter for the newspaper in Miami. They usually weren't friendly to reporters and sometimes actively despised them. But I was no longer a journalist, I was a business owner, and this was my building. Well, sort of. It was technically Dad's property, but whatever.

"Hi, I don't think we've met. I'm Lana Lewis, and I own Perkatory next door. My family owns this building." I held out my hand, and he reluctantly took it, pumping once before dropping it like a hot stone.

"We're investigating a situation involving this business. We'll inform you if we need to get in or require anything else." He turned back to the door and wrapped one end of the tape around a plastic holder that contained flyers printed with the studio's schedule.

I could tell he was being dismissive, but I didn't budge. "What's going on, anyway? Can I help?"

The guy shook his head. "You'll have to get that from the chief. I'm here to secure the scene."

"You new on the force?"

He nodded. "Just started this past week."

The gears inside my skull twisted at warp speed. What had happened at the yoga studio? Was that why Noah had canceled our date? This cop probably wouldn't reveal anything, but I could at least try to wring some details out of him.

"Welcome to Devil's Beach, Officer. Stop over for a coffee anytime. On the house. We're open tonight until nine. Lots of your coworkers and your chief come in every day. Have you talked with Raina, the owner of the yoga studio?"

He grunted in response and studied a flyer. Gah. A real talker, this one. He needed to be a lot more personable if he was going to fit in here on quirky, casual Devil's Beach.

"Well, have a good night," I trilled, then turned to walk away.

"Yes, ma'am," he replied robotically. I hated being called ma'am. I was only thirty, for god's sake.

Now I had to get into Perkatory and call Noah from the landline in my office. A burning curiosity overtook any earlier disappointment about our canceled date. Surely he'd fill me in, or someone at the café would. Probably a scandal was unfolding and gossip was winding its way around the island. If my phone had been charged, I'd have been in the know.

When I pulled open the café door, I gave the tables a once-over. There were a dozen people inside, some lounging on a robin's-egg-blue sofa and others sprawled in white wicker chairs. The rich scent of ground coffee permeated the air. A Van Morrison tune played softly in the background, mingling perfectly with the hum of conversation.

In my opinion, there was nothing more soothing than the ambient noise in a café.

My gaze landed on none other than my silver-haired father, who was sitting at a distressed white-wood table near the window. His head lifted from his phone.

"Lana," he cried, standing up.

That's when I noticed he had Stanley, my puppy, in a tie-dye-colored contraption strapped around his chest. It was similar to a baby sling. A canine carrier. A pooch pouch. Stanley's tongue drooped out of his mouth, and as I got closer, I realized he was fast asleep.

"Dad? Stanley? When did you get that thing?" I pointed at the knapsack, which had four holes for Stanley's tawny legs and a larger, oval hole for his head. He was as droopy as a soggy french fry.

"Oh yeah, I forgot to tell you I bought this. He loves it. He's resting now." Dad put a protective hand on the dog's body, which was encased in a canvas pocket sprouting straps and zippers. It didn't surprise me that Stanley was out cold. He lived his life with frenetic joy and then crashed, hard.

"Why are you here? I thought you were going home." I walked toward him.

"Sit down, sit down. I've been trying to call you." He flapped his long arms, motioning to an empty chair.

"Did you smoke weed or something? My phone died. Don't you recall?" Dad had a medical marijuana card for his "eye pressures." His doctor claimed he was at risk for glaucoma, but I also knew he enjoyed getting high. No judgment from me, but those were the facts.

"Oh, right. No, I haven't smoked in a while. I'm clean this month, remember? Sober September." He studied me over his reading glasses. My doubts about Sober September were increasing by the moment.

Barbara, our barista, waved from behind the counter. She made a motion as if she were sipping from a cup, and I nodded enthusiastically and gave her a thumbs-up. "Cold brew," I called out.

Then I turned to my father. "What's going on? There's a cop stretching crime scene tape across the yoga studio door."

As Dad opened his mouth to speak, Stanley's lids lifted. The second he saw me, he wiggled and snorted.

"Hang on; he won't calm down until he gets his paws on you," Dad muttered. For the next minute, he unzipped and unclasped a dizzying set of straps and harnesses, finally freeing the excited puppy. He handed the dog to me, and I hugged him into my body, kissing the top of his head. His fur smelled faintly of Dad's patchouli, but on Stanley it was rather pleasant. Fragrant in a doggy kind of way.

By then Barbara was at our table, and she set a tall glass of iced black coffee in front of me. My mouth watered at the sight. "Thanks." I shot her a grateful smile. She brushed a silver wisp of hair out of her eyes.

"Everyone's going crazy for the cold brew tonight," she said. "Nothing but rave reviews, and four customers tagged us on Instagram."

Cold Brew Corpse

With my arm wrapped around Stanley, I leaned over, attached my lips to the straw, and drank in. *Ahh.* I'd sourced these beans from a roaster in Miami, who'd found them in Colombia. Full-bodied, yet smooth as glass. Our cold brew tasted like heaven, and it was rapidly becoming one of our top-selling drinks. I made two batches every night and was considering adding a nitrogen gas tap to make even richer concoctions.

My cold brew recipe yielded a smooth, low-acid drink. There was no bitter tang, just a velvety, creamy mouthfeel similar to that of a dark stout and with a trace of natural sweetness.

"Did you tell her?" Barbara glanced at Dad over her rhinestone-studded pink cat-eye glasses. Her long silver-and-black hair was piled atop her head. There was a gleam in her eyes that mirrored Dad's. Perhaps his propensity for gossip was rubbing off on her.

"I was about to. Trying to get more info here, from a bunch of different people." Dad scowled at his phone.

"Would someone please clue me in?" A frisson of annoyance emerged in my chest. I hated feeling like everyone but me knew an important secret.

"It's Raina," Dad intoned in a serious voice.

"What? Who? Our Raina? Yoga Raina?" I glanced at him, confused. Raina owned Dante's Inferno, the studio next door. So that explained the officer and crime scene tape. "What happened? Is she okay? Was she in an accident?" I clutched Stanley closer.

"We don't know. She's missing." Barbara lowered her cat-eye glasses. "She up and vanished."

"She's gone; that's the rumor," Dad responded dramatically. "It's a real mess."

"What?" I yelped. "When? Last I knew, she was leaving her yoga retreat in Costa Rica. She texted me when she was at the airport, on her way home. That was the other day. Did she not make it back?"

The past several days had been a whirlwind for me, what with the arrest of the woman who had killed my barista and the coffee championship earlier in the day. I hadn't seen Raina since she'd gotten home, come to think of it. I'd figured she needed a few days to decompress after her long trip.

"She returned, right on schedule." Dad leaned in. He had that flush on his face that meant he was harboring a particularly juicy piece of gossip.

"Okay . . ." My head ping-ponged from Dad to Barbara, who was wearing a white Perkatory T-shirt under flowy, wheat-hued linen overalls. She and Dad had on matching Birkenstocks the color of dung, and I idly wondered if everyone over the age of fifty on Devil's Beach was issued a pair.

She swiveled her head. Seeing no customers at the counter, she pulled up a chair and sat between Dad and me.

"Raina made it back from Costa Rica. I saw her Friday night at the grocery store. She was buying boxed wine." Barbara pursed her lips; she was a wine aficionado.

"Hey. Don't diss boxed wine." I paused. "So she's not missing? Or is she sick? I'm not picking up what you're putting down here, guys. What does Kai say?" Kai was Raina's affable, lithe boyfriend, and he helped run Dante's Inferno. I'd always thought of him as the human equivalent of a friendly greyhound dog.

"Kai left their house today and came to the studio to do some work. When he got home, she wasn't there. Her bike, her ID, and her phone were gone." Dad took a slurp of his coffee, which had a distinctly gray-cream tinge from the soy milk he enjoyed. A few droplets clung to his silver moustache, and with the long hair and wild eyes, he looked slightly feral. Maybe that eighties mullet would be a better choice.

My face froze in a grimace. "She probably went for a bike ride to clear her head after traveling. I see her wheeling around the island all the time. Leave the poor woman alone. I don't know Kai well, but it seems as though he's overreacting. But I know he's crazy in love with Raina, so I guess it's understandable that he's worried."

I sipped at my coffee and scratched Stanley's tummy. Had Noah been called out for this? Didn't sound like a case for the chief. Seemed too low-level, even for Devil's Beach. Something wasn't adding up.

Barbara shook her head. "No, Kai swears that something's wrong. He has a feeling."

"Has a feeling," I echoed, enunciating each word. "I have a feeling too: that you've both watched too many Masterpiece mysteries."

"Hey. You know I prefer *Doctor Who*," Dad retorted. "Anyway, Kai's a perceptive young guy."

Stanley licked my collarbone. "Good boy. Only kisses. No biting." I was trying to give him positive reinforcement.

Barbara waved her hand in the air, and her stack of silver bracelets shimmied and tinkled. "Kai called here to see if by chance he'd missed Raina. Wanted to know if she was next door. Or here, drinking coffee. But I haven't seen her at all. Oops. Be right back."

She stood up and walked to the counter to serve two couples who had strolled in and were gaping at the chalkboard menu.

"Hey, why aren't you on your date?" Dad's eyebrows furrowed.

"Because Noah had to go to an urgent situation. Which reminds me. My phone's still dead—can I use yours? I need to call him. He left me a note at his condo."

Dad slid his cell across the white-wood table. "He's saved in the contacts."

I scrolled through until I found Noah. Dad seemingly had nearly every resident of Devil's Beach stored in his phone. As I was about to dial Noah, a text popped up.

"Uh, Dad? The Wolfman's trying to reach you." I showed him the device. I swear, he knew the strangest people. Fred "The Wolfman" Wolfe had been the first yoga teacher to set up shop on the island. He was also one of my father's closest friends.

"Oh, good. Some intel."

"Intel?" Goodness, the man was dramatic. This was what happened when you lived on an island and saw the same folks day in and day out. After living in Miami for years, I found the Devil's Beach gossip circles to be humorous at best, annoying at worst. "What's the Wolfman doing these days? I haven't seen him around."

"Yes, intel. About Raina. Wolfie now owns a studio. It's called Wolf Yoga. He's been busy with that."

"Ah. Right. Wolfie the yoga instructor. A known informant of all credible information. Like Serpico, only more bendy." I handed the phone back to Dad and took another sip, savoring the cool, creamy coffee. I'd outdone myself with this batch.

Dad snorted a laugh.

"When did Wolfie get his own studio? I haven't seen him around since I've been back on the island." Last I knew, Wolfie had been holding yoga classes on the sand with a ragtag group of people who liked to chant at sunrise on the beach. Mom and Dad had been among his first students more than a decade ago.

"Don't be snarky about Wolfie. He's had the new studio for a few years now. You're out of touch with the recent developments on the island. Gotta bring you up to speed." Dad tapped and nodded sagely at his phone. "The Wolfman says he's hearing that weird things went down during Raina's Costa Rica yoga retreat."

"What kind of weird things? Someone farted in class? People weren't able to do backbends? Someone's kale smoothie spilled on a bamboo mat?" I giggled. Sometimes I cracked myself up. It was hard to take some of that New Age stuff seriously, especially when earnest, well-to-do Americans practiced it.

"No, nothing like that. Real weird things. He says he's finding out more in a minute. Here, call Noah quick so we keep the line open."

He handed me the cell. Even though my dad had mostly mastered the mechanics of texting—although he still didn't grasp things like *OMG* and *LOL*—he was still unclear as to whether texts could come in while you were making a phone call. I sighed and dialed.

It went immediately to voice mail.

"Hey," I said. "It's Lana. I got your note. I'm on my dad's phone because mine died. I'm at Perkatory if you want to stop by. Or, uh, call my dad. You have his number." I paused, then shifted my body slightly away from Dad, who was peering at me with interest. "Anyway. We might be able to salvage this evening if you're done soon."

Surely if he was at Raina's, it wouldn't take him long. Could her boyfriend even file a missing-person report at this point? Didn't Raina need to be missing for a day? From the sounds of things, she'd been gone only a few hours.

I hung up and handed the phone to Dad. "The Wolfman hasn't gotten back to us yet with his intel."

I sucked down the last of my coffee. My curiosity took over, and I didn't feel like sitting around my café in a slinky black dress and sparkly silver flip-flops.

With Stanley in my arms, I stood up. If I could see Noah in person, he'd tell me exactly what was going on.

"Where are you going?" Dad asked.

"Taking a drive." I hoisted Stanley to my shoulder like a baby. "I think I'll cruise by Raina's house. I suspect that's where Noah is."

"I'll come with." Dad took a last guzzle of his coffee and jumped to his feet, not asking if he was even invited. I only minded a little, and I didn't want to hurt his feelings by shutting him out. I handed the dog to Dad and dug for the keys in my purse.

As I waved good-bye to Barbara, Dad wrangled Stanley back into the pooch pouch, and we were off.

Chapter Three

"You know where she lives, right?" Dad motioned with his arm, indicating I should head down Angelwing Road.

I flicked the turn signal and nodded. "It's that house near the Swamp, isn't it?"

"Yeah, the one that looks like a tree house. It's on stilts, set back in the woods. I went there for a yoga event not too long ago." Dad stroked Stanley's body as he chattered about the retreat at Raina's.

"You should've come with me," he said. "By the way, you need to get out more, now that you're settled."

"I was trying to tonight," I muttered. He'd gone to that yoga session right when I returned to the island. I spent the first month holed up in my house, depressed. Despite Dad's best efforts, I'd refused all invites. The last thing I'd wanted was to sit in someone's blissful, hippie-decorated tree house and stretch my tense muscles. No, I'd chosen a different path: reality TV and boxed wine.

"I sure hope Raina's okay." His voice cracked with worry. "I know she's gotten on some people's nerves, but I've never had an issue with her. I enjoyed her classes, but hot yoga isn't my thing, so that's why I practice at the Wolfman's studio." That was the thing about Dad; no matter how much he gossiped, he always found the good in everyone.

"She's probably fine. Why didn't people like her?" I had my own, private notions about Raina but chalked them up to my suspicious reporter nature.

Dad shrugged. "Raina's hyperfocused on her passion. It's her blessing and her curse, from what I've seen. She's a real champion for personal growth and yoga, but sometimes her, ah, enthusiasm can rub people the wrong way."

I let that sink in. Figured. An ambitious woman offended people.

"She's definitely an overachiever type. That's the impression I get from seeing her at Perkatory. Nothing wrong with that, though," I replied. She came in often and enjoyed our artisan tea selection. She'd been friendly, even urging me to take her hot-yoga classes a few times. I'd politely declined. She'd probably assumed I was a lost cause when I told her that my preferred yoga pose was nap-asana.

Maybe I should've been more open to her friendship. "You know, when she returns, I'll ask her to lunch at that new vegetarian place on Main Street. She'll love that."

"You should do that. Get out more. Mingle with people. You can't stay home all the time." Dad added a detailed explanation of the restaurant's menu and the new owner's culinary background, including where he'd gone to school.

While Dad chattered, I drove in silence the rest of the way, lost in my thoughts. How had I become so introverted in the past year? I hadn't been like that for most of my twenties. Was it because of everything I'd gone through with my ex? Or the layoff?

Or Mom's death? It had been a one-two-three punch in the span of three years.

Dad fiddled with the air conditioner vent. "You need to get your car checked, munchkin. This isn't working too well. Oh, look. Raina's house should be right up there, past the next curve."

I grunted in response, fully aware of my old car's shortcomings.

Because Devil's Beach was a barrier island, it was compact and easy to navigate. Twelve miles at its longest and six miles at its widest, it was ringed with picture-postcard beaches and a bustling downtown on the island's south end. I lived in a neighborhood near the main drag in a wooden bungalow that had been my parents' home until they moved to the beach house.

In the middle of the island were two things. More homes—a mix of older, modest places and newer behemoths on too-small lots—and a wild nature preserve popular with tourists and residents alike.

Angelwing Park was a lovely name, but it was a misnomer. It was better known by a nickname: The Swamp. And that's what it was—a sticky, fetid, bug-infested pile of untamed Florida muck. An elevated wooden boardwalk snaked over thick mangrove roots and tea-colored brackish water. There was a kayak launch near the parking lot, and some enjoyed paddling through the dark, silent mangrove tunnels.

I'd done it once, in high school, and found it profoundly creepy.

People also adored walking in the park on hot summer days because it was shady and cool and because they could spot a plethora of rare orchids, alligators, wading birds, and snakes. But the signature attraction was the wild monkeys.

Yes, wild monkeys.

They'd started their primate legacy at a nearby roadside zoo owned by my grandfather, but animal rights activists freed them in the 1970s. The primates fled to the preserve, and generations had lived there ever since. They were one of the top tourist attractions on the island, and the Devil's Beach Welcome Center even sold T-shirts, shot glasses, and key chains with a monkey logo.

Raina and Kai lived on the road to the Swamp, a shady, curvy street dotted with live oaks dripping with Spanish moss. In the early evening shadows, the atmosphere was moody and dark, nothing like what you'd expect of a tropical island. I slowed to take the curve, then rolled to a stop. Flashing red lights and at least six police cars greeted us. Cruisers lined the roadside, a jarring sight for such a quiet part of town.

"Whoa," Dad exclaimed.

Stanley wuffed.

"Wow. All this for someone who's been gone a few hours?" I eased to the shoulder, behind a cruiser and alongside a thicket of trees. There were only a few houses out here, set back from the road on larger lots. People here liked privacy.

I put the car in park but left the engine running, then turned to Dad. "I'm going to walk over to check things out. See if I can find Noah to get the scoop." And maybe salvage our date.

"I'll come with."

"No, you and Stanley should stay here. This isn't a social hour. Noah's working."

When I saw the hurt look on Dad's face, I sighed. "I've been to a lot of crime scenes. Cops don't like nosy people."

A sharp rapping noise on the driver's side window made me gasp. I whirled, only to find Noah peering into my car.

I fumbled with the window and lock, then gave up and pulled the latch to open the door. That's what he did to me —left me flustered and nervous. I'd interviewed serial killers, politicians, and celebrities in my previous life as a reporter, but somehow Noah Garcia made me feel like an awkward teenager with a stomachful of butterflies.

But I didn't want him to know that. Taking a deep breath, I climbed out and shut the door. The sun had set, leaving behind a fiery orange sky. Suddenly I became self-conscious about being in a silky slip dress, the night air warm against all my exposed skin.

"Hey," I breathed, twirling a lock of my hair around my finger.

"Hey yourself. Wow." His dark gaze took in my outfit.

I grinned stupidly. "Wow yourself."

Noah was wearing an untucked white linen guayabera, tan linen pants, and retro suede-and-leather sneakers. He'd rolled his shirt sleeves, exposing bronze skin. On some men, the ensemble would have looked sloppy. On him, it looked effortless and sexy. I sneaked a glance at his muscular forearms.

He chuckled. "I didn't have time to change into my uniform. I was about to fire up the grill when I was called out. I take it you got my message. How'd you know where to find me?"

"My phone's dead. Dad somehow wore down the battery, and I figured I could charge it at your place. So I owe you an apology for not getting your messages. Once I saw your note, I went to Perkatory, figuring that I could call you from there. But I ran into Dad, who already knew about Raina."

"Naturally," he replied good-naturedly.

"He said Kai called the café. So I put everything together and came here."

Noah ran his fingers through his dark hair and glanced at Raina's home.

"What's going on, anyway? Is she okay?"

He gave a subtle shrug. "She's missing. But only for about five or six hours."

Weird, because that didn't seem like cause for alarm. "Is she even considered a missing person at this point? I thought someone had to be gone for twenty-four hours before police got involved. Or is that an only-on-TV thing?"

"It's a myth. But we want to give it some time."

"But why all the commotion?" I glanced at the line of police cars. "This must be the entire island force. And then some. Is that a county sheriff's car?"

"And a state trooper, and the FDLE," Noah said. The Florida Department of Law Enforcement was a statewide investigative agency. They rarely got involved in local missing-person cases, though.

"Weird. A woman can't leave her house and spend time alone for a few hours without a battalion of cops swooping in? Maybe she's doing yoga on some beach somewhere. Or visiting a friend. Or maybe she has a lover."

Noah leaned in and lowered his voice. The smell of his spicy cologne made me unsteady on my feet. "I know that and you know that, Lana. Trust me, no one's more annoyed about all this than me. But Kai's the son of a powerful state senator here in Florida who chairs the Criminal Justice Committee. That complicates matters, and now Tallahassee's gotten involved. It's why I had to cancel our date and come here. I got a call from the FDLE commissioner himself. He sent the state agents down. Said we're too small of a department to handle such a case."

My eyes widened. My reporter antennae sprang to life. "Oh, really?"

Noah smirked. "I can tell you're writing a news story in your head already."

"Who, me?" I pointed to my chest, an innocent grin spreading on my lips.

"Yes, you." His tone was growly yet playful, and my stomach did a little flip-flop.

I studied his face, the red and blue lights of the police cruisers bouncing off his smooth skin. "Well, I'm not reporting tonight." *Or ever again, probably.* I shoved that thought aside. "Do you think you'll be able to leave anytime soon?"

The little, flirtatious smile that played on Noah's lips made my face feel hot. He turned to look toward Raina's house and pressed his hands into his hips. "I think I'm here for a couple of hours at least. The boyfriend is pretty upset, and his dad is on edge because he's running for reelection. Even got the governor to call me."

I snorted. "Justice favors the rich."

Noah shook his head. "This one's beyond my control, cupcake. We're going to stay until we find her. We're calling all of her contacts and yoga students now."

I sighed dramatically. "Okay. Fine. I'll take a rain check."

"You'd better. And you'd better wear that dress too." The corner of his mouth quirked upward.

I giggled. "I'm going to drive Dad back to his car; then I'll be home. If you finish anytime soon, call me. Or stop by. I can whip up dinner. Or we can go somewhere to eat. If you still want—"

"Lana, I'll get in touch as soon as I can." His phone buzzed, and he held it to his ear. "I'll be right there."

He tapped on his cell, then slipped it into his pocket. "Gotta run. Call you later."

With a wink and a squeeze of my upper arm, he dashed off. I slid back into the car, still feeling the heat of his fingers on my skin.

"What did you find out?" Dad leaned in eagerly.

I fired up the car and pulled a U-turn in the street, driving slowly away. "Not much. Kai's dad is some big-shot politician, and that's why Noah and all these other officers are here. I didn't get the impression that he thought it was anything serious. Raina hasn't been missing for more than a few hours. There's little they can do at the moment except try to track her down."

"Hmm." Dad's tone was skeptical. "We haven't had a missing person on the island since . . ."

His voice trailed off. He didn't need to finish his sentence, because I knew exactly who he was thinking of: my best friend in high school, the girl who'd gotten me into journalism.

* * *

After dropping Dad at his car, which was parked in front of Perkatory, I returned home with Stanley. The first thing I did was plug my dead phone into the charger. It flickered on after a few minutes, and I heaved a sigh of relief. Thank goodness Dad hadn't broken it; he had a way of doing that to electronics.

Then I climbed out of my little black dress and threw on a pair of comfy sweats and a Miami Dolphins T-shirt. It was already eight, and the chances of salvaging any kind of date with Noah were slim to none.

That forgotten mango pie, however, was calling my name. I tucked into a giant slice, not having eaten anything in hours.

"So good," I moaned aloud, shoveling another spoonful into my mouth. It was like a tropical vacation in pie form: sweet, creamy, and simple, the fragrant mango mingling perfectly with the graham cracker crust. Noah didn't know what he was missing.

As I was picking up crumbs off the plate with my fork, my phone buzzed. I walked over to where I was charging it on an end table and tapped at the green button to answer the call.

The Prince of Darkness, my caller ID said. Mike Heller had been saved as a contact that way in my phone for years, a lingering newsroom joke from when I was an intern and the reporters all feared his tough edits.

"You busy?" No hello, no pleasantries. Mike ran the *Devil's Beach Beacon*, the island's small yet scrappy daily newspaper. It was where I'd started my journalism career as a summer intern in high school.

"Nope. Just eating an entire pie. You?" Stanley zoomed past me. It was that time of night where he had to work off all his excess energy before passing out.

Mike let out a low-baritone laugh. "I thought you'd be out celebrating your win at the barista championship today. Great job, by the way. Our reporter got some excellent shots of you."

"Thanks. Had a blast. And as for the celebration, that's on hold." Stanley zoomed by again, this time with one of my socks in his mouth. I was too tired to chase after him. The contest had been only eight hours ago, but it seemed like eight years.

"Weren't you supposed to go out with a certain police chief tonight?"

"Does literally everyone on Devil's Beach know my business?"

He chuckled. "Not gonna answer that. All I can say is that I ran into your dad earlier today. And I think I can guess why you and Noah aren't out having a nice dinner together. Because of Raina's, er, situation."

"Odd, isn't it?" I sank into the sofa next to the end table.

"Indeed. That's why I'm calling you."

"I don't get it. What's the big deal? You're not doing a story, are you? She'll probably come back by the time you print tomorrow's edition."

"No, we're not writing about it tonight. I was wondering if you'd monitor it, though. If she's still missing in a day or two, I was thinking about hiring you to write an article. Figured you might want to."

"You know me too well." Mike had followed my reporting career's highs and lows and knew journalism was in my blood. I missed writing for newspapers something fierce. But jobs were scarce and freelance assignments scarcer here on Devil's Beach.

I went over the long mental list of everything I needed to do in the coming days. *Open the café, close the café, make the cold brew, order a new shipment of beans, payroll . . .*

"I guess I could do that." What the heck. I could sleep when I was dead.

"Good. Because my crime reporter's on vacation. He doesn't get back until the week after next. I want to have all my bases covered in case things go south. I don't have a big budget this month, though."

"What about that feature article you asked me to write?" He'd wanted me to do something on "reasons your barista hates you." I was lukewarm on the idea because I was more of a hard-news reporter.

"I'll take the money allocated for that and pay you for the Raina story if that pans out."

Whew. "That's fine. I'm sure Raina will return soon and I won't need to write about her at all. She's obsessed with her yoga studio and in love with Kai. What are the odds she disappeared?"

My question hung in the air, and when Mike didn't answer, my stomach tightened with anxiety. The chances were slight, but they were there. We both knew it, based on past events.

"We'll have to let it play out, Lana." Mike's normally gruff voice was uncharacteristically soft, probably because he knew who, and what, I was thinking about.

"Yeah. Anyway, thanks for asking me to help," I said hurriedly. "I'll find out what I can and let you know. Hopefully she'll turn up soon. Maybe I won't have to write anything. That would be the best-case scenario."

"It would. Say a little prayer, Lana."

We hung up, and because of Mike's somber tone, long-buried memories of another incident here on Devil's Beach flitted like ghosts around the recesses of my brain.

Chapter Four

When I was a freshman in high school, my best and only friend was a new student named Gisela Sommer. She was born in Germany but had traveled the world with her parents, who were artists. They'd settled in Devil's Beach because back then it was a hippie enclave, not a trendy tourist spot.

Gisela was geeky like me, played clarinet in the band and loved Harry Potter. We got braces the same month, adored NSync, and were trying desperately to both fit in and rebel against the popular cliques in a high school filled with jocks and girls who spent hours tanning on the island's beaches in bikinis.

At fourteen, we weren't the kind to wear bikinis. We were little kids, young and naïve for our age. Toward the end of freshman year we tried experimenting with makeup, and I have a photo of us looking like badly painted dolls, with smudgy red lips.

One week after school got out, Gisela and I went to a graduation party at a senior's house. It was our first actual party, and our parents told us we could stay out until eleven.

Neither one of us partook of the fruity, boozy cocktails mixed in a giant cooler. We also didn't take a hit of the joint when the captain of the swim team passed it to us. We spent the night hunched on a sofa, sipping sodas and gawping at the popular older boys. Because we weren't rule breakers—and since the party was in downtown Devil's Beach, close to both our homes—we adhered to our curfew.

The party was near both our homes, so we walked there and back. We said our good-byes at the corner of Seabreeze and Gumbo Limbo Streets, the halfway point between our houses. The thing I remember about that moment was how Gisela's long, golden hair looked so shiny in the streetlight.

"Think your mom will drive us to the movies tomorrow?" I asked.

"Probably. I want to see *Finding Nemo*." She spread out her arms and twirled, her melodic voice echoing in the evening's hush. She had the most unusual accent, slightly German and worldly, since she'd traveled everywhere.

"I was thinking of *School of Rock*," I called out.

"We'll see. Let's watch something light and fun. 'Bye." She took off, her long legs eating up the block. That girl was always in motion.

It was the last time I saw her. Sometime that evening—or early the next morning; no one ever figured it out—Gisela disappeared.

That night infused everything in my life from that moment on. It explained why I didn't have a wide circle of friends, because a little, nagging part of me thought they would disappear and I'd have to grieve all over again.

It was also why I became a journalist. Mom and Dad thought I needed something to occupy my time that summer, so they hooked me up with an internship at the *Beacon*. Mostly I made copies, fetched coffee, and answered the phone. Mike the editor also assigned me a column. It was called *High School Confidential*, and my first piece was about how much I missed Gisela.

I still recall the opening sentence of my article. *Gisela? If you're reading this, please come home.*

How naïve I was. Not only did Gisela not return, but her disappearance remained unsolved. And every time I've covered a missing-person case since then, I've thought of her. Gisela's memory—her ghost—made me want to give a voice to the voiceless.

Tonight, sixteen years later, was no different. I sat on my sofa, listening to the crickets hum in the late-summer air. Stanley was on his sheepskin-wrapped dog bed, snoring like a toy chainsaw. Missing-person stories made me uneasy. It was the what-ifs, and the uncertainty of them, that caused my entire body to tense.

Where had Gisela gone? And where was Raina tonight?

I glanced at the clock. Nine thirty. Although I should have been exhausted enough to fall asleep in a heartbeat, I was wired. Possibly from the coffee, or all that sugar in the pie, or from sheer curiosity and nerves. I flicked on another lamp, wanting to bathe my cozy living room in more light.

Enough of rummaging through the garage of my past. I grabbed my phone, now fully charged, and texted Noah.

Hey you. How's it going?

He responded right away, and I smiled.

Hey back. I'm at the station, doing paperwork. Crossing all my Ts and dotting my Is. Starving.
Oh! You never ate. Why don't I bring you something?

You don't have to . . .
I want to.
Well, I never turn down food from a gorgeous woman.
Be there in fifteen.

I jumped up and made a beeline for the fridge. I had the ingredients to make an incredible roast-beef sandwich. As I piled the sandwich with meat, romaine, tomato, onion, and horseradish, a fur-rumpled Stanley roared in. He looked up at me with giant brown eyes.

"No roast beef. You've had enough snacks today. I'm onto your emotional manipulation."

He wuffed in response.

"I refuse to be held hostage by your demands," I said firmly. He wandered off. "Good boy."

I wrapped the sandwich in a paper towel, then slid it into a plastic bag. The half-eaten mango pie was on the counter. Even better. I dug around under the counter until I found an adequate-size Tupperware container and lid, then carved a thick slice and nestled it into the container.

The food went into my backpack, and I grabbed my keys.

I couldn't stop smiling as I locked the door and wheeled my bike off the porch. Bringing Noah food was a perfect excuse for two things: seeing his handsome face and finding out more information on Raina's disappearance.

* * *

Bernadette, the busybody dispatcher and receptionist for the police department, greeted me when I walked through the front door of the station. So did her parrot, Max.

They were a well-known team here on Devil's Beach, tiny old Bernadette and her spirited white cockatoo. I'd known them for most of my life. She liked to gossip, and I figured she'd ring Dad the minute I was out of earshot.

"Didn't expect to see you tonight." Her voice was a smoker's rasp.

"Hello," chirped Max. He was sitting in the corner on a thick wooden perch.

"Hey, Max. Hey, Bern. Just coming by to say hi to the chief." I tried to sound professional. "Wanted to talk with him about what happened tonight."

"Mm-hmm," she responded with a skeptical hum.

My sweat pants and T-shirt didn't add to my credibility, and I shot her a tight smile as she buzzed me through the door that led to the offices and the four-cell jail.

Max let out a garbled yet identifiable swear word. That was the bird's downside. He had a vocabulary that would make a trucker blush. No one on the island cared much, although I was shocked Noah allowed Bernadette to bring Max to work while she answered police calls.

I made my way down the brilliantly lit hallway of the small station and stopped at Noah's door. It was open.

He was staring at a yellow legal pad, his dark brows furrowed together.

"Knock, knock."

He looked up, his eyes widening. A smile spread on his face. Those straight teeth and the dimples made my knees feel like overcooked noodles.

I walked into his office and plopped down in a straight-backed wooden chair, sliding off my backpack in the process. "I brought you some goodies. Hope you like roast beef and mango pie."

I half stood, setting the zip-top bag with the sandwich and the Tupperware container in front of him.

"You're kidding. Is it my lucky night or what?"

"I should've asked if you like horseradish."

"I love horseradish. Thank you. Seriously, Lana, you don't know how much this means. I was about to raid the vending machine here."

"Can't have that."

He dug into the sandwich and took a bite. Triumph surged through me when he let out a little groan of pleasure. He swallowed. "God, this is amazing."

In my mind, I was atop his desk, doing a little happy dance. "I'm glad you think so. How's it going?"

"Meh. I'm trying to finish up, but the bird's breaking my concentration." He gestured to the door.

"Max has quite the filthy mouth."

"It's only for tonight. Apparently he wasn't feeling well, and Bernadette asked, so . . ." He raised his hands in the air in a helpless gesture.

"That's sweet of you. How's Raina's case going? She turn up?"

He shook his head. "We've tried to reach everyone on Raina's phone contact list. Talked to almost all of her students at the yoga studio. No one's seen her."

My stomach clenched. "Yikes."

He slid open a drawer and extracted a long wooden box. He flipped it open to reveal a clean bamboo fork and spoon. Goodness. He even loved the environment. Could I swoon any harder?

"Listen, while I inhale this delicious food, why don't you tell me your impressions of Raina."

I settled back into the black leather chair. "You should ask my dad about her. He's connected to that yoga scene. I met her when I came back to Devil's Beach a few months ago and started managing Perkatory."

"Is she friendly? Did she have a problem with anyone?" he asked between bites.

I tilted my head. "Friendly? Yeah. You've met her, right?"

"Once, at your coffee shop. She introduced herself and encouraged me to take any hot-yoga class for free, anytime."

I raised an eyebrow. "Well. She didn't make me that offer."

He grinned. "She also called the station one time when she thought the studio was broken into."

"When was that?"

"Right before you came back. It was one of my first calls as chief. Turned out it was Kai. He forgot his keys and jimmied the back door open."

I crossed my legs, wishing I'd changed into something less slobby. "She is friendly. We had coffee together when I first took over the shop."

"But?"

"No buts. She seems like one of those type A yoga people."

Noah studied me without blinking. "Type A yoga people? Aren't you type A?"

"She's aggressive about relaxing and being fit. I met a lot of people like her in Miami. It's all about who can do what pose the best. Kind of fake." I paused. "Maybe that's mean. I've never told anyone my impressions of her until now. And, uh, I'm a different kind of type A."

"Keep going. What gave you the impression she was fake?"

I picked a pen off his desk and clicked it twice. "She made a point of letting me know that she was friends with famous yoga people. During our half-hour coffee, she probably dropped ten names of gurus. People who ran workshops in Bali, teachers with TV shows. I had no idea who they were, of course. I'd rather watch paint dry than follow the inner workings of the yoga world. She offered me a discount on my first class, but only one, then expounded about people paying their own way and owning their responsibility and truth or some nonsense. I guess that didn't apply to the island's fetching police chief, though."

Noah paused, a flush of pink creeping across his sharp cheekbones. He stuffed the rest of the sandwich in his mouth, and after chewing, he swallowed. "Did you take her up on that discount class?"

A snort-laugh leaked out my nose. "Heck no. I'm not a yoga type of person, never mind a hot-yoga person. Being in a room heated to a hundred degrees here in Florida seems like my version of ninety minutes in Hades."

Noah chuckled. "Would you say the two of you got along?"

I held up my hands. "Whoa, I have an alibi for today. I was at the coffee competition."

He was still laughing, a sound that made my insides thrum. "I know you do, Lana. You're not a suspect."

"Yeah. We got along fine. When it became clear that I wasn't going to one of her classes, we fell into a pleasant, if a bit superficial, acquaintance. She adores my dad, though. She always gushes about how authentic he is, how vulnerable. I went along with it, because that's how all those yoga people talk. You should speak with Dad. He's got connections."

"I will." Noah dug into the pie. "Thanks again for this. It's the best thing that's happened to me all day."

I smiled and tried to look as cute as possible in my sweat pants and T-shirt. "So, what's really going on with Raina?"

He paused, then pointed at the pie with his fork. "You made this?"

"I did. Why are you changing the subject?"

"Amazing. I should tell my mother about this pie. She loves mangoes, you know. When you lived in Miami, did you have a mango tree in your yard?"

"*Noah.*" His chuckle revealed his dimples, which were as sweet as the pie in front of him.

"You know what I heard?"

"What?" I leaned in, probably a little too eagerly.

"That Mike Heller was going to contact you about doing an article."

I reared back. "Where did you hear that?"

"Mike. He came by Raina's house right after you left. Said his crime reporter's on vacation."

"Oh." My shoulders slumped.

"He said I should keep in touch with you about any developments."

"I see. So what *are* the developments?" I lifted an eyebrow.

"Off the record?"

I straightened and thought about taking the notebook out of my bag, but didn't. "Totally off the record."

"Raina and her boyfriend, Kenneth, argued this morning."

I screwed up my face. "Kenneth? I thought his name was Kai."

Noah shuffled some papers and tapped on one with his finger. "Kenneth Lahtinen is his given name. Told me he took Kai as a nickname during a trip to India."

I fought the urge to roll my eyes. "So what happened after the argument?"

"Not for publication?"

"You have my word."

"After they had a knock-down, drag-out fight—his words, not mine—he left their house. Came downtown to do some paperwork at the studio for several hours. When he returned home, she and her bike were gone."

"What about her purse or ID? Her phone?"

"Gone. She often biked around the island, and it appears she took those things with her."

I nodded. "I see her around all the time."

"Same. And her boyfriend expected her to be home and figured they'd have round two of their fight. Apparently they fought a lot."

My eyebrows lifted in surprise. "They always seemed to make googly eyes at each other when they were in Perkatory together. Although, come to think of it . . ." My voice faded and I tapped my fingers on my chin.

"What?"

"I haven't seen them together in a while. Even before their retreat, she'd come into Perkatory alone and then leave. He'd come in later, alone. Hm. Anyway, what was their argument about?"

"What do couples usually argue about?"

I leaned forward, my elbow on the edge of his desk, totally unable to squelch my cheeky impulses. "Sex?"

The corner of Noah's full mouth quirked up. "Nope."

"Whether to watch *Game of Thrones* or *The Bachelor*?"

That earned me a laugh. "Come on. *Game of Thrones*."

"Agreed. Okay, money?"

"Bingo. Apparently they were in the red after the retreat. Unexpectedly."

"Whoa. Weird. She told me she was charging upwards of five grand for that retreat. She asked me if I wanted to go. I assume she was being polite. If I had five grand, I'd pay my student loans. Or put a down payment on a new car."

Noah stabbed another forkful of pie and stuffed it in his mouth. While he was chewing, I peppered him with questions.

"Did anyone see Kai come or go into the studio? Did Kai seem sketchy? Don't you think it's weird that he immediately told his dad about her being gone? Wouldn't any normal boyfriend assume she'd gone to a friend's house?"

"The owner of the souvenir shop saw Kai today and talked with him as he was coming and going. So that seems like a strong alibi."

"John, from Beach Boss?" That was the third store in my family's building.

"Yep. John. And no, Kai didn't seem sketchy, although that means nothing. He seems genuinely worried about Raina."

"Hmm. Strange. So he called the police right when he got home, when he realized she wasn't there?"

"No, he waited a few hours."

"Do you think he's not telling you something?"

Noah wiped his mouth with a paper napkin, then balled it up and tossed it in a wastebasket. "Not sure. Right now, she's not even technically a missing person. We're giving it until tomorrow morning to make that call."

"Which means technically I don't have a story for the paper. Yet."

"Exactly."

We grinned at each other stupidly. Goodness, he was adorable.

"Want me to walk you home? Or did you drive?" He stacked some papers together.

"I biked." This was my cue to leave.

He stood up. "C'mon. I'm done here, and whatever I haven't finished, I'll do at home. I'll walk you home."

I stood up and led the way out of his office. We strolled the two blocks to my house at a slow saunter, past the old Florida bungalows and the crepe jasmine bushes. The white, pinwheel-shaped flowers gave off a heady fragrance, and for a few moments, with Noah at my side, life seemed perfect. I pushed my bike and he walked alongside me, his shoes barely making a sound on the concrete.

"We've got a big week ahead of us." I figured he'd prefer some small talk.

"We?"

"Well, Stanley and I."

"Oh yeah?"

"Puppy kindergarten."

"I see. K-9 training."

I elbowed him gently. "It's not that formal. More for socialization and teaching him a command or two. I think he's going to have a tough time because his attention span is limited."

"I was a K-9 officer in Tampa early in my career. I used to have a Belgian Malinois. Bandit. He was the best dog in the world."

"Oh yeah?" There was so much I didn't know about Noah.

"When Bandit passed, I was gutted. Couldn't stay as a K-9 officer without my partner."

I watched as Noah swallowed. A brief yet definite expression of anguish crossed his face. It was the first time I'd seen such raw emotion from him. Usually he was so genial and laid-back.

"Oof. I'm sorry. That must be difficult, losing an animal after working and living with them."

He nodded and remained silent, so I steered the conversation back to my wild Shih Tzu puppy.

"You know, I could use your help on trying to teach Stanley some obedience." We were at my house, and I wheeled the bike up the walkway. Noah grabbed it and lifted it easily up the three steps to the porch.

"You have a lock?" he asked.

"Of course." I reached into my backpack and showed him my U-shaped lock. As I popped it open with a key, I could hear Stanley's distant barking from inside.

Noah reached for the lock. "Seriously, if you want help with Stanley, I'm happy to help."

"Yeah?" I gave a little snort. "I'm guessing a Shih Tzu might be a little different from a Belgian Malinois."

Noah attached the lock around the bike's frame and front wheel, then tested it. "Oh, I don't know. Dogs are dogs. They usually want to please their owners. I can give you some tips on that."

I took a step toward him. A lazy, sexy expression spread across his face.

"I think I'd like that," I said in a low tone. "You know, you could come to puppy kindergarten class with us on Tuesday."

He tucked my hair behind my right ear, and a wave of pleasure shimmied through me. "I'd love to."

"Awesome. You want to come inside for a nightcap?" *Can't hurt to ask . . .*

"I'd love to, but I'm going to say no. You're probably exhausted. I know I am. And I have more paperwork to do, and emails to send to the state agent in charge. I wish we were at my house, though, hanging out on the balcony."

A sad trombone noise bleated in my head. "Me too." We looked at each other awkwardly.

"Well, good night." I chewed on the inside of my cheek.

He smoothed my hair back and kissed my forehead. The entirety of my internal organs turned to caramel goo.

" 'Night," he murmured, then turned to walk down the steps. "Oh, and hey."

"Yeah?"

He pointed at my T-shirt. "Dolphins suck. Tampa Bay all the way."

Chortling, I said good-bye with a finger wave. My legs were so rubbery from that forehead kiss that I almost forgot about everything else, including Raina's disappearance.

Chapter Five

After a lazy morning of sleeping in, then drinking coffee and reading the Sunday *New York Times* in bed with Stanley, I got to work making a sweet treat to sell at the café. I had everything on hand for one of my all-time favorites: mint truffles.

They sounded fancy. They looked expensive. In reality, they were the easiest things in the world to make, but they were always a hit with customers. All the snacks I sold at Perkatory had five ingredients or fewer—I couldn't be bothered with complicated recipes—and these were no exception.

I cranked up an eighties station on my internet speaker and got to work, singing along to a Flock of Seagulls. I might be a millennial, but I loved older music.

The previous night's encounter with Noah was still fresh in my mind. I had a good feeling about him. About *us*.

First, I used a food processor to crumble the Keebler Grasshopper cookies. Then I added cream cheese, and when everything turned to a malleable yet sticky consistency, I carefully rolled individual balls between my palms and stuck them on a parchment paper–lined baking sheet. I slid the tray into the freezer and proceeded to step two. This was why I loved simple recipes: it was impossible to get distracted.

I melted white chocolate chips over low heat and added a few drops of green food coloring. Once it was the perfect shade of mint, I took the balls out of the freezer, carefully coated them in chocolate, and finished off with a dusting of rainbow sprinkles. They went back into the fridge to harden up while I tried to tucker Stanley out with a ball in the backyard.

Once I'd done that, I changed out of my pajamas and into a Stevie Nicks T-shirt and my favorite pair of faded, wide-leg jeans. It was time to relieve Barbara, who was working at the café until one. She had a craft class to teach, and Erica and I would handle the rest of the day.

At Perkatory, Sundays were the best. We played low, sultry jazz on the sound system, giving the airy, light-filled space a laid-back vibe. After my sweet and slightly sensual forehead kiss with Noah last night, I was in a dreamy mood, eager to listen to Chet Baker, or perhaps some Ella Fitzgerald, and brew some killer coffee.

With the mint truffles in an insulated bag, I walked the two blocks from my house to the café and spotted a throng of people even before I reached the building. A slow-moving mix of tourists and locals flopped on the white wicker chairs and sofas, drinking lattes, reading books, and staring at their phones. Most were in some form of beach attire, from board shorts and bikinis to color-ful muumuus and Hawaiian shirts.

The entire street smelled like suntan lotion mixed with espresso.

When I approached the café, I knew it wouldn't be a relaxing shift. A line stretched out the door and snaked between the five outdoor wicker tables lining the sidewalk. It was so packed that I had to walk around the parked cars, then delicately push my way inside.

"Excuse me," I murmured. "Pardon me."

A few people huffed and rolled their eyes as if I were trying to cut ahead. "I need to get through so I can make your coffee, folks," I said cheerily. "I've also got some fresh snacks for sale here."

Finally I reached the counter, where Erica and Barbara were working at warp speed. I made a beeline for my black apron and tied it on, then hurriedly arranged the mint treats on a platter and set them down.

"Why didn't you call me? I would've come earlier," I hissed.

Erica waved me off. "It's been steady all morning but got crowded about fifteen minutes ago. I think they're all from that dolphin-watching cruise. And people found out about our win at the barista championships."

"Want me to take the orders or make espresso?" I asked. Even though Erica was my employee, she was firmly in command behind the counter. And she was a better latte artist than I was, so I didn't mind deferring to her preference.

"Can you bring in another bucket of cold brew?"

"Sure thing." Grabbing two of our large pitchers, I walked to the cooler and almost ran smack into Barbara.

"The cold brew's selling like crazy today." She whizzed by, a flurry of arms and strings as she pulled her apron over her head. "Gotta run. I'm late for class."

"What are you creating today?" I called out. She was a fabulous folk artist who dispensed local lore while teaching art classes at the community center.

"Collage with driftwood and sand. First we're foraging on the beach." I pulled open the door, trying to imagine working with sand and glue. I'd surely be covered in both. For all of my writing skills, I lacked a creative gene.

I poured cold coffee into the two pitchers and hustled back to our prep area.

Erica came over. "How was your evening and morning with Sheriff Hunk?"

"I like how you assumed that we spent the night together. The date didn't happen."

"Not at all?" She opened the fridge door for me.

"He was called out to a scene."

"Barbara told me. I figured the two of you met up later."

"We did, but it was all too brief." I slid the pitchers inside and shut the door, swooning a little inside at the thought of his forehead kiss. "I'll tell you about it when the rush dies down."

For the next hour, we took orders, pulled espressos, and poured drinks. By two PM the customers had faded to a manageable trickle, and I mopped my brow with my forearm. The strains of Fleetwood Mac's *Tusk* mingled with conversational chatter.

"It's awesome to be busy, isn't it?" Satisfaction flowed through my body, similar to what I'd experienced as a reporter after nailing an exclusive story.

"Sure is." Erica handed me a shot of espresso. "So tell me about Raina. I already know a little from Barbara but figured most of that was hearsay. She's a bit of a gossip, like your dad."

"They're two peas in a pod," I agreed, wrapping my hand around the small white cup. "There's not much to say about Raina beyond what you already know. Come to think of it, I should ask Noah if he's heard anything. I'm sure she's home by now. Hang on."

I slid my phone out of my pocket.

Hey you. I'm at Perkatory. How's it going?
I'm back at the station, working on Raina's case. I'll try to come by later on.
Is she still missing?
Yes.

A chill flowed through me as I reread his one-word response. I looked up at Erica.

"She hasn't returned."

Erica's eyes grew wide. "Yikes."

"Any gossip from customers?"

Erica shook her head. "A few people came in after the ten AM class, which was taught by a sub. They speculated she visited a friend on the mainland to sleep off her jet lag."

"She never misses teaching her Sunday class." Usually Raina waltzed in, dripping with clove-smelling perspiration, after her hot-yoga class. She always ordered a passion fruit iced tea—unsweetened, of course. Somehow, even in her sweaty state, she looked lithe and ethereal, put together in her matching sports bra and athletic shorts. I tossed back the espresso and set the cup in the sink, a lock of my wavy hair falling into my face. I tucked it behind my ear.

As Erica chattered on about the alleged benefits of hot yoga, I zoned out by wiping and drying the blond-wood counter until it gleamed. Raina's disappearance was going from unsettling to alarming.

"Hey, Lana? You okay?" Erica glanced at me. "You're a little flushed."

I resisted the urge to mop my brow with the back of my hand. "I'm fine. A little worn out."

The door to the café opened, and in walked Dad.

"Munchkin!" He strode toward me.

I could tell by the gleam in his eye he was harboring a juicy piece of gossip. I moved around the counter to greet him, and he gave me a half hug. Dad was tall, at least a foot taller than me, and his limbs were long and athletic.

"What's new?"

"Over there." He motioned with his head to an empty table near the window. He had a serious look on his face, as if he were about to reveal a dark, explosive secret that would take down a global leader. We sat facing each other.

"Why the secrecy?" I folded my hands in front of me, trying not to laugh.

"I went to yoga this morning at the Wolfman's." His tone was pure drama.

"Oh yeah?"

"We shared a kombucha afterward and got to talking."

My nose scrunched involuntarily. Dad loved that fermented tea, but I thought it tasted like feet dipped in vinegar. "And?"

He leaned in and lowered his voice so much that I couldn't hear him at first.

"Dad, you can speak up. There are only three tables nearby, and they're a few feet away. I think your state secret's safe if you talk in a normal tone."

"Okay, listen. Raina's had a stalker for some time now. Well, people described him as a stalker. He was a student. Followed Raina around like a puppy. Word on the street is the guy was a real creeper while they were all on the retreat in Costa Rica."

"How does the Wolfman know this?" I narrowed my eyes. Maybe Dad's gossip connections weren't all that great. After all, we were talking about a sixty-five-year-old man who looked like a skinny Jerry Garcia and wore rainbow sweatbands.

"Wolfie knows everyone in the yoga community here on the beach." Dad sniffed.

"I'm sure he does. So who's the stalker?"

"It's a guy named Shawn Sims. He owns a personal watercraft business. Jet Skis."

"I don't think I know him. Name doesn't ring a bell. Then again, I'm not really into water sports."

Dad shrugged. "I wouldn't be surprised if he's come in here. He practices at Dante's Inferno daily."

"And yet he was her stalker? If he was creepy, why didn't she kick him out of her classes? Or why didn't Kai step in? Did she call the cops? Doesn't make sense." I made a mental note to ask Noah about Shawn.

"Well, that's the other thing." Dad drummed his fingers on the table. "Raina apparently enjoyed being queen bee. She wanted the attention of adoring students. Courted it, even. She was setting herself up to be some kind of spiritual guru. Common in the yoga world. That's why Wolfie's a treasure. He's a straight shooter. Doesn't have a good word to say about Raina, though."

"Hmm. Sounds like Raina has a bit of a complicated personal life. I wonder if anyone's talked to Shawn. Or Kai. Or any of Raina's students."

"By anyone, you mean Noah?"

I looked Dad in the eye. "No, I mean a journalist."

He scratched his beard. "Probably not. It's too soon. I haven't heard of the TV stations sniffing around. You thinking about writing an article?"

"Mike called last night. He said his crime reporter's on vacation for a few days and wanted me to monitor the story. He'd like a story if Raina's missing for more than a day or so."

56

"Lana, do it." Dad grabbed my forearms. "I can help you get all sorts of information. I'll hook you up with Wolfie. He'll tell you everything. Plus, you need to see his new studio. It's a geodesic dome and really out of this world."

I stared out the window as I pondered. Tourists in flip-flops and colorful bathing suits strolled by on their way to the beach, oblivious to the drama unfolding here inside Perkatory. As far as they knew, Devil's Beach was a casually hip island community. In reality, a scandal was brewing.

A beautiful, missing yoga teacher. A doting boyfriend with political connections. A stalker named Shawn who rode Jet Skis, probably like an extra in a satisfyingly cheesy 1980s TV show.

Any day now, the networks would be onto this story. I had to act fast.

A thought crossed my mind, one that was about as annoying as people misusing *they're*, *their*, and *there* in a social media post. It involved my ex-husband. Would he come from Miami to do a piece on Raina? I could hear his breathless baritone now.

It was the last thing I wanted.

"You really think I should write an article?" I interrupted Dad, who was still talking about the Wolfman's geodesic dome studio. "Is there even a story?"

"Absolutely." He paused. "Unless you're feeling strange about it because of what happened back in high school."

I crossed my arms over my stomach. "I got those vibes."

Dad nodded sympathetically. "I'm sure this is a much different scenario."

He was right. Just because Raina had disappeared didn't mean she was gone forever. She was probably blissed out, doing downward dog with some dashing dharma dude.

"Couldn't hurt to do a little poking around, I guess," I murmured.

"That's the spirit." Dad's eyes were positively glistening with excitement. He'd always been so encouraging of my journalism career. Part of me thought he'd missed his calling because he was so nosy.

I slid my phone out of my pocket. After a quick glance to see if Noah had texted—he hadn't—I pulled up Mike's number and fired off a message.

Afternoon. You probably already know this, but Raina's not back yet. Dad's given me some leads of some people to talk with. How about I work on a story?

A text came in almost immediately. *Sounds good. I won't expect anything for a day, even two. We need to proceed delicately, in case she left on her own. It's not a crime for an adult to skip town.*

People do it all the time, especially here in crazy Florida, I texted back. **Heck, maybe she met someone and fell in love in Costa Rica and flew back there. We don't know.**

Exactly. But I have faith that you'll uncover some good details. Keep me posted on what you find out. Gossip's flying around the island. But remember: my budget's kind of thin. I can only afford one article, so make it good.

I sent him a thumbs-up emoji and sighed.

As much as I wanted to get back into journalism and write a kick-butt newspaper piece, I had my doubts as to whether this was the best story with which to make my comeback. I'd set aside those fears when I covered crime in Miami. It was a different world, one where lawlessness was expected.

Here on Devil's Beach? It was uncomfortably close to home.

Memories of Gisela kept cropping up, of those days when the entire island searched for her. One of my enduring recollections was how my stomach churned as though I were digesting ground glass.

I'd felt that way only a few times since. When my ex told me he wanted a divorce. When I was laid off from my dream job covering crime at the paper in Miami.

And today, thinking about the missing Raina.

Chapter Six

Perkatory closed at four PM on Sundays. I'd tried staying open later but had found that most tourists wanted to go to bars on weekend nights and locals were already too drunk or bone-tired from work to want coffee that late.

After Dad left, it had been steadily busy all afternoon, and Erica had stayed a few hours extra. She locked the door behind the last customer, and I pulled up some Rick Springfield. I'd been preoccupied with thoughts of Raina, so perhaps upbeat eighties music would boost my mood.

We wiped down tables, and she sang along to "Jessie's Girl."

When the song finished, she glanced over. "What's up, Lana? You're not your usual bubbly, outgoing self. And by that I mean not doing that dance of yours."

"I wouldn't describe myself as outgoing. Or bubbly. And what dance?"

"The one where you look like a robot trying to salsa dance."

That got me to laugh.

"C'mon, Lana, what's wrong? You're always smiling and happy to see people. You have something good to say about everyone.

Well, except your ex-husband. And those kids who dumped the entire sugar container on the ground a couple of hours ago."

Those little jerks. I rolled my eyes and laughed, pushing a mop into the corner of the room. I turned to her. "It's this Raina situation."

"Why? You used to cover crime. You wrote about a lot worse at the paper."

I waved my hand in the air. "Absolutely. I could tell you some crazy stories from when I was a reporter in Miami. But this one"— I shook my head—"seems weird. Maybe because she's our age. We weren't best friends or anything, but we chatted often. Like almost every other day. I'm sure she's by herself somewhere. Still."

"You sound like you don't quite believe your own words."

I leaned my chin on the mop and let out a heavy sigh.

"Spill. What's wrong? Is it Noah?"

"I never told you about Gisela."

"No. You didn't."

I drew a deep breath, then recounted the story of my high school friend, which was now a Devil's Beach legend. It took me a few minutes to tell Erica everything, and her expression grew more somber as I explained.

"That's why I'm so unsettled. Raina's disappearance reminds me of that summer Gisela vanished. I realize it's two different cases."

Erica nodded slowly. "Don't you think her boyfriend, Kai, is a suspect in this? Or is it her stalker? Somebody must know more than they're saying. Or Noah's not telling you everything. Well, that's what your dad thinks, anyway. We had a lengthy chat about it."

"Kai? I dunno. He never struck me as the kind of guy who would kill someone. He seems so . . . gentle. Clueless, even."

She raised an eyebrow. "For a hard-boiled former police reporter, you sure have a lot of optimism about people."

"I guess." I preferred to think of myself as a realist, not an optimist. In my experience, most folks tried to do the right thing—unless they were cornered and desperate. "Yeah, it's usually the boyfriend. That's how it is on true-crime shows. And in real life. Women are much more likely to be harmed by men they know than by strangers."

"What else do you know about Kai?"

"Hmm. Let me think about it while I put this away." I walked the mop into the stock room, trying to rack my brain for information on him. When I emerged, I shook my head.

"I got nothing. When I came home after Miami, he and Raina were already running the studio. She opened Dante's Inferno about a year and a half ago. Kai came on the scene a short while after. Dad was all excited to rent the space to her."

"Hmm."

I swung open the fridge. "Hey, there's enough cold brew for two. Want to polish off the pitcher so we don't waste it?"

"Sure."

I filled the tall glasses with ice, then poured the coffee. I set one in front of Erica and took a long sip of mine. "It's strange; I don't know much about Raina or Kai. Time for some internet stalking."

"Let's get 'er done," Erica yelled in an exaggerated southern accent.

I told her to hang on and ran upstairs to my office, which was on the second floor. That was where I stored my laptop and all the coffee shop's paperwork, a tall column of extra to-go cups, and a few broken chairs. A stack of bills sat on the top of my desk, unpaid. I knew I should deal with those instead of sleuthing online, but finding out more about Raina was too enticing.

I returned downstairs with the computer and set it at my favorite spot in the café: a long table near the window. I hopped up onto the bar seat. Erica slid next to me, slurping her coffee.

"I don't know how you get the cold brew to be this smooth, but it has citrusy, honey overtones with a warm bitterness. Absurdly delicious."

"It's not my technique. It's the beans. Which reminds me, I need to make another vat for tomorrow before I leave."

She waved her hand at the laptop. "Later. This is more interesting."

I typed Raina's name into an internet search engine. Her studio, Dante's Inferno, dominated the first page of links. I clicked on the site and pointed to a lithe woman bathed in sweat and sunshine. Erica had started at Perkatory while Raina was in Costa Rica. "That's her."

"She's gorgeous. But jeez, all that perspiration. Who wants to sweat like that in Florida?"

My face screwed into a grimace. "Right? Even looking at that makes me feel sticky."

I read from the web page out loud. " 'We can't wait to see you at Dante's Inferno, Florida's premier hot-yoga studio. We have the most advanced heating system in the yoga industry. Our state-of-the-art temperature control monitors heat, humidity, and oxygen levels to ensure the air you breathe is of the highest quality.' " I pantomimed a gag. "Seems unhygienic."

"And smelly."

We both laughed as I clicked around on the studio's schedule and prices. Erica let out a low whistle. "Wow. Twenty-five bucks for a class? That's like Seattle or San Francisco."

"Yeah, her Costa Rica retreat was five K a person. Not including airfare or lodging."

"Yikes. Are there many people on Devil's Beach who can afford that?"

I side-eyed Erica. "Good question. Definitely some of the rich part-time residents. And there are some trust funders here. I went to school with a few and see them go into her studio."

I clicked over to a page titled "About Raina and Kai." A giant photo popped up. The two of them had their arms around each other's waists, both smiling serenely against a Gulf sunrise backdrop. It looked like North Beach, close to where Dad and Noah lived.

She was in her signature black sports bra and tiny shorts, and he was shirtless and in black shorts that came halfway down his muscular thighs.

Erica leaned in. "I'm always amazed when I see couples who have matching tans."

"I wonder if that's from bronzer or a tanning bed. Look, here's their bio."

We both sucked on our coffees as we read the blurb below the photo. It stated that they had both studied under world-renowned yogis. I'd never heard of anyone mentioned, but that wasn't surprising. Kai had attended a small college in California and loved apple cider vinegar and "long, yummy meditation sessions." Nowhere did it say that his proper name was Kenneth or that his dad was a powerful politician here in the Sunshine State.

" 'Raina Rose was born on a farm in Wisconsin. She's a catalyst for love, light and global peace.' " I paused, then snorted. " 'She is a yogaventurer, the founder of Dante's Inferno'—trademark symbol—'and passionate about awakening the inner chi that graces us all.' "

"Is she for real? What the heck is a yogaventurer?"

I stifled a laugh. "I think that's yoga-speak for 'I'm bendy and look hot in yoga pants while I travel the world.' Oh wow, are we mean? We're disparaging a missing woman."

"No." Erica sucked down the last of her coffee. "Not mean. We're allergic to bovine fecal material."

I cracked up. "Hey, check this out. Some articles about her." At the end of the bio were links to several yoga and sports trade publications. " 'Raina Rose inks deal for new line of athletic fashion.' "

I clicked on a story about how Raina had signed a contract to put her name to yoga wear. " 'Inferno Athleisure. Clothes for your inner fire.' "

"My inner fire can usually be quenched with gin," Erica said.

"Gin turns my inner fire into a five-alarm blaze."

Erica dissolved into giggles. "Sounds like a personal problem."

We moved to the next article, one about Raina's "Costa Rica Journeys."

" 'Dante's Inferno Journeys will take you to the edge of your comfort level, deep into the heart of the Costa Rican rain forest,' " Erica read aloud. " '*Yoga Magazine* named Raina Rose one of the top twenty under thirty in the industry. She's poised to become a guru of the new millennium.' "

"She's doubling down on that fire branding," I paused. "Oooh. Let's peek at her social. I'll bet there are pictures from the retreat."

I returned to the Google search bar and clicked through the studio's social media accounts. Erica let out a low whistle. "Yikes. Over two thousand photos? Does she live on Instagram or what?"

"Looks like it." I scrolled down. There were videos of Raina doing yoga and still images of her in various poses. Staring at the beach. Doing a headstand. Communing with nature wearing an extremely sensual expression and tight yoga attire. Those photos were interspersed with pictures of the studio. I had to admit, Raina looked flawless, making even me wonder if just doing a little yoga might make my life as smooth and picture-perfect as hers.

"That's what her business looks like? It's really cool." Erica pointed to a photo of a stark black-and-white space. The walls were exposed brick, painted white, and the floor was black cement. Which seemed as though it would be hard on the joints, even with a mat, but what did I know?

"Yeah. I went in there once to deliver a box of cake pops for their anniversary. She ended up not wanting them."

"Wait. She rejected your baked goods? You make the best cake pops." Erica looked at me with horror.

"She accepted them graciously, but Barbara later told me she threw them in the garbage out in the alley because they weren't vegan, organic, and low-carb."

Erica rolled her eyes and swore under her breath. "I would've been annoyed. You're so laid-back about it."

"We can't let our personal preferences impede our fact-finding." I channeled my inner journalist.

"You're the reporter. You need to be fair and balanced. I don't."

I snorted and kept scrutinizing the photos. They made me acutely aware of my terrible posture, and I straightened my spine. "She's exceedingly photogenic."

When I clicked on the most recent one, a photo of a group of tan people with brilliant white teeth popped up. They were all on a beach and looked like a liquor ad. "This must be Costa Rica. Look, the sand is more golden, and there's a volcano in the background."

Erica read from the caption. " 'This is what bliss looks like. Many souls, coming together in the Central American jungle. All finding their hashtag innerfire.' Huh. To me, it's a bunch of rich folks who spent a buttload of cash on a vacation."

I pointed to Raina, then a muscular, bald guy. "Okay, so there's Raina and there's Kai. There's only one other guy aside from him, so that might be the stalker dude my Dad was talking about." Everyone in the photo was tagged, and I found the only other man's name. "Here we go. Shawn Sims. Aha. That's the person Dad mentioned. Let's see what's up with him."

As soon as the page refreshed with his profile, Erica yelped. "Yikes."

"Whoa." I swiped on the laptop track pad with my middle and ring finger. There were hundreds of pictures, nearly three or four a day. Shawn staring at the sunset on a beach. Shawn beaming while riding a bike. Shawn with a parrot on his shoulder.

He wasn't alone in any of them.

"Okay, this is super weird," I said.

"I wonder what Kai thought about this. I mean, if it's well known that Shawn is her stalker, then why . . ." Erica's voice trailed off.

"Then why is Raina in almost every photo he posted? It looks like they were a couple. There are more photos of her with Shawn than with Kai."

Erica and I locked eyes. There was a story here, and we both knew it.

Chapter Seven

M onday dawned, with no news and no Raina. Tension over her disappearance ratcheted up, and the old-timers on the island whispered about the parallels between Raina's situation and Gisela's cold case, which made my stomach churn even more.

At one point, when I heard that a prenatal yoga class was getting out, I decided to take a stroll outside in an attempt to overhear any conversations. That was when I ran smack into my nemesis, Paige Dotson. We had a long and troubled history. She'd bullied me back in high school, and she was pregnant with my dead barista's baby.

She was strolling out of the yoga studio, looking glowy, fresh, and pregnant.

"Hey," I said brightly.

Her blissful expression soured. "Hi."

"Want to come over for a tea?" I pasted on a smile. We'd reached a truce after her baby daddy's death, and I was choosing to overlook that she'd even accused me of the crime at one point.

"I'm a little busy." She swept past me, and I hurried to catch up with her.

"I wanted to ask you a question."

"I don't know anything about Raina. Why don't you stop snooping and let the police do their job? Honestly. Journalists are so annoying with their *anything to get a story* mentality."

She huffed off, and I stood on the sidewalk with my hands on my hips. So much for making peace with Paige.

For the rest of the day, substitutes taught all the classes at Dante's Inferno, and whenever I pumped students for information, they either gave little detail or speculated wildly.

"I heard she's in LA, signing a reality-show deal with Fox," a woman told another sweat-drenched student while waiting for her latte.

"No, she's in Chicago for Oprah," the other student corrected.

"That is hella cool," the first student said.

But none of it was true, and the theories made little sense—especially since Kai claimed Raina had taken her bike, phone, and ID when she left. I ran every rumor by Noah when he came early for his daily dose of hot lemon water (yuck) and three truffles, and he shot them all down.

"Can't tell you much else, cupcake." He winked at me, and I let out a strangled groan. Getting info out of him was like pulling an alligator's tooth without a sedative. I was at my wits' end with the story, because there was no story.

And I had the café to contend with. The morning rush roared in like a lion. Once again we were packed, with folks clamoring to try our coffee because of the barista championship win.

It was almost too busy for Erica and me to handle, and between selling out of mint chocolate truffles and mopping up a spilled container of milk, I vowed to hire another employee as soon as possible. But I also had a newspaper article to do. When would I have time to look at applications and write a story, much less conduct job interviews?

The day smoothed out like a Parisian café au lait, with Erica pulling shots and making the drink of the week: a floral latte, made from cold brew, a splash of milk, a hint of lemon, cane sugar, and sweet orange. The best part of the concoction was the ice cubes. I'd spotted a pack of edible pansies at the grocery store and frozen the flowers. Customers went wild when they saw the delicate blooms inside the ice.

Since the floral latte was selling so well, I needed to make more ice cubes for the next day. But a half hour before Dad and Barbara were scheduled to take over at noon, chaos hit.

Bernadette, the police dispatcher, approached, with Max the cockatoo on her shoulder. I stifled a sigh, because she knew she wasn't supposed to bring him in here. She set a half-empty cup of our cold brew on the counter.

The bird let out a wolf whistle.

Bernadette's turned-down mouth and the lines between her eyebrows told me she was on the verge of a rant.

"Hey guys," I said mildly. "What's up?"

"This is terrible. Something's off, and I'm not going to drink it because I'm afraid I'll be poisoned."

Poisoned? Dramatic much? She hadn't figured this out before drinking most of it? "No problem. Can I get you a new glass, or a refund?"

"I'd like another, please. Cold brew. Black. No sugar, no cream."

"Another black cold brew, coming right up."

Max cursed me in a loud baritone, and several customers looked over. Oh, dear. This wasn't good for business at all.

Eager to make Bernadette happy—she knew the entire town and would probably tell everyone if I didn't right this wrong—I dumped the dregs, set the dirty glass in the sink, and poured her a fresh drink in a clean one. I handed it to her and she lifted the glass to her mouth.

She took a big swallow and grimaced. "No. It tastes the same. Yuck. I thought this was an award-winning café. I wouldn't serve this to my dog. If I had a dog."

"Dogs suck," Max chirped.

I frowned. Sometimes this happened, with people's taste buds being off. Nobody used the words *yuck* and *cold brew* in the same sentence around me. "I'm sorry. Sometimes the taste doesn't work for some people." I pointed to the tray of chocolate mint truffles. "Why don't I refund your money? You can also take a free treat if you'd like."

"Yes, please. And no thank you. I'm trying to stay away from sugar. Prediabetes."

I handed over bills from the register and shrugged it off. Thankfully, Max didn't swear while they were walking out.

I wrote a note to myself and stuffed it in the pocket of my apron: *Ask Barbara to create a No Pets sign.*

But a half hour later, two more customers approached, each with a bad glass of cold brew. Each customer was nastier than the last.

"This is awful. I paid five bucks for garbage water?" one guy fumed.

After the third refund, I passed Erica on my way to inspecting the cold brew stash in the cooler. In the corner, Dad and Barbara speculated in low tones about Raina, proposing that she'd either fled overseas or gotten a modeling contract in New York. The two of them had pretty fantastical imaginations, if you asked me.

"No more cold brew sales today until we figure out what's going on," I shouted as I swept past.

I went to the bucket and poured myself a glass. I'd made it last night after doing payroll. As I took a sip, I mentally ran through my recipe.

But when the liquid hit my mouth, I nearly spat it back out. Gah. It was terrible. The worst. It was like dishwater, as if I'd laced the concoction with cheap, fragrant soap. It should taste smooth and bright, with naturally sweet notes.

I dumped the pitcher down the drain, then moved deeper in the cooler, where I'd stored an extra bucket of the brew. Because of the recent surge in customers, I'd brewed two.

Putting the glass under the spout, I pressed down and poured about an ounce. I sniffed into the cup as if I were tasting wine. It smelled like it should, rich and full-bodied. I sipped, swallowed, and stuck out my tongue.

Ick. This tasted terribly too. Had I somehow not rinsed the buckets well after washing them? I popped the top and took a whiff. I detected nothing but the aroma of coffee. Drat. I'd have to part with this batch and start again. Hoisting the bucket by the handle, I hauled it to the sink and dumped the contents.

I stacked the two empty buckets and their lids and walked out.

"Wow, did we sell out of cold brew that fast?" Dad asked. "Good for you, Lana."

"No. Bad batch. Something happened." I told him about the refunds.

He stroked his beard. "Could be the beans. Or your brewing method. Did you change the roast?"

All possibilities I didn't want to consider. I'd spent a fortune on those beans from the artisan roaster in Miami. These were optimal for cold brew, and until today, I'd had a lot of success with them. Could I get a refund? I'd never asked the supplier for one before. "No. They're the same beans I've ordered all summer."

"Sometimes beans can vary, depending on which roasting batch you receive," Erica suggested.

I grunted. "I know. That's what worries me. Listen, I need to check in on Stanley. I'm taking the two plastic buckets home to scrub them good, then let them dry in the sun on the porch. I'll be back to make another test batch. Then I've got some reporting to do for the article."

Erica, Dad, and Barbara stopped what they were doing and stared at me.

"What? I'm going to write the article about Raina. Or try to. So far I've turned up nothing and everyone's clammed up."

Dad had the decency to not break out in a grin and do a little dance, but just barely. "That's the spirit, Lana." He squeezed my shoulder.

I bid them good-bye and hauled the buckets two blocks down the street. When I neared my house, a car pulled up alongside me.

It was Noah, in his cruiser. "Hey you. Where are you going? Fishing?"

I giggled and glanced down. It looked like I was carrying bait. I approached his window. "No, these are empty. I had a cold brew issue this morning, and I need to make sure these are extra clean. I wanted to spray them down at home with some organic cleaner. How're things with you?"

He shrugged. "Not bad. Raina's still not back."

The gravity of his statement hung in the humid air. "So I've heard. Hey, about that. I think I am going to do that article finally. It's too unusual that she hasn't returned."

He stroked his chin. "Figured you would."

"Would you want to give me an exclusive interview?"

He turned to look out the window, as if he were pondering something. His hand was slung over the top of the steering wheel. "I think I'd rather give you an official statement."

"That works. Any reason why you're declining an interview?"

He shifted back to me. "Oh, I don't know, Lana. Probably because that's a little unethical? Asking you over for dinner and then giving you inside information."

His words felt like a light slap in the face. Somehow I'd mingled the personal and professional in record time with him, although we hadn't gone out on a date. Yet.

"Oh. Of course. Yes. You're totally right." A ball of shame pulsed in my chest. The old me would've never blurred lines like that. But in my defense, I wasn't exactly a journalist now. Not really. Didn't make me feel any better.

"Let me know when you want the statement. I don't have a lot to say, though."

I shifted in my sneakers awkwardly. "Sure. I'll text you."

"Sounds good. Hey, you still want me to go with you to Stanley's K-9 class this week?"

A smile spread across my face out of sheer relief. My lapse in judgment hadn't bothered him that much. "Yes, I'd love that. I also like how you call it something so official. A K-9 class. It's puppy kindergarten for tiny dogs."

"That's the name? Puppy kindergarten for tiny dogs?"

"Yep."

He chuckled, hard. Then he waved, rolled up the window, and drove away.

As I was about to let myself into the house—with Stanley barking like crazy on the other side of the door—my phone buzzed.

74

"Crap." I tried to juggle the buckets, the keys, and my purse. I set the buckets down and pulled the cell out of my purse. It was Mike from the paper.

"So. About that story," he barked. "How's it coming along?"

I thought about Shawn Sims's Instagram, packed with smiling photos of him and Raina. It was early afternoon, and I had all night to scrub the buckets and make the cold brew. There was plenty of time to visit Shawn's Jet Ski business along the marina.

"I have some leads. As soon as I drop something off at home and check on Stanley, I'm heading out for an interview, in fact."

*　　*　　*

It hadn't been difficult to find out where Shawn Sims worked. It was in the bio on his social media accounts. That was one thing he shared with Raina: an innate sense of shameless self-promotion, a quality I wished I had more of, at least when it came to Perkatory.

Shawn owned one of the island's many water sports rental places. I'd heard of his company, probably because of the slightly quirky name and the fact that his glossy flyers practically carpeted the island. I'd seen them everywhere, from racks at the grocery store to the bulletin board at Perkatory.

MAKIN' WAVES, they read. *Make waves during your tropical vacation!*

The rental counter was at the marina where Erica lived on her sailboat, and I briefly thought about stopping by. But I was on a reporting trip, and this was work, not a social call. I drove by the Makin' Waves booth to scope it out. It was actually a thatch-roof tiki hut over a roughhewn wooden counter. It sat on the sidewalk near the marina entrance.

There were several similar little businesses under tiki huts here. Dolphin tours, kayak rentals, sunset party boat cruises. There was even a faux pirate ship that locals called "the booty booze cruise" because the vessel sported an oversized treasure chest on its prow. It was an attraction so popular that people were lined up to buy tickets in the sweltering Florida sun.

I had to park nearly a block away, probably because of all the tourists swarming the area. As I walked, I worked up a good sweat, winding my way through the line for the pirate boat to get to the Makin' Waves booth.

I slowed my gait to study Shawn from afar as I approached. He had a shock of thick blond hair and wore his white T-shirt tight. It stretched over his muscles. I made a mental note: conventionally attractive guy, probably in his late thirties. He appeared to be studying his cell.

There were no customers lined up for his rentals, which wasn't surprising. Who in their right minds would want to be out in the harsh daytime sun? Or perhaps tourists preferred booze cruises. I knew I did. As I approached, he peered up and set his phone aside.

"Hey there! What can I do you for?"

I was instantly annoyed. I loathed it when people said that. I slapped on my best reporter smile. "You're Shawn, right?"

"That's what they call me." He grinned and looked me up and down. "I'm gonna tell you up front, we have no Jet Skis for a few hours. They're all sold out. Folks can't get enough of the water today."

"I can imagine."

"Not as busy as the booze cruise, though." He pointed down the block and made a snorting noise.

Since I'd forgotten my sunglasses, I shielded my face with my hand and stepped closer to the counter, which was painted a jaunty coral color. "Actually, I'm not here to rent a Jet Ski. I'm Lana Lewis, reporter for the *Devil's Beach Beacon*."

His expression changed so suddenly that it was almost shocking. He transformed from warm and friendly to wary and on guard within a millisecond. I'd seen this kind of thing before and pressed my lips together in what I hoped was a professional yet sympathetic smile.

"What do you want?" he asked.

"I'm doing a story on Raina Rose."

He chewed on his cheek. Oh dear. I wanted to nail this interview, and this felt like a terrible beginning.

"She's been missing since Saturday, and I understand you were a friend." I stared straight into his hazel eyes.

"How'd you connect me with her?"

"I was looking at her studio's Instagram, and you were tagged in a photo. Figured I'd start by asking you questions because I'd heard of your business." Not entirely a lie, and I knew enough not to begin our conversation by accusing him of stalking.

A breath leaked out of him, as if he was resigned to my presence and I were an annoying yet persistent barnacle on the side of a boat. Alarm bells clanged in my head at his erratic expressions. Then again, I'd interviewed people who displayed worse behavior—much worse. Like the guy who threw a traffic cone at me in Miami. At least Shawn wasn't being openly hostile or violent. Small victories.

"Mind if I ask you some questions for the article?"

He straightened a stack of brochures and set them aside. "Guess not. What do you want to know?"

"Have you heard that she's missing?"

"Found out the other day. One of the other students on the Costa Rica retreat texted me." His tone was brittle.

"Weird, isn't it? I also work at Perkatory, next door."

He looked at me funny. "That's where I know you from. Thought you looked familiar. Do you recognize me?"

I shook my head. "Sorry. I meet a ton of people, though."

"So you have two jobs? Journalism must not pay much." He made a *tsk-tsk* noise with his tongue.

No kidding, dude.

"Actually, I own Perkatory. Journalism is . . ." I nearly replied *in my blood*, but I thought that might be a tad dramatic. "It's what I used to do in my former career. Previously I worked at the *Miami Tribune*. The editor at the paper here on Devil's Beach asked me to help with this story."

"I see." Pause.

"How long have you known Raina?"

"I met her when I came to Devil's Beach, about six months ago." He got a faraway look in his eye. "To say that day was life changing would be an understatement."

"Oh, really?" I stepped closer. Now we were getting somewhere.

"Raina's so . . ." He waved his hand in the air, and his voice faded away. The corners of his mouth turned up.

"So . . . ?" I prodded.

"She's ethereal. Physically beautiful and beautiful inside." He tapped his chest. "She's a rare being. A true visionary."

I arched an eyebrow. I'd talked to Raina many times, and while she was conventionally attractive, I'd never have guessed anyone would gush over her like this. To me, *visionary* was meant for Stevie Nicks, Christiane Amanpour, and Kaldi, a ninth-century Ethiopian goat herder who discovered coffee when he noticed how amped-up his goats became after eating the beans.

"A visionary. Wow. In what way?"

He regarded me as if I'd just asked a stupid question. "Not long after I started practicing at her studio, I took one of her workshops. It was all about goals and visions. She had us write down our goals, and one by one, she sat with each of us, asked us questions. With me, we drew up an action plan on how I could build a life that I wanted, not just a life others wanted for me."

My eyebrows sank into a scowl. I had no idea what any of that meant. "Okay . . ."

"By talking with me, spending time asking the right questions, she helped me sort through the noise and focus on the important things. She's great at figuring out what needs to be done, what's important. Because of her, I realized I was spending too little time on creating a brand. I was focused too much on here"—he tapped his temple—"rather than here." He put his hand over his heart. "And voilà, the more I spent on the aesthetic of Makin' Waves, the better my business has done financially. People are walking up, wanting an epic experience, not just a way to pass the time on vacation. Raina helped me see that I needed to sell the *experience*. She took the time and gave me her undivided attention. She's inspiring like that—you should get her to help you with your café. Maybe you could quit that second job of yours."

He winked. I wasn't sure I liked the idea of being all touchy-feely with the family business. "I'll think about it." I twirled the pen around my fingers. "Anyway, how often do you practice at her studio?"

"Nearly every day that she teaches. I love the way she leads the class through the exercises. She also infuses her teaching with philosophy. It's like a cleansing. Every. Single. Class. Hard to explain unless you've gone to one. Have you been?"

I shook my head, tamping down my revulsion. I was sweating just standing here.

"Well, they're very intense. Very sensual. Very few clothes. It's vulnerable and strong at the same time." He tapped his chest with his fist. "You should check it out sometime. When she's back to teaching, of course. The subs aren't very good."

It took everything I had not to roll my eyes. He was talking a little like my dad now, with all the New Age woo. "So you felt a connection with her?"

"Did I ever," he said excitedly. "We email and talk all the time about spirituality, books and things like that. Meaningful stuff, not superficial conversations like most people."

"How was the retreat?"

He closed his eyes and shook his head. "Incredible. The best two weeks of my life."

"Whoa. So it must have been a surprise for you to hear about her disappearance."

He screwed up his face. "It was."

"Where do you think she went?"

He again straightened a stack of brochures, stuck them on top of another stack, then moved the entire thing to the other end of the counter. "I don't think she went anywhere."

I tilted my head. "What do you mean by that?"

"Something happened to her. And I think her boyfriend"—he used air quotes around the word *boyfriend*—"is responsible. At least he's one suspect."

I swallowed hard. "Kai? Responsible for . . . ?"

"Her disappearance. And yes, I'm accusing him of something nefarious, because I'm angry. As you can tell." He clenched his right hand into a fist.

Cold Brew Corpse

I scribbled this down in my notebook. "I'm not sure we can use that in an article. I think that might be libelous."

"Of course you can't use it. But I'm telling you. Look into it. Kai resents her success. He's tried to hold her back for months now. He either did something or intimidated her into leaving."

"Hold her back how?" The phone in my pocket buzzed. I ignored it.

"Raina's a star. Kai's a rich kid with a connected daddy. He doesn't know how to run a business. Raina's going places. She's gotten sponsorships with clothing companies and festivals. The only thing holding her back is Kai." He held his thumb and finger up, an inch apart. "She's this close to being the next big breakout star of the yoga world."

"So he'd make her disappear so she couldn't succeed?" I squinted at him. "Are you accusing him of murder?"

Despite the heat, a chill hit my spine, as if someone had run an icicle down my back.

"Anything's possible. I prefer to think she might have gotten fed up. Because the alternative . . ." His voice faded, and he visibly shivered.

"Have you gone to the police with that theory?"

The muscles in his jaw ticked. "I called them this morning, and the dispatcher took a message. Said someone would call me back. Haven't talked with anyone yet, though."

"Hm." I jotted a few notes, then looked up, feeling emboldened. "You know, there are a few people around the island who thought you were a little too close to Raina. That you were even, how do I say it, stalker-ish."

He leaned over the counter with a furious look in his eye. "That's all coming from Kai, that little snake. He's got his head

81

up his butt." Shawn straightened, regained his composure, and huffed out a laugh. "Well, not really. Kai's not that flexible."

Yikes. *Yoga trash talk!*

My phone buzzed again. "Excuse me." I pointed at it. "I need to get this."

"No problem." He smiled. It was odd how his anger had flashed white hot, then vanished like a summer lightning bolt.

It was Dad. I considered not answering, but I worried that something had gone wrong at the coffee shop. Or that there was an issue with Stanley. "Hey, I'm in the middle of an interview. What's up?"

"Kai's giving a news conference about Raina at the yoga studio in fifteen minutes! The TV cameras are already rolling up with their live trucks." Dad's voice was breathless with excitement. "Want me to go check it out? I'll take notes!"

"No. I'll be right there," I barked, then hung up.

I eyed Shawn and debated whether I should tell him about the news conference. Nah. Probably for the best if I didn't.

"Hey, I need to run. Can I grab your number in case I have more questions?"

"Sure. Take one of these. My cell's on the back. I'll give you a discount if you ever want a Jet Ski too." He handed me a glossy folded brochure with laughing people jumping waves and soaring over blue water, looking like extras from *Baywatch*.

"Thanks." I was about to walk away when he opened his mouth.

"I haven't slept a wink since she went missing." His voice dripped with sadness, and for a moment my chest squeezed. "I hope they find her soon."

The weight of his words hit me. I'd been so caught up in the excitement of doing the interview that I'd pushed my emotions deep inside.

"So do I," I replied, suddenly somber.

Maybe this news conference would reveal the truth.

Chapter Eight

O n my way to Dante's Inferno, I called Mike at the paper to
tell him about the latest developments.

"Had an interesting interview with a guy who was at the Costa
Rica retreat. And, there's a news conference happening soon.
Raina's boyfriend is holding it at the studio, and I'm driving there
now." I slowed my car to a stop to allow a group of twentysome-
things to saunter across the road to the beach in their bathing
suits. Two of them stopped in the middle of the crosswalk to kiss.

I refrained from screaming at them to pick up the pace.

"Do you think she's turned up?"

My heart started thumping wildly. "I dunno. It's possible. I
sure hope so."

"Lana, that's amazing! I'll send our new photographer over.
Are you in a position to file a story afterward?"

A little surge of happiness flowed through me as the pedestri-
ans cleared and I sped away. I felt alive, back in action. All earlier
sadness about Raina and Gisela had evaporated, and I was running purely on news adrenaline.

Goodness, how I missed this.

"Absolutely. I'll write the story from Perkatory and email you."

"Excellent. Talk later, kiddo."

I parked in my usual spot in the alley with five minutes to spare, then dashed around to the front of the building. Dad was working the counter and I spotted him through the window, slowing for a second to rap on the glass with my knuckles.

He looked up from where he was clearing the table and gave me a thumbs-up. I jogged the few steps to the yoga studio and swung open the door, sweat dampening the back of my neck.

The scent of lavender, rubber mats, and body odor greeted me. My eyes went to a stark-white wall painted with giant red letters. It took a split second for the words to register.

Mystic Fire Is Within You

Hoo boy. What did that even mean? It was like word salad. Again with the fire references. If there was one thing that irked me, it was vague, meaningless doublespeak.

A woman with a severe brunet ponytail sat behind a sleek, ashwood desk. She was scowling at a laptop and didn't immediately acknowledge me.

"Hey there." I gave a brief wave as I approached.

She glanced up, and the stern expression remained. "You must be here for the press conference."

"How did you guess?"

She pointed at the notebook in my hand, then gestured toward a hallway. "It's in the Second Terrace space."

"Second Terrace. As in Dante's Inferno? Purgatory? Envy?" Gee, Raina had taken this metaphor pretty far.

"Precisely." The woman turned back to the laptop.

I wandered down the hall, marveling at how Raina had transformed the space. This had been a barbecue restaurant called the Rib Room when I was in high school. My parents had rented it to some guy from Georgia, who was a superb cook and an even better drug dealer. Last I knew, he was serving eight to ten in a North Florida prison for trafficking hashish.

I poked my head into an open door. Three television cameras were already set up, pointed to a makeshift lectern. Several reporters were here, all from the local stations on the mainland, probably Fort Myers and Sarasota. A still photographer stood front and center of the scrum. He was rakishly good-looking in that slightly rumpled way photographers tended to be. He wore a white button-down shirt, dark wash jeans, and an intense stare—he was gazing at the back of his camera as if it held the meaning of the universe.

Was he with the *Devil's Beach Beacon*? I'd forgotten to ask Mike the photographer's name. After several months away from a newsroom, I was out of practice.

I was about to introduce myself to him when four people, all in stretchy yoga clothes, filtered into the room. I recognized one of them as Kai and scurried to an empty chair next to a young TV reporter in a tight, bright-yellow dress. She was a honey blond, and pretty, and for the millionth time I thanked my lucky stars that I hadn't become a television journalist. I could never juggle looking put together *and* reporting and writing. I looked down. Already my T-shirt had an ink stain on the hem. How had that gotten there?

Kai stood at the lectern and surveyed the media with a wary gaze, one I'd seen dozens of times in my career. The women clustered behind him with bloodshot eyes, clutching tissues.

He cleared his throat, then caught my gaze for a moment. A confused expression crossed his face. He only knew me from the café and didn't realize I'd once been a journalist. We had shared no in-depth conversations beyond discussing various tea blends at Perkatory. He didn't know I was working in a freelance capacity for the local paper. Oh well, I'd tell him afterward.

"I'm Kai Lahtinen, and I'm the co-owner of Dante's Inferno." He glanced over one shoulder, then the other. "These are some of our students. Some of our beautiful, loyal students who have been such a support system for me these past forty-eight hours."

He raked in a breath and swept a hand over his bald head. "I've called this press conference not because I have any actual news, but because I need to ask you all a favor. I wanted to read a statement, and I'm hoping you broadcast it to the world. You're my only hope at this point."

A woman behind him, a tiny thing with a petite frame and a blond pixie cut who was probably in her forties, started to cry. I inched to the edge of my folding chair.

Kai rubbed his head again and unfolded a paper. "Dear Raina. If you can hear this message, please get back here. I miss you and need you. *We* miss you and need you. Devil's Beach isn't the same without you, and we need your sunshine in our lives. You're our sunshine girl. Please come on home."

He cleared his throat and looked at the back wall. It was easy to see that Kai had been raised by a politician; his voice was steady and firm, and when he punctuated the end of a sentence, he made a fist and rested his thumb on top. Called "the Clinton thumb" after President Bill Clinton, it was a way to appear less aggressive without pointing or shaking a fist.

I knew these things because I'd once written an article on politicians' body language. It was an interesting choice on Kai's part, or perhaps a learned gesture from his father.

All of the women next to him sniffled and wiped tears from their dewy, makeup-free faces. Kai produced a pack of tissues from his pocket and passed them around. I scribbled away, trying to figure out why everyone was getting so emotional so quickly.

He continued, and I could easily imagine him at the age of fifty, running for some statewide office. "If it was something I did, I'm sorry. Please come back. And if someone has Raina, if someone's kidnapped her or harmed her, this is a warning to them. We will find you and bring you to justice. I promise you that. We may seem like peace lovers, but I guarantee we will not be kind if we discover that you have our precious Raina. It's been forty-eight hours since she was last seen, and we are begging you, the media, to broadcast and print our message. Raina, we love you. Please come home."

He paused. "I'll take questions, I guess."

There was a hush over the assembled press. Back in Miami, the TV reporters were so aggressive that I'd rarely gotten in a word during news conferences. Here, that didn't seem to be a problem.

I raised my hand, thinking it better to be polite, especially since he was my neighbor. He pointed in my direction.

"I know you and Raina recently returned from a retreat in Costa Rica. Can you tell us about that trip, including how many people were there with you?"

His face fell into a confused scowl. "Lana? Don't you run Perkatory next door?"

"I'm working for the local paper also."

He mustered a weak smile and gripped the lectern, which made the muscles in his arms flex and ripple. "Okay. Uh, what was the question?"

I repeated myself.

"Right, right, the retreat. Every year Raina goes to Costa Rica and brings a group of students. She started that even before she came to Devil's Beach. It's an amazing two-week trip, with hiking and surfing and, of course, yoga and meditation. It's her signature event, and it's outstanding."

Jeez, could Kai use more superlatives in his sentences? "Who all was there?" I probed.

"Well, let's see. This was my first year. We've only been together for six months." He pressed his fingers against his breastbone, then put his hand on the arm of the woman from the front desk. "Jennis was there."

She smiled, but it didn't reach her eyes, which were flinty and appraising. I had to admit that she was exceptionally fit looking in her tight blue unitard, with that high, raven-hued ponytail and those sharp cheekbones. I briefly mulled how she handled going to the bathroom in that outfit. She also had matching blue toenails and fingernails. An impressive and coordinated fashion sense. I glanced down at my worn black Converse All Stars.

He turned and looked at the redhead and the woman with the pixie cut. "Molly, she was there. And Heidi. Oh, plus two other women from out of state who knew Raina from years ago. They don't practice here on Devil's Beach. It was a small group."

I arched my eyebrow. What about Shawn? Had Kai conveniently forgotten to mention him? "Those were the only people on the trip?"

Jennis elbowed his arm, and his lips thinned. "There was one other student on the retreat, a local guy. He's not here today."

I scribbled some notes. It was difficult not to think about what Noah had told me the other day, about their fight. "Can you tell us about the last time you saw her, Kai? Was everything okay between the two of you?"

"It was at our house on Saturday morning, and we'd, well. Gosh. How do I say this?" He clutched the lectern and looked down, gulping in a breath. "I might as well tell you. I've got nothing to hide. Raina and I argued."

"About what?" The eyes of the TV reporters swung to me, then back to Kai. The women behind him were all sniffling, although a couple glared at me through their tears. I wasn't intimidated, though. People needed to know these details. Besides, Kai was the one who'd called the press conference.

"Stupid stuff. The business. Raina was taking on too much, and I felt that she should give herself a break. Focus on teaching classes instead of building her brand. She was obsessed with getting her name out there and increasing her reach on social media."

I hesitated, wondering how much I should pry. Aw, heck. This could be my only chance to talk with him.

"Did she say that she wanted to leave you?"

Kai looked over my head, toward the back wall. His eyes brimmed with tears, and he blinked. "That's all for the questions." He slipped his cell out of his front pocket, then stalked out of the room. The three women circling him stared in my direction with shocked expressions, as if I were personally responsible for Raina's disappearance.

Guess I'd blown my shot. Great.

The woman with the severe ponytail stepped into his place and gestured toward the door. "Thank you all for coming. We've got a class in this room in an hour, so you must clear out right away." I leaped from my seat, eager to get the names of the women standing behind Kai. Something told me they knew more about Raina.

"Excuse me," I piped up. The trio glanced at me, then kept moving toward the door. Ugh, I'd messed up bad. I should've been more folksy and less Miami.

"Ladies, may I ask you a question?" My head turned toward the deep, masculine tone. It was the photographer, camera in hand. The women stopped in their tracks and swiveled, almost in formation, at the sound of his voice.

"I'm with the *Devil's Beach Beacon*. Can I get your names, please? Spelling, too. And your titles or what you do for a living. We like to have all that for the paper. Y'all were extremely photogenic." He smiled, and the trio of students made a beeline toward him. Oh, brother. Everyone thought women reporters flirted for information. Newsflash: men did it too, and I was witnessing a prime example.

Still, I breathed a sigh of relief, because it meant I didn't need to chase everyone down individually. Maybe these women would all sit for an interview later, if I brought Hottie McPhotoGuy with me.

The raven-haired receptionist went first, and I noticed a smattering of freckles on her nose. "I'm Jennis Hudson. Yoga instructor, with a specialist in Ashtanga. I'm twenty-five, I live here on the island, and this is my full time-job, managing the studio. I'm a Devil's Beach native."

She spelled her name with crisp precision. Odd; I was from here too, but didn't recognize her. She was five years younger than me—that was probably why.

"Where do you think Raina is?" I piped up.

Jennis turned her gaze on me. It was a thousand-yard stare, and it felt like she was looking right through me. "If I knew, I wouldn't be here. No ifs, buts, or coconuts about it. I don't know anything."

She quickly stepped aside, and the redhead woman took her place. She was tall and reedy, with a heart-shaped face, green eyes, and pink lips. Everyone who practiced at this studio was obviously a former supermodel or something. Between the yoginis and the TV reporters, I felt like a short, chubby troll.

"I'm Molly Wayne. I'm a student here." She spelled her name. "I'm twenty-eight and a server at Bay-Bays. Was just hired. You know, the restaurant across the street?"

I scribbled furiously. Bay-Bays was a popular place, one of my favorites. She and the photographer smiled at each other, and then she pulled the third woman close.

In a wispy voice, the woman with the pixie cut stammered, "I'm Heidi Torrance. Let's see. I'm forty-three, married, and also a student. I'm an empty nester as of this year, and I'm new here to Devil's Beach, been here two years. Um, I considered Raina a dear friend. One of my best friends."

Everyone in the media paused, and the TV reporters waved wildly at their cameramen to keep rolling.

"What else can you tell us about her?" one of the TV reporters asked, her voice dripping with fake empathy as she shoved a microphone closer to Heidi's face. I hung back, watching the entire scene.

"She was so wonderful. A jewel of a person. She's helped me through a lot of difficult emotional things lately, and I can't imagine why she'd up and leave." Heidi wrung her delicate hands. "I've never met a more spiritually brilliant teacher."

More gushing adjectives. Why had I not picked up on all that greatness when I chatted with Raina? I scrawled furiously, flipping a page.

Heidi dissolved into racking sobs, and the redhead slid her arm around her thin shoulders and ushered her to the door. Jennis folded her arms and glared at us.

"We're leaving in five minutes, Jen," the photographer called out, lifting his camera and strap over his head.

"It's Jennis," she snapped, then stalked out of the room.

Yikes. I threw my notebook in my bag and was about to introduce myself to the photographer, but Molly the redhead was back and had cornered him. He said something I couldn't hear, and she laughed. It was a high-pitched, breathy sound. I studied them from afar, watching as he showed her the display on the back of his camera.

She laughed uproariously, sounding a bit like a dolphin. He held out his notebook for her. She scrawled with a pen and returned the pad to him.

Source building? Or a hookup? Who knew. Who cared? Molly turned and bounced out of the room, her long, curly red locks swaying from side to side. I approached.

"Hey there. I wanted to introduce myself."

He pushed hair off his forehead, and that's when I realized why all the women were gaga over him. He was actually quite cute, with a tan face, hazel eyes, and golden stubble on his jaw. Not Noah Garcia handsome but charming enough.

"You must be Lana."

"Did Mike tell you I'd be here?"

"He did. Asked me to look out for you. Said you'd have the wild, dark hair and matching intense eyes. He wasn't wrong."

I opened my mouth, wondering about a comeback to that. I didn't have one, so I scratched my forehead and plowed on. "Thanks for that question about the names. Good call. I was worried I'd have to scramble after them, since they ignored me."

"Anytime. Happy to help. So, you're kind of a legend in these parts. Award-winning *Miami Tribune* writer and all." He picked up a black bag at his feet.

"Pfft. I was laid off, like half the reporters in Florida. I'm helping Mike by doing this story. You walking out?"

"Sure am."

We were silent as we made our way through the dark corridor and waiting area. We waved to Jennis, but she was on the phone and ignored us. Outside, we squinted in the blinding sunshine and immediately began sweating in the oppressive humidity.

"I didn't catch your name." I pulled at the collar of my shirt, trying to get some air on my chest.

"Cody Graves. It's good to meet you. This is my first assignment with the paper. First week, actually."

"What happened to the other photographer?" It was only recently that I'd seen a lanky guy snapping photos around the island.

"Left to do public relations in Atlanta. He also got into a screaming match with Mike in the newsroom, according to what a sports writer told me this morning."

Ah, journalism. Always a revolving door of layoffs, firings, and dramatic exits. "Wow. Well, nothing like diving right into a tough story."

He smirked. "It's not that interesting, really. I was a freelancer over in Iraq. This is small potatoes."

"Oh!" My eyes widened, but inside I bristled at his smarminess. "How'd you end up here?"

"My grandparents retired here, and my grandpa died recently. I'm here to help my grandma. Came back about a month ago. Plus the freelance budgets have all dried up. So I figured I'd take a staff job here for a while and chill. You know, soak up some sun, get out in nature."

Empathy replaced my annoyance. "Don't blame you. I'm sorry about your grandpa. I mean, that's very sweet of you to be there for your grandmother. Welcome to Devil's Beach."

"Thanks. It's a bit of a culture shock, y'know?"

I didn't, but played along by nodding. "Listen, I own the café next door. Perkatory. Well, my family owns it."

"I know. Mike told me." He grinned, which turned his face from cute to devilish. Warning bells clanged in my head, but for the sake of camaraderie, I pressed on.

"Do you want to file your photos there? I can hook you up with the best cup of coffee you've ever had in your life."

He paused, then chuckled. "I'm sure it won't be better than the coffee I had in Turkey."

This guy was way too arrogant. Foreign correspondents often were, in my experience.

"Try me."

"Oh, I will." He licked his bottom lip, and I narrowed my eyes. I was sweaty, hungry, and on deadline. Flirting was the last thing on my mind, and I stifled a sigh.

Now I wished I hadn't invited him into the café. He obviously knew he'd overstepped, because he shifted back to his professional demeanor. "Hey, did you notice something strange back in the press conference?"

We walked down the block, toward the coffee shop.

"This is Devil's Beach, and I grew up here, so sometimes I don't pick up on the obviously strange. The bar is high for weird here."

"Did you catch what that Heidi woman said?" Cody held the door open for me.

"Thanks. I guess I didn't. I was in the zone, writing everything down."

"She referred to Raina in the past tense. She was so wonderful. *Was* wonderful. Doesn't that seem odd to you?"

I shrugged and hoisted my bag atop a vacant table. "Maybe. Maybe not. People say strange things when they're upset."

He pulled out a chair and set his bag on the seat, extracting an expensive-looking Apple computer. "I suppose. She seemed beside herself with grief. So, how's the cold brew here?"

Gah. I needed to make more after yesterday's debacle. I'd scrubbed the buckets and vats last night and wanted them to air-dry before making a fresh batch. "Normally delicious, but we're out today."

"Then I'll take a regular black coffee, hot. Nothing fancy. You sure you don't want money?"

"Of course not." I waved him off. "I'll grab our drinks."

Dad emerged from behind the counter. "What's the latest?" He rubbed his hands together. "Did she come home?"

"Unfortunately, no." I gave him a brief rundown, omitting Cody's theory on the older, sobbing woman's use of the past tense. I also didn't mention how Kai had walked abruptly out of the news conference.

"Yikes, sounds heavy." Dad winced, then glanced at Cody. "Who's that with you?"

"New photographer for the paper. We're going to file our stories and photos from here. Hey, can you grab us two black coffees?"

"Sure thing, munchkin. Oh, and don't forget. You need to resolve that issue with the cold brew tonight. Customers are disappointed that it's not on our menu. One woman left in a huff and mentioned Island Brewnette."

"Figures," I muttered. Island Brewnette was the other café in town. It was owned by my nemesis Paige Dotson's father Mickey, who was a grumpy jerk. I didn't have time to think about that right now. As I walked back to the table, my mind churned with details of the story, the press conference, the earlier interview with Shawn . . . and my Perkatory duties.

Cold Brew Corpse

Even though I missed journalism, there was no way I could neglect Perkatory. I'd worked too hard over these past few months to let it slip away. It had been my mother's coffee shop, and I had to make it succeed beyond her wildest dreams. That was part of the reason I'd come home after the layoff. Well, that and wanting to be near Dad.

I glanced at my watch. It was four in the afternoon, and I was already behind schedule.

Chapter Nine

"Well, that's done." Having sent the story to Mike, I snapped my laptop shut and stared at Cody. His thick hair was the color of coffee with two creams.

"Wanna see my pics?" He angled his computer so I could view the screen and scrolled through. Most of the pictures were medium-to-close shots of people at the podium. A few were of the students' reactions as Kai spoke, crisp and poignant images. He clearly knew how to take a decent photo.

"I like that one." I pointed at a close-up of Heidi brushing tears from her cheeks. "Lots of emotion in that picture."

"Thanks." Cody smiled.

"It was good working with you. Feels awesome to be part of a newsroom again. And you can hang out here as long as you'd like. I need to do some stuff around the café, though."

"I'm wrapping up here too." He stretched and his shirt rode up, revealing bronze skin covering six-pack abs. I averted my eyes, and he leaned in. "Wanna grab a beer sometime?"

I paused. On the one hand, it would be nice to have a drinking buddy at the local paper. On the other, I got the impression he was looking for more than a night of knocking back beers. Even if I'd been single, Cody was the kind of man I was trying to stay away from.

"Oh, I get it. You have a boyfriend," he said with a teasing smile, shutting his laptop and stuffing it into a bag.

"Sort of?" I wasn't sure. Noah and I were so close to . . . something.

"Doesn't sound very solid." He flipped to a blank page in his notebook and scribbled some digits, then ripped it off. "Here. Call me if you're sort of available."

With a smirk, he rose and gave me a one-finger wave good-bye. Yuck. I squinted as I watched him swagger out of the café. I'd seen his kind before—hotshot photographers who liked danger, hard liquor, and easy hookups. No thanks. I didn't need friends that badly. I had Stanley.

Cody was too cocky, sort of like my ex-husband. Younger me would have been intrigued. Older me was wary.

Plus, there was Noah. Lovely, kind Noah. Even thinking about him made my heart flutter. But I didn't have time for fantasizing about my future with him. I needed to get a move on.

After saying good-bye to Dad, I walked home and fed Stanley. Then I returned to Perkatory—it was closed by now—with the clean buckets and prepared to assemble a vat of cold brew for the next day.

The process was oddly meditative. First, I laid out all the components: the stainless steel container, the valve, the filter, a long, oversized spatula, and most importantly, the coffee beans. Using a gasket, I screwed the dispensing valve into the side of the vat, then attached a hose to the valve.

Then I had to grind ten pounds of beans. I used the Colombian blend that had been so popular, pouring scoop after scoop into our commercial grinder. Tonight I was following the recipe to a T, so much that I'd dug out the notes from my meeting with the roaster two months ago.

I inhaled deep, savoring the rich, earthy-chocolate-tinged scent. There was nothing in the world that smelled better than freshly ground beans.

I removed the lid and poured gallons of water into the stainless-steel vat. After that, I took out a contraption that looked like a metal pancake with holes. It was called a platform, and it was about the size of a manhole cover. I slipped a filter around it. It had the texture of the kind you'd see in a home coffeemaker but was similar to a large envelope. I settled the filter-covered disk into the vat.

As I was about to grab the bag of freshly ground coffee to pour it into the vat, my phone buzzed.

I groaned and reached for my cell, then brightened when I saw it was Noah.

Nice article

I grinned. **Thanks**

You at home?
No, I'm at Perkatory, making cold brew.
Mind if I come by?
Not at all. I'm here for a while.
See you soon.

Because I was a stickler for hygiene, I washed my hands again. Huh. Noah wasn't usually that curt in his texts. These past few days though, our communication had dwindled. Why did he want to see me so badly tonight? Perhaps he was dropping by to tell me something about Raina.

Had she turned up? Nah. If she had, Noah wouldn't be coming here. He'd be far too busy.

My arm muscles strained as I hoisted the bag of coffee and poured half of it into the vat. Maybe I should take some yoga classes. I could stand to put on a little muscle; all the women at Dante's Inferno had impressively sculpted arms.

I added more water to the vat, this time pouring in a circular motion, making sure I was wetting all the coffee grounds evenly.

Now came the fun part. "Bubble, bubble, toil and trouble," I whispered, taking the long spatula and dipping it into the vat so I could mix the moist grounds, which looked like mud. I plunged downward and gently pulled the grounds toward the middle until everything was well combined.

To ensure quality taste and adequate quantity, I added more water and more grounds, then reached for the spatula again. I'd just dipped it into the heavy, fragrant mix when there was a loud rapping sound against glass.

I looked up. Noah was on the other side of the front door, peering in. I set the spatula down and ran to undo the lock.

"Hey," I called out. "Sorry, I'm at a crucial moment in the brewing process. C'mon in."

I quickly washed my hands for a third time and went back to stirring the coffee. He walked over and peeked into the vat.

"This is how you make cold brew," I explained. "I have to mix it now, and again in thirty minutes, to allow any trapped gases to escape."

He nodded. "Then it'll be ready to drink?"

I laughed. "No. This is a long process. It needs to sit overnight so the coffee bean oils can mingle. This is why cold brew is a lot smoother. I'll come in tomorrow morning and drain this"—I patted the aluminum vat—"into that bucket." I pointed to the food-safe plastic containers that I'd scrubbed three times at my house. "Hopefully this will do the trick. The last batch tasted weird, and I'm troubleshooting."

"So that's why the cold brew costs a little more," he said. "It smells amazing."

"Indeed." I peered into the vat. Everything looked and smelled perfect, and I lifted the spatula from the container and set it in the sink. "There. I think it's good for now. How's it going with you? Anything new with Raina's case? Please tell me she's been found."

Nervous, I wiped my hands on a towel, then covered the vat with a wide, stainless-steel lid.

"About that." Noah leaned against the counter and folded his arms.

I clutched the towel in my fists. "What?"

"Interesting press conference, don't you think?"

"It was. I take it you saw the article."

"Saw it? Pfft." He snorted. "I was shocked. I'd specifically told Kai not to speak with the media. And what does he do? He calls a news conference. I got an alert on my phone from the *Devil's Beach Beacon* and then watched it on the six o'clock news out of Tampa."

I lifted a shoulder. "That's his right, no? You can't tell him not to talk."

Noah sighed. "Of course not. And yes, it is his prerogative. But considering we're officially calling this a missing-persons case,

I'd like to have a little more control over what information gets out to the public."

I chewed back a smile. "All cops are control freaks with information."

"I wouldn't call myself a control freak. Just being prudent."

I studied Noah's face. His full lips were set in a line, somewhere between smirk and scowl.

"Someone's annoyed."

"I wish I'd have known about it, that's all. Wish you would've told me, at the very least."

"Me?" I pointed to my chest and laughed. "Um, Noah? I'm a reporter. Okay. A freelancer, but Mike asked me to write the article. I was doing my job, and it's not a reporter's role to tell police what they should already know."

He rolled his eyes. "I know that."

"And yet you're annoyed." I paused, trying to diffuse the tension. "You want something to drink?"

He tugged at his hair. "I'm frustrated with the entire situation. There's a lot of pressure on me with this case because of Kai's father. Everything has to be done by the book. We're up for reaccreditation, and his father controls the purse strings in the legislature, so to speak. The FDLE is making noises about taking over the investigation entirely. Which I think is inappropriate, since we can handle a missing-persons report."

"Ah, so that's why."

"Yeah. Sorry. I didn't mean to be a jerk. You have any iced tea?"

"In fact, I do. Mind if it's raspberry flavored? It's not exactly fresh brewed, and I'm sorry about that."

"Works for me."

I filled a glass with ice and pulled open the fridge door. There was enough left over from the day for a single serving. I poured and handed it to Noah. He took a huge gulp. This was a bit of a triumph; in the three months I'd known him, I'd seen him drink only hot water with lemon and, once, a boozy coffee concoction.

"It's good, actually. I expected it to be sweeter."

"You want sugar? I have some simple syrup here." I reached for a squirt bottle.

"No, I like it like this. I'm not much of a sugar person, except for your baked goods. They're my weakness."

I stopped myself from rolling my eyes. Noah was one of a growing population on Devil's Beach: the exceedingly fit. I was not in that cohort.

"Do you mind if we talk while I make a second batch of cold brew?"

He shook his head and took another sip. I readied the next vat. Noah's brows were still furrowed, and the iced tea hadn't seemed to improve his mood.

"So, what's stressing you out here about this case? Are you worried Raina's in danger?"

"Off the record?" He stared at me warily, a reminder that cops and reporters had vastly different needs and goals. This would be a difficult relationship to navigate if I continued to do more journalism.

I smirked. "I guess. For now. The article's finished and published online. It'll be in tomorrow's newspaper as is, barring any last-minute developments."

"Unfortunately, there are zero developments, and that's the problem. To answer your question, yes. I'm stressed out about this case. This has the potential to blow up, which is the last thing I want. It'll be bad for the department, bad for the island. The mayor and city council are about to spend a ton on a nationwide tourism campaign."

I poured the water into the vat. "Why would it be bad for tourism? Because she's an attractive white woman and the national media can't resist falling all over themselves when someone like that is missing, while ignoring people of color in the same circumstances?"

He grimaced. "That sums it up, yeah."

I nodded slowly. He had a point. I'd covered enough big, national stories involving missing or murdered white women. Not that the reports weren't newsworthy, but I had noted that when I wrote about missing Black or Latina women in Miami, the networks and the New York papers didn't swoop in for the story.

"So you're worried about negative publicity for the island?" I poured one scoop of ground coffee into the vat, and he walked over and peered in.

"Interesting," he murmured into the container. "Yeah, I'm concerned about it all. I'm disturbed about Raina, mostly. From what I know, she's diligent and punctual, and she's very involved with her students. My gut tells me she wouldn't blow off her classes, several days in a row, telling no one. And I'm worried about the publicity it could cause if she remains missing, or if she turns up dead. I also don't want the FDLE to take this case away from my department. I have a competent team."

I wiped my hands on the towel as a surge of adrenaline shot through me. "You think she's dead?"

"No. I don't know. I have nothing to indicate that she is, and I really, really don't want to see my conjecture in the newspaper, Lana." His tone was stern.

"It's okay. I keep my off-the-record agreements. But surely you've handled cases like this before."

"Oh, sure. Absolutely. Bigger cases than this." He mentioned a few infamous crimes out of Tampa. "But that was when I was a detective. I wasn't chief. And now I'm trying to reform this department and get it accredited. And keep the people who hired me happy."

"I don't get why those things are mutually exclusive." I poured myself a glass of water, my mouth parched from our intense conversation.

"Usually they're not. But because of my history in Tampa, I need to be careful with the accreditation bureau."

I frowned, not following his logic. I knew he'd been an internal affairs investigator back in Tampa, and a K-9 officer.

He sighed. "Sorry. I'm not explaining myself. I was a bit of a hard-ass on corrupt cops in Tampa. I got several rotten apples disciplined, for good reason."

"Oh, so you earned a reputation for being an ethical cop. You're worried that the accreditation board might hold that against you?"

"Bingo."

"And you think any publicity about Raina's case could exacerbate that?"

"You got it."

He was definitely in a pickle, I had to admit. "Now I understand."

"I pray she comes back soon."

"I do too."

An insistent buzzing noise came from his belt. He set the glass down on the counter and unclipped his cell, holding it to his ear.

"Hey. Where? Okay. Is the scene secure?"

I stood straighter as little prickles ran down my arms. This seemed significant. Had she turned up?

"I'll be right there," he barked, then clipped the phone back to his belt. "Lana, I'm sorry. I need to go."

My brows shot up as he stepped close. Close enough to detect his spicy, intoxicating aftershave. We locked eyes. "News about Raina?"

He broke into a grin. "No, silly. It's a burglary at Alligator Allie's. Someone tried to get in and steal the baby gators. Or set them free. Not sure which. A couple of them got loose."

"Hmm," I muttered. "Those gators might be better off in the wild."

Alligator Allie's was one of the island's more questionable businesses. It rented out live baby alligators for birthday parties. People could pay fifty bucks and voilà! A baby alligator would paddle around your pool for an hour.

I thought it was cruel to the gators. But tourists who rented some of the single-family homes with pools on the island ate it up with a spoon.

"I've wondered what happens to the gators when they get bigger," he mused.

"You can probably find the answer in the belts they sell in the store."

He laughed, a rich, adorable sound. Finally, he seemed more relaxed than when he'd arrived. "What time is puppy kindergarten tomorrow night?"

"Seven. It's at One Lucky Pup, the dog bakery and groomer on the south side. They have a kennel and training space."

"I'll pick you two up around six thirty, okay?"

I grinned. "Perfect. See you then."

He kissed my cheek, and my knees nearly buckled.

" 'Bye," I whispered. He walked out, and I spent the next fifteen minutes tidying up, making sure everything was ready for the morning rush. As I was locking up, a figure coming from Dante's Inferno approached.

"Lana?" The voice was deep.

Instinct told me to shrink away, but then I realized who it was. Kai Lahtinen, Raina's boyfriend.

"Hey there." I used a soft, sympathetic voice.

"I was over at the studio, paying bills, when I saw you coming out. I wanted to say, great article today. You were super respectful. Thank you for that." He held his hands in front of him in a little prayer gesture.

"You're welcome. Any news about Raina?"

He shook his head mournfully.

Most people in my situation would have given him a hug, squeezed his shoulder, or offered words of condolence. But I was a journalist at heart, which was why I took a deep breath and asked him the only thing on my mind.

"Kai, how would you like to do an exclusive interview with me?"

Chapter Ten

Kai rubbed his bald head. Part of me figured that he might want to talk more after the brief news conference. Then again, I'd asked him that tough question earlier, and on top of that, opening up to a reporter went against every natural human instinct. I braced myself for a no—or worse.

"I dunno. I guess I could. Have nothing to lose at this point." He sighed heavily.

The muscles in my body relaxed. "We could go inside my place." I jerked my thumb over my shoulder, toward Perkatory.

His nose scrunched. "I don't really drink coffee."

Oh blergh, another one. It was a miracle Perkatory was even in business. "Tea? Water?"

"Tea would be good."

"Perfect."

We shuffled the few steps to the entrance. I unlocked the door and let him in, then locked it behind us. When I saw his expression of alarm, I smiled reassuringly.

"If people see lights on, they'll try to come in. I always lock up after hours."

"Right! Sorry. I'm so distraught, my reactions to things are all out of whack."

"Understandable. We have a lot of different teas." I rattled off our selection.

"Raina likes the chamomile, so I'll have that. Thanks." He settled in a chair at a table and laid his head on his folded arms. Tonight he wore a loose black tank top cut low on the sides, which exposed his muscles, and tight black workout shorts. He was also in flip-flops.

I made us two cups—I was well caffeinated by this point and doubted I'd be able to sleep anytime before midnight, which was three hours away—and brought the mugs to the table. "Sweetener?"

He shook his head. "I don't do sugar."

Oh dear.

I sat facing him and adopted a professional air. "So, I did that one article for the paper, on the news conference. I was thinking about doing a profile of Raina, which is why I wanted to talk with you."

Not that editor Mike knew I was doing another article. I had pitched nothing yet. But I wouldn't let an opportunity for a key interview pass me by.

Kai nodded. "That's fine, I guess."

"Do you mind if I record this on my phone and take notes?"

"Not at all."

"Great." I pulled the phone out of my purse and pressed the red dot, then took out my notebook and a pen. "Tell me about where you met Raina and how you two landed on Devil's Beach."

He launched into a story about how he'd started doing yoga in college and somehow sounded exactly like a small-town politician reciting the ins and outs of a wastewater treatment spill. That is to say, Kai made what should have been interesting, boring.

His tale was long, and detailed, and frankly, not all that engaging. He'd been teaching at a studio in Fort Lauderdale and had come to Devil's Beach for a yoga retreat. His tale was interspersed with revelations on what he ate (mostly raw vegan), the yoga he practiced (hot Ashtanga), and the varying levels of difficulty of the poses (muscle busting).

I was about to stifle a yawn as he took a sip, his long, tapered fingers gracefully lifting the cup to his mouth. "And then I walked down to the beach, and there was Raina, in *utthita trikonasana*."

I blinked.

"Triangle pose. And she did it perfectly. Like an exact expression of the pose. Her long blond hair was blowing around her face, and she looked so serene, so perfect. She was like a tropical goddess. I fell in love with her that very second."

"Well, that's quite a story." My muscles ached from hearing about all that activity, and I massaged my forearm. "Then you moved to Devil's Beach to be with her?"

"Yes. We were inseparable after that. We talked after class and connected. It was a magical bond, something that only two people share when they're in love."

"Mm-hmm." Finally, a good quote. I jotted it down in my notebook.

"We kept talking all that weekend, and one thing led to another; she asked me to teach at Dante's Inferno. I'd come into a bit of money from my grandfather's inheritance." Kai sniffed. "He was president of Sun Harvest Citrus, you know."

"I didn't." But I'd been in Florida long enough to be familiar with the name. Sun Harvest was one of the state's biggest orange growers. No wonder his father wielded power in Tallahassee.

"Yes. My family's legacy in the state goes back generations."

Mine did too, but my kin's claims to fame included smuggling rum from Cuba to Tampa during Prohibition, owning a roadside zoo with monkeys, and starting a kumquat farm. Dad was the only successful one of the bunch, and even he was eccentric. "Go on." I motioned to Kai with my pen.

"I invested in the studio because I liked the vibe here on Devil's Beach and because I believed in Raina. There's something really special about her." He stopped, as if lost in thought.

"I understand she's quite charismatic in class," I offered.

"That's exactly it. When she turns her attention on you, it's as if the warmth of a hundred suns is directed only on you. It's . . . it's captivating." He swallowed hard, as if overcome. Finally, a crack in his exterior. "Anyway. I moved here and helped her run the studio. Of course, we were lovers too."

I wasn't sure why, but that phrase—*we were lovers*—made me cringe. So cheesy. I nodded encouraging him to continue.

"Our relationship was perfect at first." He took a sip of tea. "We did yoga together, cooked together, spent hours kayaking and biking and jogging. I thought she was flawless. She was Claudine to my Honza."

I scowled. "Who?"

He waved his hand dismissively, and my eyes keyed on a blue, marble-veined ring on his right ring finger. "A famous yoga couple on Instagram."

He went on for a while about their favorite macrobiotic meals, and I felt myself zoning out. People's food habits did not make great copy.

"She has a wheat sensitivity. Not diagnosed by a doctor, but she's excellent at that. Listening to her body. Listening to others' bodies and souls, figuring out what they need."

"Sounds like you were a match made in heaven. Did she give you that ring? It's stunning." I pointed to his hand.

"We are perfect together," he cried, slapping his palm on the table, which made everything shake. A splash of tea erupted over the side of my cup, and I quickly wiped it with a napkin.

He fiddled with the ring and cleared his throat, seemingly annoyed that I'd interrupted his dissertation on Raina's eating philosophy. "Well, usually perfect. And no, I got this somewhere else. Anyway. Raina became more popular, and that's when things started going sideways. More requests for endorsements, more offers. Which is natural, because she's an incredible teacher. Like one in a million; she has that magic. And she's beautiful. That doesn't hurt. But I want us, well, the studio, to stay small and true to our roots. She wants to expand. She's looking to buy a piece of land here on the beach so we can hold retreats. She's relentless in pursuing her dream to make this the most popular yoga retreat in Florida."

I bit my cheek, wondering if this was a classic case of a man being threatened by a successful woman. "Okay. And?"

"And she's taken out loans."

"Loans? Plural?"

He sighed. "Multiple loans. I'd put my entire inheritance into the studio, so I was broke. After that, she took out even more loans from the bank and asked the wealthier students for help. I didn't mind her dealing with the bank, but I felt it unethical for her to take money from clients like that. It seemed as though it could open up some sticky situations. And sure enough, it did."

"What do you mean by that?" Finally, this was getting interesting. "How sticky?"

"Well, she recently accepted a healthy five-figure sum from a guy who had a massive crush on her."

"Tell me about him. If you can."

Kai's face grew red. "He's a student."

I arched an eyebrow. "By any chance, is it Shawn Sims?"

A strangled groan escaped his throat, and he threw his head back. "Does everyone know about him? What a jerk. That guy won't leave her alone. And she encourages his affection, if you catch my drift. So disrespectful." He whispered a swear word, and my eyebrows shot up.

"Please explain, if you feel comfortable."

"They're together a lot. During the retreat in Costa Rica, they'd go off hiking together. When I question why he's supporting her so much, or ask why she's spending all that time with him, she tells me I'm being jealous and that I need to purge that toxic emotion from my life. She says things like, 'If you love me, you'll support me in this,' and 'If Shawn doesn't give us money, we'll have to close the studio, and I'll be devastated. Do you want that?' That kind of thing."

"Hmm. Sounds complicated." And emotionally abusive, but I didn't say that aloud.

He grunted. "Raina's complex. She's an excellent yoga instructor. A so-so businesswoman. But she can be explosive."

"Oh dear."

"Yeah. She's fantastic at getting students, teachers, anyone in her orbit, to fall in love with her. And do her bidding."

I wondered if Kai was being a bit extreme. It was hard to tell because he was so upset. Erratic, even, in his tone and expression. My earlier sleepiness gave way to deep skepticism.

"What do you mean by that?"

He stared at me straight in the eye. "She flirts with her male students if she thinks they might benefit her financially. And she cozies up to the women, pretends to be their best friends, in case they'll help her. She's shameless."

I frowned. "Interesting."

When he snorted, he looked exactly like a horse. A bald one. "When she heard you were coming from Miami, she was all excited. Figured you could introduce her to some media people. Assumed you might have money. Then she found out you'd been laid off from your job, were broke, and had no interest in yoga. That's why she always was superficially friendly to you but kept you at arm's length. You couldn't do anything for her."

I reared back. That was what she'd thought of me? To think I'd wasted my cake pops on her. "Wow."

"Yeah. That's how she is."

"And yet you still adore her? You want to be with someone like that?" I couldn't understand his rationale.

Kai hung his head sheepishly. "Yeah. I love her despite it all. My dad thinks that she walks all over me. Thinks she's tried to separate me from my family."

"And yet he's worried enough to come here and pull strings to get the state agents involved."

Kai snorted. "Because of his image and reputation, that's why."

A clearheaded assessment if I'd ever heard one. "Why do you still love Raina, anyway?" This interview was quickly veering into therapy-by-reporter. I leaned in.

He gulped in two deep breaths and looked closer to crying than he had in the news conference earlier in the day.

"I guess I keep hoping that the Raina I met on the beach will come back. Those first months were idyllic. That sweet, kind, soulful person is in there somewhere, I can feel it, and I get glimpses of it when it's just the two of us."

"But?"

"But even when things are bad, I keep holding out hope. I know I should walk away, but I can't. I'm too in love." A miserable expression clouded his face, and for the first time, I had sympathy for him. I'd felt the same about my ex-husband—for years I'd hoped he'd return to the affable goofball I'd met while covering a story. Instead he'd morphed into a caricature, a cross between a news anchorman and a used-car salesman.

Raina was a classic emotional manipulator.

"I'm sorry," I said softly. "Do you know if she's planning on paying back the money she got from students and from Shawn?"

His right shoulder lifted into a shrug, as if that was an afterthought. "I suppose. She avoids all of my questions. She has a way of doing that while making me feel terrible for even asking. Take Costa Rica, for example. She insisted on organizing the trip, doing all the financials, even though I have a business degree. Then we arrive, and I find out that she'd spent some of the deposit money before we left on expensive video equipment for the studio. She wants to start streaming classes online. But then we didn't have cash for the hotel, and she asked Shawn, and it was all a big mess."

"Why was streaming online such a big deal?"

He snorted. "Because that other yoga guy on the island's offering online classes. The Wolfman."

"Aha," I said, writing Wolfie's name in my notebook and circling it twice. Maybe Dad was right and his friend *did* have some intel.

"But that's Raina, always worried how others will see her. Always wanting to be better than anyone else—that Wolfman guy's using an iPhone propped against a yoga block and broadcasting on Facebook Live. Raina bought pro equipment so she could film a whole web series. She has plans to hire a part-time videographer, but we can't afford it."

I stared at my phone, which had recorded everything, then glanced at Kai. "This might all make it into an article, you know."

He licked his lips. "I'm beyond caring. I mean, I'm so worried about her. But I think her behavior and attitude has led to what's happening now. Even if it's the end of our relationship, she needs to face the consequences." He paused, eyes downcast. "If she hasn't already."

Yikes. Ominous much? "What do you think has happened to her?"

"She's gone. And I'm truly concerned she's in danger. Clearly she is, because she hasn't turned up. She's too much of a show-off to go somewhere and not broadcast it on Instagram. I keep waiting for her to post a long, passionate screed accompanied by a beautiful photo. I'm both worried and angry and I can't get a handle on anything. I'm super overwhelmed."

I could tell, and let the magnitude of his statement hang in the air. "So why are you telling me all this? Usually the friends and family of a missing person are a little, I dunno, kinder."

He scrunched up his mouth. "If she did just run away and is trying to get sympathy out of me, or more money out of someone else, I want her to own up to it. Know I'm not going to be manipulated anymore. But . . ." His voice faded.

"But?"

"If someone who's been giving her money got fed up and did something terrible to her when they found out they were being used, well, I want that out there too. Because I don't want her physically hurt either. Obviously."

117

I arched an eyebrow. "Who would hurt her? Anyone you can think of?"

"Turn that off and I'll tell you." He pointed to my phone.

I swiped the off button and put the phone facedown on the table.

Kai took another swig of his tea and grimaced. "Sorry. Your tea's delicious. This whole subject's giving me heartburn. My stomach hasn't been right for days. I probably need a detox."

"I can imagine."

He leaned in, a fierce gleam in his eyes. "I'm going to ask police to investigate Shawn. He's a total stalker. Never leaves Raina alone. He's consistently on the phone, always texting her. And check out his Instagram. Or interview him in person. I'd be curious to learn what he has to say for himself."

I was about to tell him I'd already done exactly that when he continued. The words tumbled out of him.

"I know for a fact that he gave Raina ten grand for upgrades to our website. An online reservation system. And then he settled that shortfall we had with the hotel in Costa Rica. And he's paid for Raina's head shots, business cards, a second photo shoot . . ." Kai ticked off several other items.

It sure sounded like Shawn had maintained Raina. And that Kai was the loser in this situation. And terribly jealous. But jealous enough to make Raina disappear? Or was Shawn the culprit? I needed another interview with him, that was certain.

"So you've told the police all of that?" I wondered if any of this would make it into a newspaper story. Probably not much, since Kai's allegations bordered on libel of Shawn.

"Not yet. I've been hoping Raina would return. Now that it's been a couple of days, my father's going to hire that famous search-and-rescue group. Texas EquuSearch."

"I've heard of them." They were a well-known outfit and had been involved in several high-profile missing-persons cases.

"Look, I have to go home and feed the dogs." He pushed his chair back and stood. I did the same.

"Same here," I replied. I hadn't seen Stanley in three hours, which seemed like an eternity.

With his index finger, he jabbed at the air in my direction. "And I know police will be all over Shawn when they look into him. I'll make sure of it."

My hand found the back of the white wooden chair. I was skeptical of Shawn's involvement, having interviewed him and detected nothing sinister, but I had zero doubt that Kai was going to use his father's influence to bring a world of hurt onto the other man. Jealousy was a heck of a drug. He seemed like he was all over the place with his emotions, and after learning more about Raina, it was understandable.

"Hey, can I get your number in case I have follow-up questions?"

He rattled off his digits, and I scribbled in my notebook. "Thanks. I really appreciate this. I hope everything turns out well."

He had a faraway look in his eye. "Me too. Me too."

"One more question. Why do you think Raina's like that? Kind and sweet, then manipulative?"

We trudged to the front of the store, and Kai ran both hands over his bald head. "I think it all goes back to her childhood. She's the middle child of three kids and was a really talented gymnast in high school. She realized her parents, her friends, and all the adults at school valued her for how well she performed. And her beauty—she was always praised for that too. We did an inner-child workshop together, and she admitted she doesn't think she deserves love and feels like she needs to earn affection. She always has to feel valuable to everyone around her."

I could empathize with that feeling, needing to feel valuable. The realization that I might be a little similar to Raina left an uncomfortable metallic taste in my mouth. I gave Kai a sympathetic smile as we stood near the door. "Interesting. Thanks again. Drive safe," I said softly, unlocking the door.

The minute he left, my discomfort evaporated, and I dove for my phone to call Mike. I simultaneously locked up, then power walked down the street to my house. The crickets were out tonight, screeching so loudly that I could barely hear the voice mail message.

He had to be sleeping. Mike was an ultramarathoner, and I knew he usually got up at the butt crack of dawn. Still, I couldn't wait to tell him about my chat with Kai.

"You're not going to believe what I just found out," I said breathlessly, then launched into every detail of the interview.

Chapter Eleven

I t was Tuesday, my one day off. We didn't have deliveries scheduled, and it was the slowest on the island, businesswise. Which meant I could sleep in, run errands without getting caught in tourist traffic, and take Stanley to the dog beach while avoiding throngs of sunbathers.

It was ten in the morning and I'd just rolled out of bed. I had a fuzzy plan to make no-bake chocolate peanut butter bars while drinking a mug of Perkatory House Blend.

Like every other treat I concocted for the café, the recipe had five ingredients or less, which meant I could throw it together in no time. I mixed melted butter, graham cracker crumbs, and confectioners' sugar, then stirred in some peanut butter and spread it all into a pan. Two more spoonfuls of peanut butter went into a bowl, along with a few handfuls of chocolate chips, and I microwaved that sucker until it was nice and gooey.

Stanley waited patiently at my feet, craning his neck as I started to screw the peanut butter lid shut.

"Fine. Only a teaspoon." I gave him a little dollop on his special treat plate.

Then came the fun part: drizzling the chocolate over the peanut butter–graham cracker mixture in the pan. The recipe needed several hours to chill, and I leaned against the counter, licking a spoon clean of chocolate.

Stanley barked once, which meant he wanted to go outside.

"What is it, buddy? C'mon. Let's go soak up some sunshine."

It was so pleasant, temperaturewise, that I figured we should hang outdoors for a bit. The Florida sky was a deep, clear blue, without a cloud in sight.

I stood in my backyard in my robe, drinking coffee and tossing a mini tennis ball to Stanley. He plucked it out of the grass and bounded over to me on his stumpy legs. We'd been working on playing fetch in recent days.

He had part of it down, and loved to bound after the ball and retrieve it. He pressed the small, fluorescent yellow ball into my shin. I tried to take it from him, but he growled softly. "Leave it," I warned.

He dropped it, and I knelt, reaching to pet his soft, gold-and-white fur. "Good boy!"

That's when he started to wuff, bark, and growl. Anyone overhearing this exchange would have thought he was trying to murder something. Instead, he was jumping on his front legs, then rearing up like a tiny Ewok. I'd learned that this was his signal that he wanted to play more, but I worried that it would appear as aggression to another dog.

I'd address it tonight at puppy kindergarten. Egad. A zing of awareness went through me. It wasn't only a dog-training class; it was a date with Noah. I needed to figure out what to wear. No sexy black slip dresses tonight.

Pocketing the ball, I walked to my back door and whistled. Stanley trotted after me, and once inside, I poured myself a second cup, pondering whether I should return to bed. Maybe I had to make another deposit into the ol' sleep bank.

As Stanley messily lapped water in the kitchen, I glanced at my phone, which was charging on the counter. A message flashed on the screen. It was Noah.

Hey. Get down to The Swamp if you want a big scoop.

The text jolted me awake like a shot of the best Italian espresso. Noah was giving me a tip, but about what? My stomach tightened when I remembered that Raina lived near the Swamp. This was significant. I could feel it.

I rushed to my bedroom and threw on khaki capris, a long-sleeved thin white T-shirt, and a pair of sneakers. As I ran out the door, I grabbed bug spray, sun block, and a hat embroidered with the logo of my old newspaper. On second thought, I nixed that idea. They'd laid me off. The *Miami Tribune* didn't deserve the publicity.

I located a ball cap in a drawer that must've been Mom's at one point. It was light blue and had the words TROPICAL VIBES and a palm tree on the front. Worked for me.

It took me ten minutes to drive from my door to the Swamp. On the way, I slowed past Raina and Kai's home. A lone police cruiser sat in the driveway, and I thought I spotted that new officer inside, the one who'd strung the crime scene tape over Dante's Inferno the other night. I considered waving but didn't want to call attention to myself, so I chugged down the road in my Honda.

The Swamp was owned by the island's city government, not the state, and there was no guard shack or tollbooth. The road ended in a parking lot, one that was usually half-full with tourists and local kayakers.

Today it was overrun with officers. I pulled into one of the only available spots at the far corner of the lot, then got out and went around to the passenger side. I opened the door and did my usual reporting-outdoors ritual: first I sprayed my exposed skin down with sunscreen, then layered bug spray on top of that, bathing my clothes in a fine layer of mist for good measure. A cloud of chemicals surrounded me.

I grabbed my cross-body purse, which contained my phone, notebook, and stash of pens. As I powered toward the boardwalk entrance, I counted ten cop cars, a county sheriff's wagon, three fire trucks, and an ambulance.

There was a second van parked in the spot closest to the entrance.

Medical Examiner, it said on the side.

"Oh, crap," I whispered to myself. This definitely wasn't good. Every dark scenario about Raina flashed through my mind. There was no way she was alive. Not if all these officers and the ME's van were here.

I swallowed the thick lump that had formed in my throat and walked faster.

An officer was stationed at the entrance. I didn't recognize him as being one of the local cops, and sure enough, his badge indicated that he was with the county sheriff's department on the mainland.

"Park's closed today, ma'am." He folded his hands over his belt. Since he wore mirrored sunglasses, like a cop from Central Casting, I couldn't determine if he was a friendly officer or a frosty one.

Cold Brew Corpse

"Good morning," I said in a cheery yet professional voice. I tried to subtly look around his wide shoulder, but all I could see was a thicket of saw palmetto bushes, their pale silvery-green spikes concealing whatever was happening back there.

"My name's Lana Lewis, and I'm with the *Devil's Beach Beacon*. I got a tip that I should come here because I'm working on a story about a missing woman."

"Know nothing about that, ma'am. You're going to stay right here, because I don't have authorization to let you back into the scene."

"Can you tell me if Raina Rose has been found?"

"Can't tell you anything, ma'am. That was an order from the Devil's Beach police chief and the Florida Department of Law Enforcement. Just doing my job, ma'am."

He'd called me *ma'am* so many times I felt like I'd aged twenty years in two minutes.

"Okay. Thanks a bunch," I murmured. Long ago, as a rookie reporter, I'd realized that it paid to be polite even when I was annoyed.

I fought back a sigh. It was common for reporters to not be allowed close to the crime scene. Normally I'd try to charm my way past someone like this. Today, I had an in. Or so I hoped.

I wandered a few paces away and pretended to inspect a sign instructing people not to feed the wild monkey colony while I slipped my phone out of my bag and dialed Noah.

"Garcia," he barked.

"Hey, it's me. I'm here at the park. The officer here won't let me back."

"I'll come to you. But Lana?"

"Yeah?"

"You need to be prepared for what you're about to hear, okay?"

"Absolutely," I agreed swiftly, even though I wasn't prepared in the slightest. My stomach clenched into a small, hard rock.

"Hang out in the shade near the trail map, and I'll meet you there. It's to the right of the entrance. Oh, and did you bring water?"

"Yeah, I have some in my car."

"I'll be there in five."

I smiled at his thoughtfulness. We hung up and I crossed the sidewalk, acknowledging the officer along the way. I wasn't about to rub it in his face that Noah was coming to get me, so I nodded and smiled, tight-lipped.

Even under the shade of the canopied trail map, I was working up a sweat something fierce. I texted Mike, the thrill of adrenaline coursing through my veins. It felt like old times, covering crime back in Miami.

I think there's a break in Raina's case. I'm at The Swamp. ME Van here.

Whoa. Keep me posted. We'll send a breaking news alert and a push notification for the web. You okay to hang out there for a while, or do you have to get back to the coffee shop?

It's my day off:)

Perfect timing. I'm going to send Cody to get photos Probably a good idea.

I'm waiting for Noah to give me more info now

I spotted Noah coming toward me in his crisp blue uniform. **I'll have something for you soon,** I texted.

I slipped the phone into my bag. As Noah came closer, I saw the lines of worry etched on his handsome face. He walked up to me and stood close. Close enough that I could sense the heat of his body and smell his spicy aftershave and his man scent radiating off his skin. It was a little heady, here in this humidity.

"It's her," he declared in a low voice.

"Oh my god," I whispered. "In the water? Or where?"

He inhaled and put his hands on his hips, looking around. "Yep. The first tourists in the park found her. A family from Ohio. Came here to see alligators and monkeys, stumbled on a corpse instead."

I gulped in a few shallow breaths. The realization that my next-door neighbor was dead, in a swamp, hit me hard. Still, I had a job to do. A story to report. "I'm ready to go back there."

Noah shook his head. "There are too many state agents. Since Kai's dad has crawled up the butts of every law enforcement agency in Florida, I can't take the chance. They're taking over the investigation."

"Crap. I'm sorry." I inhaled slowly, trying to figure out a way to pump him for more details. "What else can you tell me. On the record?"

He licked his lips and glanced at the boardwalk. "Okay. I'm giving you the exclusive."

I raised an eyebrow. "I should hope so."

The corner of his lush mouth lifted. "Only the facts, ma'am. Nothing more, nothing less."

I took out my notebook. "Shoot."

He stood back, and it was as if he were a different man. "Today at zero-eight-hundred hours, a family of tourists was walking along the boardwalk at Angelwing Park on Devil's Beach."

"My, how formal," I murmured.

"Only the best for my favorite reporter," he said in a tone that matched mine, then snapped to attention. "The witnesses were in the back of the preserve, where the mangroves meet Devil's Creek, when they saw what appeared to be a human form."

He paused, and I scribbled each word madly. I looked up and nodded once.

"The body was that of a white female, in her twenties. We're unable to say how long she has been in the swamp, or the manner and cause of her death. We're classifying it as a suspicious death. That's about all I can tell you."

I raised my pen. "Is it the body of Raina Rose?"

Noah looked deep into my eyes. "I cannot confirm the identity at the moment. The medical examiner, along with the Devil's Beach Police, the county sheriff's office, and the Florida Department of Law Enforcement, will work to identify the individual, and then we will notify next of kin. When that happens, we'll send out a news release with the identity. We found the body with multiple, obvious marks on the skin."

I furiously scrawled these details. Suddenly I was as awake as if I'd mainlined a pot of Italian espresso. I hadn't felt this alive since . . . since leaving the *Tribune* in Miami. As much as I loved my coffee shop, breaking news made my adrenaline pump.

"Marks? What kind?"

"It's hard to say right now. There seems to have been some degradation from the elements."

I narrowed my eyes. "Because she, er, the body, was in the water?"

"That and other elements, yes. But there is bruising. An extensive amount."

My heart rattled around my rib cage. "Can you tell me if there's any obvious foul play? Gunshot wounds? Where are the marks located? Any other details I should know about the body? The identity of the witnesses who found her? Was there any other evidence nearby?"

He shook his head, a little grin dancing on his lips. "No more questions, cupcake."

My nostrils flared. I needed *more*.

"Seriously. I can't tell you anything else right now. I should have something for you later today. You have enough to call Mike and impress him. I'll let you know when we have further details. Listen, I need to get back. I want this crime scene wrapped up as early as possible. Time's of the essence."

I clicked my pen. "Why? What's the rush?"

He winked at me. "I've got a hot date tonight."

My jaw dropped a little. He was rushing on a potential homicide for me?

"Kidding, Lana. Sort of. It's sweltering out here. Now I really gotta run."

The officer at the entrance whistled, and we both looked over.

"Chief Garcia." The cop yelled and waved.

"Go, go," I urged. "Thanks, Chief Garcia."

He winked, and I watched him jog away. As I was punching in the numbers for Mike, a well-worn black SUV drove up. It had a bright-yellow kayak strapped to the top and several dents on the body.

It was Cody.

"Hey, little girl, you lost in the swamp?" he called out.

Ew. I waved and pointed at the phone, then pushed call. Cody drove off and parked a few spaces away from me. Mike answered on the first ring.

"What have you got for me, kiddo?"

"Body found. Noah's not confirming it's Raina—yet. At least, not on the record."

"What about off the record? On background?"

I watched Cody climb out of his SUV and go around to the back, extracting a long, expensive-looking lens.

"Well, Noah told me off the record that it was Raina," I replied to Mike. "How do you feel about using him as an anonymous source?"

"If the source is Noah, I'm fine with it."

"Let's run with it." Nearby, Cody popped off several shots of the ME's van. Two people in white hazmat suits pulled a stretcher from the back. "Give me the basics now so we can get something on the website; then you can write a longer version for print."

My heart felt like it might beat right out of my chest. I took a deep breath and dictated everything that Noah had told me.

Chapter Twelve

A three-hundred-word story with the headline *Body Found in Nature Preserve Likely Popular Yoga Teacher* was posted on the paper's website not long afterward. A pop-up alert also flashed on my phone's screen, and as I studied the words, a surge of pride settled in my chest. That emotion was quickly overtaken by another, darker mood.

Fear.

On the one hand, I was thrilled to be back in the game of breaking news. I adored the energy rush of writing and crafting a story on a tight deadline.

On the other hand, a person I knew was dead. And it was highly doubtful that a healthy, fit young woman would crawl into a swamp and die of natural causes.

A sharp rapping noise on the passenger window startled me, and I gasped. Oh. It was only Cody. I unlocked the door and cleared a dog blanket, an empty coffee cup, a notebook, and an overdue library book off the seat.

"Come on in." I deposited everything into the back, where it mingled with other junk. "Sorry about the mess."

He snorted, holding his camera gingerly on his lap as he eased his strapping frame into my little Honda hatchback. "Is there a reporter alive who doesn't have a sloppy car?"

I arched an eyebrow. "No need to judge."

He shrugged. "Only an observation. I've worked with reporters in three states and four countries. It seems like all of them have poor vehicular hygiene."

"Oh, so your car is pristine?" I teased.

"Heck no." He grinned, and I started to like him a little more. "Anyway. I heard the ME techs talking. They were speculating on how the paper—that would be you—learned about Raina so fast."

I shot him a triumphant smile but didn't answer.

"I'm impressed at how quickly you nailed down the info. You dating the police chief? Is that how you got the details so quick?" he asked. From the tone of his voice, I suspected he was being playful. But a pang of guilt moved through me because of what he was implying.

I gaped at him and pressed my hand to my chest. "No. No! My goodness. Of course not."

"Listen, I'm only teasing. All's fair in love, war, and journalism." He said in a gentle voice, "The other thing I heard them say was that they're going to bring her body out in about a half hour. Dunno if you want to hang out for that."

"Why wouldn't I want to be here for that?" Cody had a touch of macho arrogance that grated. I narrowed my eyes.

He shrugged. "You might not wish to see it, since she's your friend and your neighbor."

"I saw plenty of dead bodies in Miami," I huffed.

He held his hands in the air in a truce motion. "Okay, okay. Don't get touchy. I'm going to send some photos from my car. Oh, and check this out."

He flicked a few buttons and dials on his Nikon, and the screen on the back of the camera came to life. "Here's what I shot."

He tilted the camera's viewfinder to me and scrolled through, stopping at a close-up of the ME's van with a tall, white ibis in the background. "I like this one the best."

"Yeah, it's good," I agreed. "I'm sure we'll get more if we hang around here for a while. Good lord, it's crazy hot." I fanned my face with a notebook. Hanging out in sweaty cars in parking lots used to be routine for me when I was in Miami. I'd gotten used to the air-conditioned comfort of my coffee shop.

But at a crime scene, nothing ever happened on time. A half hour ticked by, then an hour. A TV crew from the mainland arrived with a live truck, and I watched the blond reporter from the other day do a stand-up in the sun. She looked uncomfortably warm, and I had to hand it to her. She turned on the professional charm when she was doing her live shot. I probably would have punched someone if I had to stand in heels in the middle of a swamp parking lot in the early September Florida heat.

When I saw three uniformed officers emerging from the swamp, all wiping their brows and swatting away mosquitoes, I hustled out of my car so I could get a better look. By the time I got there, they had roped off half the lot with yellow crime scene tape.

Cody was already out of his SUV, firing his camera with that long lens, leaning over the tape.

"Stay back," hollered one officer.

"This is public property, and we have every right to be here," I yelled.

The TV reporter strode past me with her tall heels. "Yeah, did you hear that? Public property. You can't kick us out," she spat.

Her moxie impressed me. A few moments passed, and no one else emerged from the swamp. I sidled up to the TV reporter.

"I'm Lana Lewis."

"Oh! Nice to meet you." With manicured pink nails, she squeezed my hand in a vise grip. I marveled at her perfect hair; I'm sure I looked like I'd rolled in the swamp.

"I'm Kate Bernstein. You're the owner of Perkatory, right? I love that place. My wife and I sometimes come over on weekends for your coffee. I just adore the atmosphere there. And such a glorious name for a business."

"Thanks," I said shyly. I wasn't used to people recognizing me from the café, especially when I was in reporter mode. I also felt a little awkward about my freelance status, as if I were a rookie or someone unable to get a job. Which wasn't far from the truth.

"That's my family's café. I manage it and do some reporting on the side."

"Our station mentioned Perkatory last week. In our dirty dining segment."

I stopped breathing for a second. No one had told me that the café was on the local news. "Your . . . what?"

She laughed. "You got an A. We listed Perkatory and the other businesses on Devil's Beach that passed. Well, right after we did a report on a sandwich shop for having a frozen iguana in the cooler. They got an F."

I let out the breath I was holding. "Oh, thank goodness. You scared the daylights out of me. The last thing I want is to be on a dirty dining segment."

We spent the next few minutes chatting about the cleanliness of the restaurants in the region. When her camera guy snapped to attention and hurried to the far end of the tape, our conversation faded. Cody popped off several shots, his shutter making a fast clicking noise.

In the blink of an eye, the hazmat-suited workers emerged, carrying a stretcher. Atop it was a black body bag, immobile from two red straps. I shielded my eyes from the harsh midday sun, watching as they carried Raina's corpse to the van.

The back doors were open and waiting, ready to whisk Raina on her last journey to the afterlife.

*   *   *

I had hoped Noah would come out soon after, but he didn't. After phoning in the latest developments to Mike, I walked over to Cody's SUV. He was on the driver's side, with his seat all the way back and his laptop on his legs, wedged against the steering wheel. I tapped on the window with my index finger.

He rolled it down, and I peered in.

"What's up?" he asked.

"Wow, this is a mess. Worse than mine." I spotted fast food bags, various tools, and what looked like busted-up auto, bicycle, and motorcycle parts. A spark plug and an orange plastic reflector were nestled inside a giant, empty coffee cup. It appeared that he loved a particular brand of beef jerky, if the dozen or so wrappers were any indication. "Want to follow me back to Perkatory and we can work there? If you have time to spare, that is."

He pushed out a breath and closed his laptop, setting it on the passenger seat next to some trash that looked like a stainless-steel arm attached to something black, plastic, and mangled. "Yeah, that would be more comfortable, wouldn't it?"

We caravaned back downtown, parked, and walked in together. A few regular customers glanced my way, probably not accustomed to me appearing so sweaty and disheveled. I gave them a little wave and retied my ponytail.

The minute the sweet air conditioner hit my face and evaporated all the sweat, I let out a satisfied groan. I swept my gaze around the blue-and-white café with the white wicker furniture and shabby chic white-wood accents. My shoulder muscles instantly lowered about two inches. This was my happy place.

Erica was behind the counter, and she lunged at me. "What's going on?"

"You're not gonna believe the day we've had." I inhaled a soothing noseful of coffee aroma.

She glanced at Cody and raised a thin, black eyebrow.

"Oh. This is Cody. He's a photographer for the *Devil's Beach Beacon*." I turned to him. "You want an iced coffee?"

"Nah, I'll take a regular cup of black. Hot." He wandered over to the table we'd sat at the other day while I dashed behind the counter to wash my hands.

"Where were you? I tried calling, but you didn't pick up," Erica said.

"At the Swamp." I kept my voice down because I didn't want to alarm customers. As much as I loved talking about news, chatting about a dead body wasn't best for business. Even I knew that.

"The Swamp? Why? Are you doing some nature article?" She scurried around to pour our coffee.

I grabbed both mugs, then motioned with my head to the far table in the corner. "Thanks for this. C'mere and I'll tell you."

She wiped her hands on her apron and followed me. Cody had already opened his laptop and was laser focused on his screen, probably editing photos. I set his coffee down in front of him.

"Look at this one." He twisted the laptop toward us.

"Is that a body bag?" Erica pointed at the screen.

"Thanks much," he murmured, holding up his mug. "And yeah, that's a body in a body bag. What else could it be? You must not watch many crime dramas."

Erica, sharp as a tack, glanced from him to me with a flinty expression on her face. She had no tolerance for arrogant men and no qualms about telling them off. I set my mug down and pulled her a foot away from the table, hoping to diffuse her annoyance. "Tourists found Raina's body in the water," I whispered in her ear.

Her ruby-red lips formed an O shape. "Whoa, that's awful," she breathed.

"Isn't it? I've already got a story out online, but Mike wants a longer version that will run in the print paper tomorrow. Did you see the first story that came out a couple of hours ago? The paper put out an alert and everything."

She shook her head. "I gotta confess I don't read the news that much."

I shot her a glare of reproach.

"Okay, okay. I'll subscribe to the paper today. Congrats on writing the article so quickly. Hey, is that photographer a jerk or what?"

"Yeah, a little. I'll explain later." I untied and retied my ponytail. "We're going to hang out here for a while, do some work."

Erica rested her hands on her hips. "Cool. Cool. Do the cops know what happened to her?"

I shook my head.

Erica paused, chewing on her cheek. My phone pinged, which meant I had an incoming email. Probably from a reader already. Or maybe it was a story tip!

I slid into the seat opposite Cody, and Erica strode away. A quick check of my cell revealed it was a press release from the Devil's Beach Police. Weird. I figured Noah would've given me a heads up about any announcements.

ATTENTION ASSIGNMENT DESKS

A positive identification has been made of the body found at Angelwing Park, and next of kin has been notified. An autopsy and full investigation are underway.

NAME: RAINA ROMERO, aka RAINA ROSE

AGE: 29

RESIDENCY: Devil's Beach, Florida

FOUL PLAY SUSPECTED? (y/n) YES

OTHER DETAILS: Body was found clothed. Police are seeking the help of the public. Anyone who was at Angelwing Park or on Angelwing Drive on Saturday from approximately noon until midnight should contact CrimeStoppers or the police station.

All media inquiries should be directed to Chief Noah Garcia. No news conferences are scheduled at this time.

So Rose wasn't her real last name. Interesting. Both she and Kai had renamed and reinvented themselves.

"Well, there it is." I tapped on my screen with my nail. "It's official. Raina's death is definitely suspicious."

Cody snorted. "I could have told you that."

I lifted the screen of my computer and stared at him over the top. I liked him less by the minute. Eh. Whatever. Not my circus, not my monkeys.

I had a story to write.

Chapter Thirteen

Six hours later, I'd no sooner stepped out of the shower than my phone rang. It was Noah.

"Hey, you," I said in a chipper voice. I was running on caffeine and purpose. I'd filed a long and decent news story for the first time in months and hoped I'd fixed the cold brew problem. Before I'd left Perkatory, I'd made two vats to sit overnight, one using the previous recipe and the other with more ground coffee.

"Lana. I'm afraid I'm not going to make it tonight. I'm working to get out of here, but I don't think I'll be there in time to pick you up." His voice was clipped.

"Aw." I paused. "I kind of figured as much. You have your hands full."

"Especially now that everyone's wondering how the paper got Raina's ID before we officially announced that it was her."

I swallowed. "Oh. Well, we didn't quote you."

Silence.

"Are you mad?" I asked.

He let out a sigh. "Lana, we'll need some boundaries here if you continue to report for the paper and if we're going to . . ."

"Going to what?"

"Do whatever it is we keep dancing around."

"Hmm." I wasn't sure what to make of his reproachful tone. "I'm not a particularly impressive dancer."

"Me neither. That's why I want things nice and clear between us. So we don't step on each other's toes."

I chewed on the inside of my cheek and thought about how Cody had insinuated that I'd slept with Noah for more info. "Yeah."

"Have any thoughts on what those boundaries should be?"

"Not particularly. I'm kind of focused on getting ready and taking Stanley to class." For all my confidence as a reporter, I was inept with confrontation in my personal life. The end of my marriage had made me allergic to fighting. Even now, talking to Noah, I wanted to curl into a ball.

I wasn't sure how to respond to him when his tone was stony and almost accusatory.

"Gotcha. Well, I guess I'll talk with you later."

"Okay." I'd barely gotten the word out when he hung up, and I stared at the phone for a couple of long seconds. Had I been in the wrong?

I hadn't named him as a source in the paper. There were so many officers from different departments there that it could have been anyone who leaked the news. Although, on Devil's Beach, people could put two and two together, since everyone knew Noah and I had been, as he phrased it, *dancing around each other*.

I blow-dried my hair, still with the uneasy pit lodged in my stomach. Part of me thought it was unfair for him to call me out like that. Another part wondered if I'd been overzealous to nail down the story and jumped the gun. Was I bringing my Miami news sensibility to Devil's Beach? Or maybe, since my divorce, I'd gotten so used to doing things my way that I was being selfish.

Ugh. What a terrible thought.

I reflected on this and so much more as Stanley and I drove to class. It wasn't how I wanted to start a relationship. Noah deserved an apology. I'd put on my big-girl panties, call him after class, and hash it out. I was mature enough to admit when I was wrong.

Taking a deep breath, I pulled into the lot. Since Stanley was so little, I carried him inside. The black asphalt was still too warm for his tender paws.

He was one of four puppies in the session, and the smallest. The owners all took seats with their leashed dogs. Three of the dogs strained to reach each other, and Stanley sat at my side, staring at the door. He remained there while the instructor told us what to expect and wouldn't budge when she tried to tempt him with a spoon dipped in peanut butter.

And while all the other dogs made an effort during each exercise, Stanley wanted to either play or nip at my hands or the leash. Apparently I had a wild animal as a pet. One who ate anything and everything at home but repeatedly snubbed the instructor and her peanut butter.

"I don't know what's gotten into him. Normally he loves peanut butter." I scooped him up at the end of the hour-long class.

"All the other dogs liked it." The instructor shook her head. "But sometimes it takes a while for them to warm up."

"He's a little stubborn," I replied. Possibly like his owner.

I walked out with Stanley, feeling defeated. He licked my hand while I buckled him into his car seat in back. "Listen, buddy, we're going to have to both be flexible here. Me with Noah and you with puppy school. Trust me on this."

We took the scenic route near the beach as I drove home, rolling down the windows and breathing in the nighttime salt air. I tried blasting my favorite Fleetwood Mac playlist, but that only conjured melancholy because I remembered how Mom had loved the band. Which made me think about how much I wished I could talk to her and ask her advice.

She'd have known how to handle this Noah situation. When I was younger, she'd been a coffee buyer in the Caribbean, and I'd gone on trips with her. While buying Blue Mountain in Jamaica and Pocillo in Puerto Rico, she'd charmed everyone with her beauty and gentle wit. I was more like Dad: curious and goofy and sometimes careless in my enthusiasm.

I yawned and turned down the music. Goodness, I was exhausted. Writing that story about Raina wasn't as satisfying as I remembered news to be, probably because of how I'd betrayed Noah's trust. And because I knew her personally. She was about the same age as me, and now she was dead.

Top that off with my puppy's inability to socialize or even eat peanut butter, and I felt like a colossal failure.

I turned onto my street and spotted a familiar police cruiser in front of my house. My heart soared a little as I pulled into my driveway. When I got out, I was assaulted with a roar—my next door neighbor was leaf blowing his property. It sounded like the loudest blower in the history of power tools.

Noah walked up with a sheepish smile on his face. His hands were stuffed into his pockets.

"Hey," I yelled.

"How'd puppy class go? Man, that blower's powerful." Noah glanced up and squinted at my neighbor.

"No kidding." I opened the back door and freed Stanley from his car seat. "It didn't go that great. He's not really a people dog. It takes a while for him to warm up."

Noah smiled and held out his hands. "He'll do fine. The first lesson's always difficult. C'mere, little doggo."

Stanley immediately lapped Noah's chiseled jaw, then nuzzled into the hollow of his neck. Lucky pup.

I shut the door, and we walked up my porch steps to retreat from the noise. With my keys in hand, I turned to look at Noah. Gah. I felt terrible about our earlier spat but didn't want to rehash it. Especially not over the sound of the leaf blower.

I twisted the key in the lock. "Can you come inside?"

"Only if you want me to."

"Of course I want you to. Don't be silly."

Noah set Stanley down, and he made a beeline for his food dish in the kitchen. I shut the door, and the blower noise faded. We stood facing each other, awkwardness crackling in the silence.

"I'm sorry," I blurted.

"No, I'm sorry," he declared, nearly at the same time.

"I was just trying—"

"It's been a hard day—"

I swallowed, fearing that the thick lump in my throat was about to turn into tears. Why was I being so emotional while looking into Noah's soulful brown eyes?

He took a deep breath and stepped closer to me. I licked my lips.

"I should've told you I wanted to put that in the paper," I said softly.

He brushed a lock of my hair back, then tucked it behind my ear. "I probably could've guessed you were going to jump on that detail."

I nodded. "I got carried away. I apologize."

"And I shouldn't have called you with an attitude. I'm sorry. It wasn't that big of a deal. I'm under a lot of pressure with this case. The state's riding me hard to find a suspect." He paused awkwardly, and I played with the hem of my shirt. "Sorry it didn't go well with Stanley. We'll get him trained. I promise."

I released my shirt. "Stanley loves people he knows. But tonight he was thrown off his game. There was a Chiweenie that took two poops during class, and Stan got overwhelmed. I also discovered that he doesn't want to be told what to do."

"Like dog, like owner." Noah smiled.

He stepped even closer and wrapped his arms around me. The hug felt so good, so nourishing, and then I realized it was probably just as necessary for him. We inhaled and exhaled in tandem. For a second, I thought we were going to kiss, but we broke apart and blinked at each other.

"Want something to drink? I have wine."

"Yeah. I could use that right about now." He ran his hand over his short hair. It was then that I noticed he was in jeans and a plain black T-shirt. Noah looked effortless and sexy no matter what he wore.

He followed me into the kitchen and slid onto the stool at the eat-in nook. I took out the Merlot, the bottle Dad had brought over the other night, and uncorked it.

Making sure my two good wineglasses were clean, I poured us both a modest amount, then handed one to him.

We clinked glasses. "What should we toast to?" I asked.

He smiled. Lord, he looked exhausted. "To boundaries in a personal-professional relationship."

"An excellent toast. I definitely don't want to step on your toes."

I plopped myself on a seat and took a sip.

"Lana, I think we should have a rule. I'm going to treat you like any other reporter and answer your questions during news conferences, formal phone calls, and through news releases. When we're together, alone, work is off the record for publication."

I laughed. "Formal phone calls?"

"You know what I mean."

I pondered this. "But I want you to talk freely when we're alone. About your frustrations or concerns. And I don't want to violate that trust."

He sighed. "Oh, believe me, I have a lot of frustrations and concerns right now."

"Talk to me. I promise I won't put this in the paper. Girl Scout honor." I held up three fingers.

He lifted an eyebrow. "Were you actually a Girl Scout?"

"Well, for a few months. In third grade. My father worried it was a paramilitary organization. So then I joined a local group called the Islanders. It was a bunch of kids who wanted to save the whales and protect the environment. We'd pick up trash on the beach. We were like an unpaid cleaning crew. We disbanded when a brick of marijuana washed ashore and one of the older girls tried to sell it at school."

The corners of Noah's eyes crinkled, and I could tell he was trying not to laugh.

I gestured in his direction. "Anyway. Never mind. Back to your frustrations."

He took a sip, then set his glass on the table, twisting the base. "I'm worried there's a killer here on Devil's Beach."

"That's a concern, right? But realistically, most women are killed by people they know. Raina probably was."

"True. But if there's a slight chance that it's not someone she knew, if it's some guy who is targeting women . . ." His voice trailed off.

"Are you worried about that? Really?" I scrunched up my face. "You know, during my days as a crime reporter in Miami, I wrote about a serial killer who targeted women. All the profilers told me that was statistically a rare thing. Those stories led to a big arrest. Perhaps it was because I was in a city, or perhaps because I was aware of my privilege, I never dreamed I'd be the victim of the killer."

"Things are always more personal in a small town." We stared at each other for a long second.

"That's true." Memories of Gisela broke through the waves of my thoughts.

"What I'm trying to say is, I hope it's not someone going after women here on the island. I'm tasked with keeping people safe, but I now have a vested interest in keeping one woman in particular safe. One extremely nosy woman who doesn't mind getting into a bit of trouble by snooping around."

"Who, me?" I fluttered my eyelashes, and he snorted.

"Yeah, you. And I'm also under a lot of pressure to solve this case from the state agency and Kai's father."

"That's a bigger concern, in my book. Do they think the police force here isn't up to the task because it's so small?"

He smirked. "That, and the fact I upset so many people in Tampa. The thin blue line is thick in some quarters."

I winced. "I'm sorry."

He shrugged. "It is what it is. I know I have the full confidence of the mayor and the council here, though. Which is a positive thing."

I hummed an agreement. Noah was in a pickle, it seemed, and I wasn't sure how to reassure him everything would be okay.

It was one of those situations he—and the entire island—would have to endure.

"This is the worst part of a random murder, don't you think?" I said. "That nebulous, nervous time between the finding of the body and the arrest. That's what puts a community on edge."

"Sure is."

"I remember when Gisela, my high school friend, went missing all those years ago. We lived in this limbo for an entire summer, waiting for something to happen. Waiting for her to be found. Waiting for news. It was awful. Resolution never came, though."

"You know, when Raina disappeared, I looked at Gisela's file. It's still technically open. All the evidence was in storage. Had to hunt for it."

The wine mixed with all the coffee churned like my stomach was a washer on a spin cycle. I nodded. "Why did you do that? Did you think they were linked?"

He shook his head. "No, not at all. I remembered you telling me about her and wanted to see if there were any obvious similarities. There weren't."

"Yeah, Raina seemed to have many issues," I muttered.

"Like what?" His dark eyes flashed.

A coy smile played on my lips, and I drained my wineglass. "Are we having a personal, or professional, conversation? And do you know about her loans?"

He sighed, and sounded so defeated that I decided to share a few details with him. I'd put everything that wasn't libelous in the paper, so as far as I was concerned, this exchange with Noah was pure gossip and would never make it into print unless confirmed somehow.

"From what I'm hearing, she'd accepted a lot of money from her students so she could expand her business. For building her brand." I made air quotes when I uttered the word *brand*. "And Kai seems to think one student in particular is shady."

"Shawn Sims?"

"Yep. Him. Have you interviewed him?"

Noah nodded. "We talked with him before she was found, though. I'm going to take another crack at him tomorrow."

"Out of curiosity, why didn't you speak with him today, or tonight? What if he's a suspect and he flees the area?"

Noah smirked. "I've asked one of my patrol officers to keep an eye on his home and business in case Shawn tries to Jet Ski off the island."

I nodded. "He didn't seem too sketchy to me. That's my opinion, though."

"You talked with him?"

"Yeah, the other day. I try to be thorough. Plus, I have yoga sources through my dad. I have a whole other list of folks to chat with tomorrow." I paused and batted my eyelashes. "We have boundaries for the information you tell me, though. What are my boundaries? What are you going to do with any information I let slip?"

He squinted one eye and grinned, then slid off the stool and crossed the kitchen, grabbing the bottle of Merlot.

"Dating a reporter's going to be difficult, isn't it?" he mused, pouring a splash in my glass, then a little in his.

"We're dating?" A zing went through me.

He set the bottle down and turned to me, placing his hands on my knees. He was tall enough that when I was seated on the stool, we were eye to eye.

"I'd like to think we are. What do you say?"

He cupped my face with his hands. "What do you say?" he repeated in a low murmur.

I answered him with a soft kiss. Possibly the most unusual kiss I'd ever had, because it wasn't only exciting, it was reassuring and tender, exactly at a moment when I needed those things. He probably did too. Maybe it was how we'd talked out our differences, or the news about Raina. Noah was someone I could trust, and I could sense it in every cell in my body.

"You know I'm going to have to leave soon," he murmured.

"Then I guess we'll continue this conversation another night." I slid my arms around him, and we hugged each other hard.

Chapter Fourteen

The next morning I raced around the café, serving customers, fielding phone calls from suppliers, and wiping down tables. I even hummed a little as I swept.

"Someone's in a good mood." A sly smile spread across Erica's face.

I grabbed a gently used copy of today's *Devil's Beach Beacon* off the table and spotted my story. I wasn't sure which was better: my kiss with Noah last night or the fact that I had a byline on the front page of a newspaper.

"What do you mean?" I asked.

Erica shrugged. "You look all glowy. And you can't tell me it's because your name's in the paper. Great story, by the way."

I let out one of those little sighs, the kind teenagers do when they see the Instagram feeds of their favorite K-pop boy band.

"Did you just swoon?" she yelped, then clamped her fingers over her mouth when two customers looked up, startled.

I pressed a hand to my chest. "Perhaps."

"You were supposed to go to puppy kindergarten with Noah last night, right?" She used air quotes around the words *puppy kindergarten* and cackled. "Is that what the kids are calling a hookup these days? Puppy kindergarten?"

"He didn't make it to class." I paused, then laughed at her expression, which made her look like an owl. "He was busy with the homicide. But he came over later."

She nodded slowly, a salacious grin spreading on her face. "Nice."

I rolled my eyes. "We kissed. Once. In the kitchen. Very chaste and sweet."

"Like teenagers! He stole a kiss!" Erica was positively gushing.

"It was"—I took a deep breath—"romantic."

She reached for her iced coffee stashed under the counter. "I'd normally say it was strange for a couple to smooch after a murder, but with you two, it kind of makes sense."

"Occupational hazard."

"Anyway. Did you have any pillow talk about Raina's case? Any new clues?"

I moved closer to Erica so I could speak in a low tone. I didn't want any of the customers to hear me. "He's worried that people on the island are going to freak out and that eventually national media will get involved and it will hurt tourism. The island's gearing up for a big tourism campaign, so they don't want any bad publicity right now."

"And what about you? Did he tell you not to snoop around and report more on the case? Did he disarm your sleuthing skills with his kiss?"

"He didn't, in fact. Which means I'm going out to do an interview today after my shift." I tossed my ponytail saucily. "And even if he did try to get me to stop investigating, I wouldn't."

"Sweet! Can I come along for the interview?"

I briefly pondered this. At the *Miami Tribune*, I'd rarely taken anyone with me during my reporting trips. Unless it was a photographer. Usually I'd knocked on doors and approached strangers all on my lonesome. Devil's Beach was a much more relaxed place, though. And I wasn't a staff writer at the paper. Freelancers had a lot more leeway, and Erica was an awesome sidekick.

Why not bring someone with me? Erica had great instincts. "Sure. We'll head out once my dad comes to relieve us at noon. I haven't asked Mike at the paper about doing another story yet, but I'm sure he'll want one if I—er, we—get some good material. No need to get Mike's hopes up just yet."

"Excellent. Who are we interviewing first?"

"A guy named the Wolfman. He owns a studio here on the island. He was Raina's main competitor and is privy to a lot of yoga gossip. You'll like him. I've known him since I was a kid. He's one of Dad's best friends."

"We can't pass up someone whose nickname is the Wolfman. Should I be prepared to take photos? Carry your notebook? Be a bodyguard? Will there be a fracas?" She cracked her knuckles and flexed the muscles in her thin arms. Even though she looked fragile, I suspected Erica could kick butt if needed.

An image of Cody's arrogant smirk came to mind. "Nah. The paper has a photographer. And who uses the word *fracas* in a sentence?"

"Not enough people." She pointed at me. "Oh, yeah. That photo dude. Who I think is interested in making you his Mrs. Right Now. He kept staring at you with googly eyes."

I stuck out my tongue. "Not my type. He reminds me too much of my ex-husband. Hotshot journalist. Arrogant. Smarmy."

"That's what I figured. And anyway, you're already smitten with Sheriff Hunk Hot Lips."

"That I am." I eyed a group of slow-moving women, all wearing flip-flops and beach cover-ups. One after another, they burst through the door, talking loudly. They stopped about ten feet from the counter and gaped at the chalkboard menu above.

I leaned into Erica. "I meant to ask you, how was your date with Joey?" Joey was the owner of the Square Grouper, one of the most popular restaurants in town. I'd set the two of them up recently.

"Oh my god, cold brew," a woman squealed in a thick Boston accent.

"I'll tell you later," Erica muttered. "Did you know his dad used to be in the Mafia? This island has some crazy secrets. The longer I stay, the more I fall in love with it."

I couldn't help but smile as I took the first order. Yeah, I knew about Joey's dad. And yes, Devil's Beach had secrets, many of them. With the mystery of Raina's suspicious death, it was likely there were new ones swirling around the island at this very moment.

* * *

" 'Wolf Yoga. Get your howl on.' " In a deadpan voice, Erica read the words on the sign, which featured a little cartoon wolf on a yoga mat, howling at a moon and doing an upward-facing dog pose. "So this is where your dad practices. He talks about it all the time."

I snickered. "Yeah, it's definitely his special place. Wolfie got my parents into yoga. Years ago he invited people to practice with him on the beach, down that path over there. It was an informal thing, and that's how Mom and Dad found him. They were walking along one morning at sunrise and joined a class. That was before Wolfie built this studio."

We climbed out of my car and meandered down a slate-rock walkway flanked by bushes that were positively rioting in pink blooms. For a fraction of a second, a wave of nostalgia washed over me, and I paused to touch a flower.

"What?" Erica asked.

"I haven't been here in years. Mom used to come often. She loved everything about this place: the quiet of the tropical foliage, the beach, the quirky atmosphere."

"It's the little moments when you really miss someone." Her voice was soft.

I took a deep, bracing breath and nodded. "C'mon, let's do this."

After a few paces, the yoga studio came into view, nestled in a thicket of lush plants.

"Whoa," Erica exclaimed. "Can't say I've seen a building like this anywhere."

"Dad says it's the only geodesic dome on the island. Maybe on the west coast of Florida. And the beach is behind it, on the other side. I vaguely remember my dad telling me when Wolfie built the thing. I was living in Miami and he called, all excited. The Wolfman built it to withstand hurricanes."

"Smart," Erica replied, moving aside a giant leaf blocking the walkway.

We passed by several effigies of the Buddha, a stone statue of (I think) Bigfoot, and a bronze figurine of a howling wolf before we arrived at a door leading into the dome. I pulled it open, and a light-filled space greeted us.

Under our feet was a shiny, blond wood floor. Toward the front of the dome—I guessed it was the front because it was opposite where we entered—were several clear triangular panels overlooking a white sand beach and a palm tree. As a place to relax, I had to admit, it was stunning.

A man with a buzz cut was standing near the clear panels, watering a potted elephant-ear plant. He turned and grinned.

"Lana? Is that you? I haven't seen you since, what? Your mother's funeral?" He set the green watering can down and walked in our direction. Wolfie was a trim guy in his seventies, with a posture that would have impressed a Marine.

I didn't recall him being at Mom's funeral, but that wasn't surprising. I'd blocked out so many details of that entire month. "I think so. Hey, Wolfie, why haven't you come into the coffee shop to say hi since I've been back?"

I crossed the dome and met him in the middle. We embraced, and I realized he smelled exactly like Dad: patchouli mixed with Colgate toothpaste. I guess that was the scent of the over-sixty set these days.

We broke apart, and he thumped my shoulder. "Good to see you. Your dad told me you'd be coming by today. Sorry I haven't been into Perkatory. I stopped drinking coffee because of my adrenals."

"Gotcha. Well, I'm glad we came when you weren't in class. Oh, this is Erica. She works at the café and is my"—I glanced at her—"reporting assistant."

I'd never in my life had a reporting assistant. Wolfie was unfazed and wandered over to pump Erica's hand.

"Nice grip you got there, woman. And you're sporting a proper set of muscles in those arms. We gotta get you in here for some power yoga."

Erica scratched her neck. "I dunno, man. I get my exercise on the boat."

Wolfie and Erica immediately began chatting about her live-aboard sailboat while I stood in the middle of the dome. It felt a little like being at a planetarium, and my instinct to lie flat on the ground and stare up at the sky was strong. I glanced up, and my stomach swam with wooziness.

The dome and its high, curved ceiling made me dizzy, as if I were looking up while standing on a ladder. It also had triangular panels, which gave it a trippy, M. C. Escher vibe. My stomach did another flip. I was afraid of heights, so this feeling was entirely unwelcome. I edged toward Erica and brushed her shoulder with mine.

"Yeah, so we're here to discuss Raina and her death." I interrupted their conversation about the fish-greedy pelicans at the marina.

"Oh, right. Fiddlesticks! Let me get some pillows and we can sit. Would you like some iced green tea? I received a special stash today."

"Sure," I said.

"Why not?" Erica replied.

Wolfie scurried around, setting three black pillows in the middle of the space. I fanned my face with my notebook.

"It's steamy in here," I whispered to Erica, while Wolfie fiddled with a mini fridge near a desk at the far end of the room.

He hustled over to us with plastic bottles of tea. "Sit, sit." He pointed to the cushions. "Sorry about the temperature. I usually only blast the AC when I have a class. You want me to crank it up now?"

"No, I'm good," I answered, and Erica said the same. We plopped down and he followed, so we were all sitting in a triangle. I cracked open my tea and took a long sip.

"Nice," I nodded. "Delicate."

Erica guzzled hers, then smacked her lips. "Doesn't have the usual overpowering grassy taste."

"Exactly," Wolfie said. "So let's get to the point."

"Yes. Let's. About Raina. What can you tell us about her?" I opened my notebook and clicked my pen. Then I tapped my phone to record the interview; I enjoyed having a backup system.

"She was a total, unmitigated witch."

A tiny dot of spittle landed on my chin, and I recoiled.

Chapter Fifteen

*D*on't hold back, Wolfie. Tell us how you really feel.
My eyebrows shot up, and I scrawled all his words down. Well, that wasn't particularly Buddha-like. The Wolfie I remembered from my teenage years was an easygoing guy. Today, his blue eyes flared with anger.

"Yikes," Erica whispered.

"Can you tell us why you feel that way?" I asked. Guess the concept of not speaking ill of the dead didn't apply here.

"Pfft. Honey. How long have you got? I could talk all day about that one."

"We'll take as long as you need." I settled into my seat, knowing this had all the hallmarks of a great interview.

He inhaled. "Okay. For starters, we were friends at first. As you know, I'm the longest-running yoga teacher on the island. Been here for fifteen years, here with this studio for about three. She came along about eighteen months ago, and I was the one who suggested she rent from your dad. She wanted a studio downtown, near a lot of foot traffic."

I nodded as I scribbled. "Go on."

"She came to class here while she was fixing up her studio space. I thought that was groovy. I'm all about helping young people and newcomers to the scene. She was so . . ." He waved his hands theatrically in the air.

"So . . . ?" I prodded.

"At first she was sweet and genuine. After class she'd stay behind and organize the prop area." He pointed behind me, and I twisted in my seat. Near the door was a tall, cubby-like bookcase filled with rolled-up mats, foam blocks, and blankets.

Wolfie continued. "After classes, students can get impatient, and they just chuck stuff into the shelves and on the floor. People can be pigs. Raina always stayed and made sure everything was orderly. She'd also do things like bring my wife and me bags of oranges, thoughtful gestures. But that all changed when she opened her own studio. It was some Jekyll and Hyde stuff, and I realized she was just using me."

"How so?" Erica asked.

"When she opened Dante's Inferno, she stopped talking to me. At first I thought she was just busy and overwhelmed, so I thought I'd give her some space, but when I ran into her downtown, she brushed me off. I figured she'd be back to her sunny self eventually. Then she stole my newsletter list. That was my tip-off that she was nothing but a money-grubbing bottom-feeder."

"Okay. What does that mean? The newsletter part, not the money-grubbing part." I licked my lips.

"She wanted a copy of my list, of everyone who had signed up for my newsletter. I never sell addresses. Been collecting them for years. And I get a lot of them, because I livestream events. Tons of tourists come here. And locals, of course." He puffed out his chest.

"Are you sure she tried to steal it?"

He snorted. "My wife and I sometimes stay here in the trailer out back, and I use it as an office. The rest of the time we live in a condo downtown. One day we came here and caught her inside the trailer. She was at my laptop with a thumb drive. She knew I never locked the place."

"She broke into your office?"

"Yep."

"Did you file a police report?"

"Tried to. But the old chief, he was useless. Chief Noah would've taken it seriously." Wolfie waved his hand. "And Raina, as you know, was beautiful. She won that cop over in seconds. All she had to do was invite him to her studio and strip down to her little shorts and sports bra."

I cleared my throat and locked eyes with Erica. "So I take it she didn't get your email records."

"She did. When I walked in on her, she was snapping the laptop shut and had a thumb drive in her hot little hand. She smirked at me and left. I coulda killed her, I was so mad."

I let his words hang in the air.

"Wow. Sounds shameless," Erica prodded.

He shook his head. "Outrageous. And criminal."

"What did she do with that list?" I asked.

"She emailed everyone to invite them to her studio opening. Then kept emailing them, giving them discounts on classes. Even offered them a free yoga mat for joining."

"Ugh. So did you lose clients?"

"Absofreakinlutely." His voice rose and bounced off the convex roof of the geodesic dome. "My classes were down by two-thirds for months. They're still not back to where they were before she opened."

I winced. Raina had done a number on his business, it sounded like.

"And then she spread rumors about me. First, it was how I had poor technique in doing headstands."

I glanced up from my notebook, and Erica butted in. "How is your technique? I mean, some people teach headstands in a way that's hard on the neck."

When had she become a yoga expert?

"I teach the safest way of doing a headstand. Here. Let me show you."

Erica and I watched as he moved through each step, doing a pose called the dolphin, which looked suspiciously like a push-up to me. Then he set the crown of his head on the floor and walked his feet toward his face so that his body was in an upside-down V.

"You use your core strength to lift your legs up, and boop. Headstand." He lifted his legs, and indeed, he was balancing on his head and forearms.

I wasn't sure if we should applaud or what, so I settled on, "Very nice."

"That's exactly the best technique," Erica cried out, clapping her hands. She was a constant surprise with her obscure knowledge.

Wolfie untangled himself from the headstand and returned to sit next to us on his cushion. I needed to get the interview back on track.

"So she was wrong about your headstand teaching. What else?"

"Her allegations became more nefarious. She claimed I was inappropriate with my students. Which was absolutely not true. I am one hundred percent respectful of my students. And I've been married for forty years. Your parents and my wife and I have been friends for decades."

He had a point. Every time Wolfie and his wife, Sadie, came to visit when I was a kid, they had seemed so in love.

"Inappropriate how?" I asked.

He threw his veiny hands in the air. "I have no idea! It was allegations and veiled rumors."

"Did she offer any proof?" Erica leaned in.

"None at all. She started a whisper campaign. People mentioned she'd drop little comments into conversations. She never came out and gave details. Every time I asked someone, they said it was insinuations and half-baked lies."

"Did she say you harassed *her*?" I asked, needing to be clear on this point.

"No. Because she couldn't. I've never been alone with her. My wife has always been with me when Raina was around. Not on purpose; it just happened that way. Sadie helps with my yoga classes and does the books for the business. Raina told people she'd heard things about me. Nothing substantial and nothing anyone could ever confirm. She was trying to destroy my business, pure and simple."

"When were those rumors?"

"Well, the headstand allegations, that people were getting neck injuries from the way I teach—that happened about a month after she opened her studio. Then things died down for a while. The other rumors cropped up about two months ago."

I nodded slowly. The fury in his voice left me with more questions than answers. In my experience, people usually tried to say something nice about a dead person, even if they hated them. Wolfe hadn't done any such thing. He'd launched into his tirade

162

immediately and hadn't let up. Come to think of it, Kai's description of Raina hadn't exactly been glowing either.

"Can you think of anyone who wanted her dead?" I asked.

"Pfft. The way she took money from people and used them? I'd say the list is a mile long."

"Who did she take money from, and why?" I suspected this part of the interview wouldn't make it into an article because it veered into hearsay territory. But this was the fun part of interviewing: probing people who might give up a detail that could later be confirmed.

"She wanted to expand her brand," he said bitterly, echoing almost exactly what Kai had told me. "She wanted to be an international yoga star. Oh, she told people many stories; it was hard to decipher what was real and what was a lie. She needed that image, you know? She was hiring a top TV production crew to do videos on the beach. She was going to build a new, freestanding studio here on Devil's Beach and make it a yoga mecca in Florida. She needed money to buy land for the freestanding studio. That she had an offer for a partnership with a clothing company. On and on and on."

"It seemed like she had some brand partnerships, from what I've read."

"Yeah, she had a few. Because she was photogenic. And she was excellent at yoga. As much as I hate to admit it, she did all the postures perfectly. Some people are born with flexibility."

Even sitting in a cross-legged position on this cushion, my lower back and hamstrings ached a little. I straightened my spine. "So, if you could point the police in any direction to her killer, who would be your top suspects?"

He scrunched up his face and tilted his head to the left, then to the right. "Well, there's Kai. The boyfriend's always the first suspect in these sorts of situations, at least if you watch any crime television."

"Exactly what we were thinking," Erica interjected. I narrowed my eyes at her and willed her to be quiet.

"But Noah said Kai had an alibi," I piped up.

The Wolfman lifted a lone gray eyebrow. "Murder for hire, perhaps. And there's also her stalker."

"Shawn. The Jet Ski guy," I offered.

"Yeah, him. Apparently he's been slavishly following her around for weeks."

"Okay, who else?" Erica asked.

"I heard that she got into a blowout in Costa Rica with one of her students. Molly Wayne. And one of her teachers was also pretty disgruntled."

"What's her name?"

"You didn't get it from me. It was Jennis Hudson. She used to practice here but jumped ship to join Raina. You can probably catch both women at the studio this week." He also mentioned three other people, all students of Dante's Inferno. "Those students didn't have a problem with Raina but could probably tell you more about her in general."

I carefully wrote the names down, then underlined Jennis and Molly. They'd been two of the women at the news conference. And I knew exactly where to find them. The other three people he mentioned wouldn't be difficult to find, not with names like Petal and Shakti and Gia.

"Where were you Saturday afternoon?" Erica asked, leaning in. I looked up, eyes wide.

"Me? You talking to me?" Wolfie pointed at his chest. A twinge of a long-buried New York accent emerged.

"Yeah." She stared him down. Yikes. This wasn't how I wanted to end this interview. We were here for information purposes only, not to make a citizen's arrest.

"I was with my wife. We were going to stop by that barista competition. Your dad invited me." Wolfie's flashing eyes turned on me. "But we went off island and took a hike near the Little Snake River on the mainland. The wife's gotten into searching for rare ghost orchids in the swamp."

I frowned. "You know they have those at Angelwing Park, right?"

Wolfie stared at me for an uncomfortable beat. "Of course we know that. My wife gives tours there. She knows where all the ghost orchids are in that park and when they're going to bloom. There aren't any right now. That's why we went to the Little Snake River area."

"Snakes?" Erica's face puckered. I ignored her and sensed Wolfie was going to launch into an explanation about reptiles, so I cut him off.

"I see. Well, thanks for this." His alibi was definitely worth checking out, although I didn't want to accuse my father's oldest friend of murder, at least not yet. "I think this is all we need. I'll call you if I have any other questions."

The three of us scrambled to our feet. Well, I scrambled while grunting. Erica and Wolfie popped up.

"I have an alibi," he cried, walking us to the door. "You can check with my wife. I also think she has a receipt for our lunch that day. We ate at that place with the great waffles."

"Well, thanks. Why don't you give me her number?"

"Aw heck, I don't know it off the top of my head. Here, let me get my phone."

"Perfect. That sounds pleasant. Let's hit that up."

She shifted in her seat, a flush creeping over her cheekbones. "Can't. Gotta date with Joey. He's coming over to the sailboat."

I smiled, then turned down the road leading to the Swamp. "No worries. I can go alone. Hey, let's go check something out. You have time, right? It's only three."

"Yeah, I'm not meeting him until six thirty. We're doing cocktails and he's bringing over his lasagna. What have you got in mind?"

"Lasagna. Sounds serious." We whizzed past Raina's house. "I want to check out the crime scene. You up for that?"

Erica turned to look at me, sliding her glasses down her nose much like Horatio Caine in *CSI: Miami*. "Heck yeah, babycakes. You know I love a little intrigue."

Chapter Sixteen

When we drove into the Swamp, there were only a couple of cars in the lot. "This isn't a popular place in midday." I eased the car under the shade of an oak tree.

"Probably because it's the temperature of the devil's den."

We got out, and I immediately started to sweat. "Wish I'd brought a hat."

"No kidding."

Erica, as usual, was in all black. Black tank top, black shorts, black sandals. I was in my unofficial uniform as well: well-worn jeans, Converse sneakers, and a light-pink Perkatory T-shirt.

We stopped at the map billboard and studied it.

"I think they found her right about here." I pointed to the far bend, indicated by a yellow squiggly line. "It's not as far as it looks. The entire boardwalk is only a mile, and in a loop. See?" I swept my finger around the map, indicating the oval-shaped trail.

"I've never been in here. Let's check it out."

We plodded along the boardwalk in silence, our shoes making muted thumping noises. On each side of the wooden rails were tall mangroves and, below, murky swamp water the color of sweet tea.

"This is where the monkeys live, right? Your grandfather's monkeys?"

"Well, their descendants, yeah. He lived in a property south of here." I waved my hand in the direction I believed to be south. "But back then, this wasn't even a nature preserve. It was a big, undeveloped plot of land. The city bought it shortly after the monkeys took it over."

"I wonder if we'll see any," she mused aloud.

"Usually not in the middle of the day. It's too hot for them. They like to take siestas in the trees where it's cooler. Probably best to spot them in the early morning. I've also heard that they're easier to spot if you're in a kayak. See those little breaks in the trees? Those are kayak trails through the mangroves."

"Cool. We should definitely come back in a boat."

I shot her a skeptical look.

"What?" she asked.

"I'm not big on water sports."

She punched me in the arm lightly. "Aw, come on. Let's have an adventure. What could be better than paddling at dawn and seeing monkeys?"

"Staying in bed. Reading the paper. Basking in the air conditioning."

"And you need to get over your boat phobia. I want to have you over to my place sometime."

"I don't have a boat phobia. Maybe a dislike of kayaks in swamps." We both laughed and walked on. I was going to remark again about how hot it was, but there was no use in even expending the energy. When we got to where the boardwalk curved, I slowed.

I paused, looking over the wooden rail at the sepia-colored water. Erica stood next to me, and we watched as an alligator floated by. It went under the boardwalk, beneath our feet.

Erica shuddered. "See you later, little gator."

"He wasn't so little," I said.

"Are there snakes in here?"

I shrugged. "Maybe little ones, but no."

"Good." She blew out a breath. "So this is where she was found?"

"Yeah. At least this is where Noah described it. Look." I pointed at a mangrove, where a short snippet of crime scene tape clung to a branch. It flapped in the wind, the only evidence of the horror discovered here.

The silence of the swamp overtook us. All we could hear was a hum of invisible bugs and, every so often, a soft splash in the water.

I glanced around, from the mangroves to the sun-soaked wooden boardwalk. "How did she end up here?"

Erica leaned with her back to the rail, propping her elbows up. "Right? Did someone kill her and then bring her out here? Or was she killed here?"

"Excellent question. You'd think if she was killed elsewhere, there would have been evidence on the boardwalk coming in. Blood or something."

"Unless the person brought her here by boat."

I nodded slowly. "Or brought her nearby, and the current carried her here."

"That's a possibility too."

We stood for a few more minutes while I took the notebook out of my bag and scrawled a few notes. *Desolate. Isolated. Quiet. Mangroves and cicadas, harsh sun, tea-colored water, the smell of dirt and sunshine.*

I closed the notebook and jammed it in my bag. "Let me snap a couple of photos too. It'll jog my memory while writing."

I took a few with my cell, from all angles, then waved at Erica. "That's all I need. Want to go back the way we came or go all the way around? We're about halfway."

"Eh, we might as well continue on. Who knows? We might spot a monkey." Erica flashed me a wan smile. It was admirable how she was trying to put a positive spin on this scene. In reality, it was depressing, seeing Raina's watery grave in a swamp.

We had cleared the second bend and were bearing down on the straight boardwalk when we saw someone jogging toward us.

"Jeez, who would go for a jog in this heat?" Erica muttered.

"Only a crazy person."

The figure came closer, and I realized it was a guy. A familiar-looking one. He was about twenty feet away now, and I could see his face clearly. "Holy crap, I think that's Shawn."

"Who?"

"The guy who allegedly stalked Raina," I hissed.

I'd no sooner gotten the words out than he turned and sprinted in the other direction.

Erica and I glanced at each other. "Let's get him," she cried.

We took off running. I wasn't entirely sure why, or what we'd do if we caught up with him. All I knew was that it seemed pretty heckin' weird for him to be here, of all places, in the middle of the day.

* * *

We tore down the boardwalk, our shoes slapping against the wood.

"Shawn!" I gasped in as loud a voice as I could muster.

Erica was far more forceful, or her lungs were. "Hey! Hold up! We wanna talk to you."

He didn't stop. Within a few seconds he was out of our sight. Shawn and his physically fit legs were too fast for us. This didn't shock me, although I was impressed at how quick Erica could sprint. She was several paces ahead of me.

By the time we reached the parking lot, a white car was driving away.

"That was him," Erica said.

I doubled over, trying to take in more air. "I'm really out of shape. Blergh. I've got to get my act together, fitnesswise. And with this story."

"Yoga tonight will do you some good."

I straightened, still gasping. "Why did Shawn run from us?"

"I dunno. But it's awfully suspicious."

It sure was. It was all I could think of while dropping Erica off at her sailboat, while feeding Stanley his dinner, and while talking to Dad. He called to give a full report on the latest cold brew batch, and I put him on speakerphone.

"It still tastes terrible, munchkin."

I let out a long groan. This again? "I'll try a different recipe. It has to be something I'm doing wrong."

When I hung up, I avoided thinking about that mystery and turned to the other one that was percolating in my mind: Raina. I launched into a deep dive on Google into Raina and her real last name: Romero. Because I still had my old paper's log-in information to the state's criminal records database, I could check there too.

ROMERO, RAINA R
DOB 12/10/1990
RACE: CAUCASIAN

"Bingo," I whooped as I clicked on the hyperlink. I leaned forward. There was one charge, when she was twenty-two.

Felony fraud, in Jacksonville.

"Well, well, well." I tapped the pen against my chin. The records didn't explain the case, only the resolution: she'd pleaded the charge to a misdemeanor and been levied a five-hundred-dollar fine.

I clicked over to my email and sent a message to Sheila, a former colleague of mine who worked as an editor at the paper in Jacksonville.

I will give you my firstborn if you can find this case for me at the courthouse, I wrote.

Her reply came almost immediately: *I'd rather have a bag of your coffee, if you don't mind. Seriously, I should have this for you early next week.*

Yass. This was the best feeling, tracking down information. I promised Sheila a few bags of coffee.

Emboldened, I Googled Kai. Didn't find much, other than mentions in yoga studio newsletters and some high school track team rosters. His father, though, was a different story. Kenneth Lahtinen Senior had no fewer than four ethics commission complaints against him, all for campaign-donor-reporting problems and a lack of financial disclosure forms. He'd beaten all of them, unsurprisingly.

In my experience, Florida politicians weren't exactly sticklers for ethics. And neither was the state ethics board, which was supposed to police the politicians. I dutifully made notes on everything, though.

I turned my attention to the names Wolfie had given me earlier in the day. Since I knew where to find Jennis and Molly, I didn't bother looking for them.

However, I located Petal, Shakti, and Gia, and for a solid hour I messaged with them back and forth, peppering them with questions. All three expressed sadness over Raina's death and adoration for her yoga.

I loved her classes! They were so hard and I always felt great after them, Petal gushed.

It's so sad she's gone, wrote Shakti. *I had to stop attending when I moved to New York. I miss Devil's Beach so much.*

Yeah, she was a bit of a saleswoman, but the yoga was epic. And I liked her hustle. It was inspirational. Her boyfriend Kai runs a great class on the weekend. You should come, typed Gia.

I thanked them all and shut my laptop. The interviews with the students hadn't yielded much other than effusive quotes. Which were fine, but they wouldn't move the story forward. Raina's fraud arrest was potentially more promising.

I'd have to double down on my efforts to interview more people in person, including Jennis and Molly. I also wanted to locate Heidi, the woman who'd cried the most at the news conference. She seemed like she'd known Raina intimately.

With any luck, I'd run into all of them at yoga class tonight.

Chapter Seventeen

I settled on a safe and, most important, comfortable ensemble: gray workout leggings, a black sports bra, and a slightly off-the-shoulder white T-shirt that read SURELY NOT EVERYONE WAS KUNG FU FIGHTING.

Stanley tried to climb my leg by standing on his back paws, and I scooped him up and planted a giant smooch on the top of his tawny head. The older he got, the more he looked like a mini Ewok.

I put him in the kitchen, penned in with a baby gate. Dad had advised me to keep him there while I was gone, so he wouldn't destroy stuff or poop everywhere.

As I walked out, I remembered a key part of yoga. The mat. *Drat.*

I could probably rent or use one at the studio. From my limited experience with yoga—granted, my last encounter had been about eight years ago in Miami with my ex—I knew that studios had extra mats for students to use. Lying on a piece of rubber that someone else had stepped on with their bare feet and probably sweated on made my stomach curdle. I'm a bit of a germophobe.

Since I was living in my parents' old place, I knew there was a bunch of junk in the garage. Probably Dad and Mom had stowed a mat or two in there. They'd always bought new things and stashed the old crap there. I'd been meaning to clear it out but hadn't had the energy.

I checked the time. I had exactly fifteen minutes to get to yoga. Dante's Inferno was next door to Perkatory, which meant it was only two blocks away. I sprinted into the garage and flicked on the light. My eyes scanned the stacks of stuff collected by my parents over a lifetime.

Then I spotted it: a rolled-up purple mat, still in plastic. "Bingo," I whispered, sidestepping a treadmill.

Someday I'd really have to come in here and assess the contents. There was no need to have this much excess stuff.

While unwrapping the mat, I flew back inside, stuffed the plastic in the trash, and called out a good-bye to Stanley. I sailed out the door. Since I was running a little late, I took off at a soft jog. For the first few steps, I felt triumphant and hoped my neighbors were taking note.

Look at me! I'm exercising on my way to exercise!

Soon my breath grew short, but I pressed on. No pain, no gain. As I grew closer to my family's building, I picked up the pace, not wanting the customers at Perkatory to see me dragging and gasping. A few looked up and pointed, and I casually waved. In my mind, I was bouncy and light on my feet.

In reality, I was probably plodding like a sick elephant. But at least I was trying.

I yanked open the door to Dante's Inferno. For some reason, there was no one at the front desk. Odd. How would I register for class and pay? Didn't they want me to fill out a release form in case I was injured?

I stood for a second in the middle of the lobby, trying to catch my breath. My gaze landed on a flashy, orange, blown-glass sculpture of what looked like flames. At least I thought it was flames. It was abstract enough that I wasn't sure.

The front door swung open. A muscular guy I didn't recognize walked in. He nodded and walked past me, down the corridor, and into the room where the press conference had been held.

Crud. I should've asked him about registering and paying. He sure looked like he belonged here, with his blue shorts and perfectly fitted white tank top.

There was a clock above the empty desk, and I glanced at it. Two minutes to seven. Yikes. I had to claim a space with my mat. Needed to get into the room and calm my nerves before class started. I'd pay afterward. I walked down the hall and spotted a line of shoes. Mostly flip-flops. That's when I remembered from my few classes years ago that I had to take off my shoes before going into the yoga room.

I toe-heeled my sneakers off but left my socks on. Or, ew. Maybe not. It was hot yoga. Grimacing at the thought of swaddled feet and the blazing temperatures of a hot room, I stripped off my socks and stuffed them in my shoes.

As I gently eased the door open, I plastered a sheepish smile on my face. One that suggested, *I'm new here and not bendy at all, so please be nice.*

But my grin, and my entire face, plummeted when I got an eyeful of what was inside.

Naked men. At least two dozen of them. They all turned to me. Some chuckled; others groaned.

And there, closest to me, was the man I'd spent weeks lusting after. The top cop on Devil's Beach. The man I'd kissed the night before.

"Noah?" I blinked, trying to focus on his muscular chest and not, well, anywhere below.

"Lana?" His hands cupped his privates. My eyes landed on his hands. My brain stopped working, and not only because of his physical, naked beauty. I was still stuck on the obvious question.

What were all these men doing in their birthday suits? My feet began to sweat, and I was seemingly attached to the wooden floor. Someone familiar was in the front, gaping at me. Oh no . . .

"Oh, hey, Lana." Kai gave me a casual little salute. He was also naked as the day he was born. My jaw dropped. A nervous giggle slipped out of my mouth.

"Lana, I think you're in the wrong room. This is men's candle-light nude yoga," Noah said in a gentle voice.

I dropped my mat, and it half unfurled at my feet. Noah and I locked eyes, and my face felt like I'd dipped it into a vat of ghost peppers.

Noah bent in the direction of my mat.

"No, no. I've got it. Stay where you are," I cried. Mortified, I bent down and scooped up the mat, which rolled out even more. Letting out an unladylike grunt, I tossed the mat over my shoulder like a scarf, turned, and fled.

I sprinted outside. When the door shut behind me, I paused to roll up my mat, which was severely hampering my ability to run to where I intended to go—the next continent, preferably. Once it was in a nice, tight roll, I took off again, jogging past Perkatory's windows without a glance inside.

As I was rounding the corner of the building, I nearly ran smack into a thin, dark-haired woman.

"Oof," she cried. "Be careful."

I'd stabbed her stomach with my yoga mat. As she rubbed her midsection with her right hand, I realized she looked familiar. She was clad in what appeared to be a tight red unitard. It was fabulous on her; I would've looked like a tomato.

"Oh, god. I'm so sorry." I wrangled the yoga mat to my shoulder. Then it hit me: it was one of the women who'd been at Kai's news conference. "You're the studio manager at . . ." I motioned toward Dante's Inferno but couldn't utter the name aloud because I was still so embarrassed.

"It's okay. And yes, I'm Jennis." Her eyes were a pale hazel, striking against her dark hair. Like the other women in Raina's orbit, she was super fit and willowy, as if she'd jumped off the pages of *Yoga Magazine*. She squinted at me. "You own Perkatory, right?"

I glanced at the window. "Yep. That's me."

"But you were also at the news conference." Her eyes went to my mat, which I was holding like a bayonet against my shoulder.

"I'm also a reporter. I've been writing about Raina's case." An idea came to me. "Hey, I was hoping to talk with some of the teachers at Dante's Inferno about Raina for another article. Do you have a few minutes to join me for a coffee? Step into my office and we can talk?"

She shot me a funny look, then scowled at her Apple Watch. "Your office?"

"I was joking. I meant the coffee shop."

She blinked, not getting my lame attempt at humor. "I've ignored the phones at the studio long enough. Mind if we do it in there?"

I flinched, thinking about Noah and all those naked guys bending and twisting. Jennis tapped her flip-flop-covered foot.

Her pedicure was the same color as her unitard. So was her manicure. The red polish popped against the single ring on her right middle finger. It was unusual, blue and veiny, as if the band itself was carved from an unusual marble.

"Okay. It shouldn't take long. But if you'd ever like to try one of our excellent coffee drinks, feel free to come over and I'll hook you up. We source our beans from Ethiopia, Jamaica, and Guatemala."

She ignored me, moving toward the yoga studio while I blathered on about our various coffee blends.

We marched inside and she slipped behind the desk, opening the laptop while glancing everywhere but at me. "Okay, so what do you want to ask me?"

I set the yoga mat down and reached for my notebook, pen, and cell phone, setting them all on the desk next to a brochure with a picture of Raina in a pose that seemed physically impossible.

Then it hit me: I'd never actually cleared all this additional reporting with Mike. He'd published that first, short story after Raina's body was discovered, then the longer print story the following day. After that, I hadn't heard from him, and I'd gone on my merry way, chasing leads and doing interviews. I wanted to make sure I had enough for an article before I pitched him another story. I'd call Mike tomorrow, and he'd surely give approval for another article since I was getting such great material.

"I hope you don't mind if I record our interview."

She had a perpetually distracted gaze that made me feel like I was taking up too much of her time. "I guess not. Hey, were you just in class?"

My face grew hot. "Uh. I stopped by. Then I realized that particular class wasn't exactly my style. I'll try again some other time."

"Cool. We have a lot of great offerings."

Like a roomful of naked men. I nodded, praying I'd wrap up this interview before Noah and the class ended.

"Candlelight nude yoga isn't for everyone."

"Definitely not as the only woman."

She pressed her lips together. "You walked into the men's nude yoga?"

So there were two nude yoga classes? What in the world had Erica been thinking? I swallowed hard. "Uh . . . I think there was a mix-up."

A little tinkle of laughter escaped her mouth, and for the first time, she looked me in the eye. "People do that all the time, mix up the classes. Either intentionally or unintentionally. It's a great way to remove the toxins in your body, though."

I nodded, hitting the record button. We needed to steer this conversation into more useful territory, before my face became a Flamin' Hot Cheeto. "Right. So tell me about Raina."

She tapped her short, perfectly manicured red fingernails on the wooden desk and sobered. "Gosh. Where to begin? She was great at two things: sun salutations and emotional blackmail."

Goodness. In all my years as a reporter, I'd never interviewed so many people who had such terrible things to say about a dead person.

Chapter Eighteen

"Wow. That's a serious allegation. But I guess you'd know, since she was your boss and all."

Jennis huffed a breath out of her nose. "It's awful to speak ill of the dead. But I'm still salty from what happened at the retreat."

"Tell me."

"It was all to do with money. Initially, Raina told us that the teachers had to pay for airfare and incidentals. Then we arrive, and boom! We were told we had to pay for our hotel and food. A couple of the other teachers were fine with it, claimed that Raina was going through a tough time and we should be honored to teach at her seminar. But I called her on it. This is my only job. I don't make a lot."

"Wow. That must have been quite a shock."

She snorted. "And so, after I threw down my credit card, she took me off the schedule and left me to teach one meditation class. I traveled there for nothing." She blinked.

"So what did you do for ten days?"

"Hung out on the beach. Hiked in the jungle. Looked at monkeys and sloths. Don't get me wrong. It was a great time. But it was awkward, embarrassing, and financially devastating." She paused and looked down at her hands, which were folded in front of her. "I'm not proud of this, but I kind of blew up at Raina on the flight home."

"Really? What happened?" I glanced at the ring again. It looked familiar. Where had I seen it?

"I had three of those little bottles of vodka and went bananas."

"Oh dear. How did she react?" I couldn't imagine this in-control woman exploding in such a public place. But even in retelling the story, she was obviously upset, judging by the way her hands shook as she gestured.

"With that fake piousness. Told me I needed to work on myself and my toxic behavior. But it was her who was toxic. I was ready to quit working here. But she begged me to stay."

"When did she do that?"

"The morning she disappeared." She paused. "We had a long text thread."

"Mind if I see it?"

"I erase all my texts immediately. Sorry."

I chewed on my cheek. "I see. So where were you on Saturday, the day she disappeared?"

"Teaching a daylong workshop." She flipped through a stack of papers and, with a flourish, set a flyer on the counter in front of me: *Hot Yin Yoga Workshop with Jennis Hudson: Only $50!*

"There were twenty-five students." A tinge of pride laced her tone.

"I see. May I keep this?"

She slid the flyer to me, and I studied the blue stone ring again. "I appreciate your interest in all this," she said breezily, gesturing to my notebook. "But I really have to do some work.

183

Kai's asked me to continue on as studio manager, and we have a lot to organize here. Raina was great at branding but terrible with organization. Apologies that I couldn't be of more help. I started here a few months ago. I was a huge fan of hers before the retreat. I even defended her against her many haters. Or did, until Costa Rica."

"Did she have a lot of enemies?"

Jennis sneered and stared to the left. "Pfft. Is it hard to do a crow pose on the first try?"

I wasn't sure how to answer that, but I assumed it was, indeed, difficult to do a crow pose on the first try. Crap. If only we had more time for this interview. I was sure she knew a lot more than she was letting on. It was worth trying to eke out a couple more questions.

"Here's what I don't understand. If she was so awful, why did people flock to her? I've seen dozens of people stream in here every day of the week. Clearly they loved her; otherwise this place wouldn't have been so popular and your classes wouldn't be so packed." I gestured to the room where a couple dozen naked men were doing yoga right this very second. My face grew hot.

Jennis leaned in. "She had that special sauce. That quality."

I lifted my hands. "What quality?"

"She made you want to be around her. Like she was doing the coolest, most exciting things, even when she was just hanging out at the yoga studio. And when you first meet her—well, met her—she was attentive and friendly and, like, sparkling. It was only later, when you got to know her, that she became difficult and manipulative. She had a way of first finding out your deepest, darkest secrets, then exploiting that information."

"Like blackmail?" I hissed.

"Yes, like emotional blackmail. If she knew you were trying to set goals and be more disciplined, she'd remind you of that when she needed something done. For instance, she'd say, 'Jennis, can you come in on your day off to clean the studio? I know you're trying to be more attentive with your routines.' " She mimicked a high-pitched voice.

"Couldn't you have just said no?"

"Yes, but . . . no. She always somehow twisted it around so that it seemed like a good idea for you, when really it was only benefiting her. Kai got the worst of it, poor guy. He never knew whether he was coming or going with her. Talk about a toxic relationship."

"Wow. Okay." I took a deep breath. "Do you know who might have wanted to kill Raina?"

Jennis blinked with rapid fire. "The list is a mile long. She upset so many people with her money shenanigans and her fake friendliness, and she probably manipulated those people into supporting her. The police sure have their work cut out for them."

She leaned in and lowered her voice. "I even heard she was a convicted felon. Something about fraud. Don't know any details, though. I never asked and it was just a rumor. I was grateful to have a job. It's not like there are a lot of opportunities for yoga teachers here on the island. That's also why I stuck around, and her promises to turn this studio into a retreat. See? There I go again—even after all this, I believed she'd do something great."

That charge out of Jacksonville!

I heard the creak of a door coming from one of the studio rooms, and my heart rate sped up. Yikes. Was class over already? I wasn't about to stick around and find out, because I didn't want to face Noah. My eyes landed on Jennis's hand again.

"Thanks again. Oh hey, pretty ring." I pointed at her finger.

She smiled. "Thanks. I made it. I'm a jewelry designer in my spare time. Not like I have a lot of it these days, though."

I stuffed everything in my purse and grabbed my mat, which somehow unrolled. Crud. I scooped it up like a blanket just out of the dryer and tried to exit with as much dignity as possible.

I took my time walking the two blocks home, going over the interview in my mind. Jennis's story made me more suspicious of everyone and everything. And I finally remembered where I'd seen a similar ring: on Kai's finger. What did that mean?

Now I was more confused than ever about what had happened to Raina.

*　*　*

Stanley barked like crazy the moment I stepped inside. While cooing and praising him for being a good boy, I freed him from his makeshift prison in the kitchen and brought him to the backyard.

Stanley nosed around in the grass and spotted a squirrel on the trunk of a palm tree. The squirrel was almost as big as him, but that didn't stop him from zooming to the tree, sending the creature climbing into the fronds. For good measure, Stanley peed on the trunk.

I sank onto the porch steps. The weird, brief interview and the humiliating scene at the yoga studio swirled in my mind, competing for meaning. Of all the embarrassing moments in my life—of which there had been many—crashing a men's candlelight nude yoga class topped the list.

When I shut my eyes, all I could think of was Noah. And his nakedness. And his look of wide-eyed incredulity that I was standing there, yoga mat in hand, while two dozen naked dudes stared back at me.

I burst out in a laugh. Yikes. I was a goofball.

Still laughing, I reached for my phone and dialed Erica.

"Hey, shouldn't you be in class?" In the background, I heard the pop of what sounded like a bottle of champagne. Joey must be there.

"I was about to go to class, but you sent me to men's nude candlelight yoga."

There was a pause, then a scream of laughter and a gurgle. "Hang on while I wipe my face. I shot champagne out of my nose. No. Stop. You did not."

"I did."

"You walked in on a bunch of naked guys?"

"Yes. There were two classes tonight. One for men, one for women. Both were nude candlelight yoga sessions. I picked the wrong room."

"Sounds like the right room to me." She was in near hysterics.

"Funny."

"I wonder why they don't hold them together? Seems unfair to segregate by sex."

I rubbed my temples with my free hand. "But wait, there's more."

Erica snort-laughed. "Hang on, Lana. Joey, I'm okay. Muddle the mint with the raspberries. Then put the champagne in with the bitters. It's Lana. Hang on, I'll be right there. She's telling me the craziest story about naked yoga. Lana, you still there? We're getting cozy in the kitchen with our cocktail concoctions."

I sighed, too keyed up to argue about whether Joey should know about my embarrassing evening. "Yes. I'm here. So guess who was in class?"

"Your dad?"

I grimaced. That might have been the only way tonight could've been worse. "No. Noah. Chief Noah Garcia."

I had to wait fifteen seconds for her to stop laughing.

"You're killing me. Noah? Was he naked?" she asked, gasping.

"Yep." I made the *p* pop.

When she snort-laughed again, I had to cut her off. "It's not hilarious. It's mortifying. I've only seen one man naked in my life, and that was my ex-husband."

"Well, now you've seen two dozen of them." She paused, giggling. "And you got to check out the goods with Noah."

"Gah. Erica? Would you stop? I'll let you go. Have a fun night. I'm going to hide under a blanket for the next several years. This is going to be all over the island by morning."

"Don't sweat it," she said. "You did it in the pursuit of truth and justice."

"Yeah, I guess. I also ended up getting an interesting interview."

"Tell me about it tomorrow, okay? And hey, sorry for steering you wrong. Honestly. I guess I missed the nude part on the schedule."

"Definitely. Okay, have fun tonight."

We hung up. I quickly checked the Dante's Inferno website on my phone, and it appeared as though the nude part of class was downplayed in small print. Well, that was some bad branding. Even I knew that.

Stanley bounded over to me, a small, dirty tennis ball in his mouth.

"Let's exchange this for a fresh one, okay, buddy? It's getting dark." I wrestled the little ball out of his mouth—I'd bought him the size for small dogs—and he followed me inside. When I tossed it in the trash, he let out a whimper, but then I opened a kitchen drawer.

"Don't worry, Stan. I've got the stash." He did a little dance when I flashed the new fluorescent yellow ball, and I tossed it into the living room. He scampered after it.

No sooner had I poured myself a glass of wine than there was a knock on the door. Weird. I wasn't expecting anyone. I padded to the door and looked out the window panel.

It was Noah. Fully clothed, perfectly handsome. His eyes met mine and he smiled, his lips pressed together as if he was suppressing a laugh. My face burst into flames, and I flung open the door.

"Hey." I stared down at his sneakers.

"Lana."

"Sorry," I mumbled.

"Why are you apologizing? Can I come in?"

I stood aside, and he walked in. My heart sped up. "Is yoga already over?"

"Yeah, it was only an hour-long class."

Stanley raced in at the sound of Noah's voice, dropped his tennis ball, and barked once. Noah crouched, and my puppy launched himself at his best buddy, making that growly play noise.

"Little monster." Noah grabbed and tickled him. Stanley was overjoyed. I stared at the top of Noah's head and winced as I recalled the scene in the yoga studio.

"Want some water? Or wine? I'm indulging." I was eager to do something, anything, other than look him in the eye.

Noah stood. "Water would be great, thanks."

I scurried off, fetching him a glass. It took me a few minutes to dig out a lemon from the fridge and cut a slice, because I was procrastinating. How was I going to explain why I'd stumbled into men's nude yoga? When I looked up, he was in the doorway, smiling.

"So, want to tell me why you showed up at class tonight?"

I handed him the glass and focused on his chin. "I could ask the same question of you."

"I was trying to get some information on Raina. I've never attended a nude yoga session before. To say it was awkward was an understatement. But sometimes you need to be uncomfortable to get information."

I raised an eyebrow and stared at a chair. "You're telling me. Gives a new meaning to undercover police work."

He laughed. "I take it you were doing the same thing?"

"Erica and I were hanging out today, and she told me about the class. Only she didn't say it was for men only."

"There's a women's nude class in the other room. Maybe she accidentally sent you to the wrong class? Accidentally on purpose?"

I swallowed, even more mortified. "The website isn't really clear. And it was my fault. There was no one at the front desk. Some guy walked in, and I figured I'd follow him into the room. And then there you were. There you all were. Nude. So awkward. So naked."

"A little awkward, yes. Nothing we can't overcome. Why aren't you looking me in the eye?"

"A little awkward? No, a lot, Noah. You might think of me as some crazy, freewheeling reporter, but I am actually a prude. I was not prepared for all of"—I waved my hand in the air, over Noah's body—"that."

Noah chuckled. "I don't know that freewheeling comes to mind when I think of you."

"You know what I mean. Yikes. I've never seen that many naked people in my life." I wasn't about to tell him I'd seen only one man naked prior to tonight.

"Didn't you live in Miami? Weren't there nude beaches over there? Clubs where people wear next to nothing?"

I shrugged. "Yes. But I never went. I'm not hip at all." Then I paused, and a titillating yet terrifying thought came to me. "Do you go to nude beaches?"

"No. Never been to a nude beach." He set the glass of water on the counter and moved in my direction. I flattened myself against the wall, and a little grin spread on my face. I couldn't help it. His expression was too adorable.

"I'm not a secret nudist." He smoothed my hair back, and little tingles flowed through my body. "And I take it you're not either."

I shook my head. "I was hoping to talk with some students for my article after class. It was a giant fail."

He pressed his lips to my forehead. "Maybe this serves you right for snooping around. Oh, Lana. What am I going to do with you?"

"Let me report the news, unhindered. Without judgment. And tell me when you're going to be naked outside your own home."

He cupped my face while chuckling, then pressed a soft kiss to my lips. "I can do both of those things."

"Okay then," I murmured. Finally, my shoulders were unsticking from my ears. Noah's kisses had a way of hypnotizing and relaxing me. "Want to stay and watch a movie?"

He shook his head. "I have to get back to work. So much paperwork."

A disappointed growl rumbled in the back of my throat. "Too much paperwork."

"I promise we'll have an official date once this week's over. Once this case is over," he said, stroking my cheek with the back of his fingers. "I'm sorry."

Tara Lush

"No, I get it. I totally understand." How many times had I stood my ex up because of a story in Miami? Too many to count. Then again, he was also a reporter, so he didn't mind.

And, honestly, after the night I'd had, I didn't mind that Noah had to return to work. I wanted to transcribe my interview with Jennis anyway.

"No frowning, okay?" He kissed the space between my brows.

" 'Kay. Coffee tomorrow?"

"Absolutely."

After one long, lingering kiss that made my entire body tingle, Noah and I said our good-byes. I held Stanley and moved his little paw in a waving motion as Noah walked down the steps.

"Make sure to lock up, cupcake," he called.

"Stay clothed," I replied.

I locked up and sauntered into the kitchen. That had been some conversation with Noah, and I was glad he wasn't annoyed that I was snooping around. Or that I'd seen him in the buff. That he had a sense of humor made me appreciate him even more.

Still, I was keyed up from tonight. Whenever I was nervous, I needed to do something with my hands to calm down. In my less productive moments back in Miami, that had meant doom scrolling Twitter on my phone. Here on Devil's Beach, I tried to channel my anxiety into something more positive. Like making snacks.

I opened all the cabinet doors to assess my options while Stanley looked on, wagging his tail. "Let's see. We have apricots, chocolate chips, and"—I rummaged through my baking supplies—"coconut."

Chocolate-dipped apricots rolled in coconut. Three ingredients, lots of mindless repetition. Perfect. I puttered around the kitchen, melting the chocolate and preparing a parchment work space.

As I was dipping the twenty-fifth apricot into the chocolate, my phone buzzed insistently. Gah. It was probably Dad, having heard about my yoga faux pas. After a quick roll of the chocolate-covered fruit in coconut, I wiped my hands on a towel and snatched my phone off the counter.

It was a local number, one I didn't recognize. I answered.

"Lana?" came the gravelly male voice. The background sounded busy. Voices and the clinking of glasses and music. Like a bar or restaurant.

"That's me," I chirped, my curiosity piqued.

"Hey, girl. This is Cody. The photographer. Remember?"

Oh dear. I raked in a breath. His tone sounded entirely too hopeful. Would this get awkward? Rejected men always turned weird. "Hey, Cody. How's it going?"

"It's not bad. I'm here at the Dirty Dolphin and was thinking of you."

I scrunched one eye closed. Was this a booty call? I winced. "Yeah?"

"Yep. Was sitting at the bar here and they had a copy of the paper, and I was reading the article you wrote. I think I might have a news tip for you. It's pretty juicy. Someone who knew Raina real well."

My eye snapped open. "How long will you be at the Dolphin?"

"Dunno. Just ordered another beer, so for a while, I guess. Until you get here."

"I'll be there as soon as I can."

I hung up and scooped a drowsy Stanley off the sofa. Probably I should leave him at home, but I figured it would send a message to Cody if I toted my dog along. After I grabbed the tie-dye carrier Dad had bought, we made our way to the car. Something told me Cody was using information as a ploy to see me.

But I couldn't resist those two sweet words: *news tip.*

Chapter Nineteen

I t didn't take long to reach the Dirty Dolphin, the island's largest beachside watering hole. After dark, the scene at the Dolphin ranged from typical tourist weirdness (bawdy bachelorette parties, drunk frat boys, exuberant family reunions) to something more dangerous.

Go to the Dolphin on vacation, leave on probation, used to be the slogan.

It was still early enough, thankfully, to be tame. With Stanley tucked in his carrier and suspended against my chest, I strode in as if I owned the place. Because I was a Devil's Beach local, not much fazed me. And the place was quirky enough that no one— even the bikers in the corner—batted an eye when I wandered through while carrying the cutest Shih Tzu on the planet on my chest in a pooch pouch.

I spotted Cody almost immediately, his tanned, muscular limbs taking up space at the far end of the bar. I slid onto the stool next to him.

"Hey, you." His smile was lazy and a touch flirtatious. He looked like a quintessential beach bum and was seemingly harmless. But I knew otherwise; those foreign correspondents were love-'em-and-leave-'em types. I spotted a colorful and sexy mermaid tattoo covering one of his biceps.

"I see you're getting acquainted with the local scene." My gaze swept around the room, taking in the table of bikers and a group of middle-aged women in tank tops and tight jeans. When one of the women winked at the bikers, I refocused on Cody.

Stanley wiggled in the carrier at the sight of a possible new friend.

"Sure am. Not a bad place, this Dirty Dolphin." Cody reached to give Stanley a scratch on the head. "Who's this little guy?"

I told Cody the story of Stanley and how I'd adopted him.

"Sounds like you hit the jackpot, doggo," Cody said.

The bartender wandered over, and I ordered a beer. Cody and I made small talk until the bartender returned with my drink. I took a sip, the crisp, cold liquid sliding down my throat. "So what's going on? What's the hot tip? I'm eager to find out."

He leaned in, and he smelled exactly the way I'd have expected him to: like coconut-scented suntan lotion mixed with beer. "I got here about an hour ago. Sat right here, ordered my drink. Started reading the paper."

"Okay." He'd better get on with it, because Stanley was a couple of minutes away from being too wriggly to control.

"That's when a woman sat next to me. She was cute. Really cute, like a naughty Strawberry Shortcake. And I recognized her from the press conference. It was Molly. You know, the redhead?"

"I remember. She was sweet on you." I rubbed my forehead.

"Yeah, she was. She's not as cute as you, although you've got a sort-of boyfriend." He winked.

I stared into my beer bottle.

"I put the paper down, ready to chat her up. Because that's what I do, y'know? I get into the game." He rapped on the bar with his knuckles.

"Mm-hmm." He'd better get into the story soon.

"Your article was on the front page, and I could see her eyes scan the words. I thought that was my cue, so I made a comment about the article. About how unfortunate it was that Raina died."

"Cody, talking about a homicide investigation isn't the best way to pick up women."

He scrunched up his nose. "You don't think so?"

I shook my head. "Anyway."

"Molly was like, I'm not sad at all. And I was like, whoa, dude."

Now I perked up. Yikes. Raina was admired and loathed almost universally. Well, except by Shawn the stalker. And Heidi. "That's weird. She looked pretty upset the other day at the news conference."

"Right? But apparently that was all for show. She talked about how Raina played fast and loose with the class passes. At first it seemed like an error that Molly had fewer classes on her pass. Then it happened again and again. Raina blamed it on a computer error, but Molly always felt shorted. Then prices shot up. There was the pressure to join in on private meditation, private instruction, products. Raina tried to get her to buy lots of stuff. She went to Costa Rica because she'd always wanted to see the country."

I frowned. Not exactly reasons for murder. "Seems odd, I guess."

"Then she started talking about how Raina was different with the men in her class. How she was stringing a guy named Shawn along. And how Kai was jealous and often had screaming matches with Raina in a massage room at the studio. Molly called the yoga studio a rotten cherry on top of a poop sundae."

Eek. Now this was interesting. "She used those exact words?"

"Yep. I thought they were kind of poetic."

I had to agree and wondered how I could work the phrase into a news story. "Does she think Kai's responsible for Raina's death?"

"I didn't have time to ask her. She was only at the bar to buy a pack of cigarettes and leave. I tried to get her to stay for a drink. Said she had to get back home."

"A yogi who smokes?" I raised an eyebrow.

Cody chuckled. "I was a little surprised myself. But listen, she lives close to here, a couple of streets over. I got her address for you. Check it." He reached into his pocket and took out a napkin. "She thinks I'm going to stop by later tonight."

"Are you?" I couldn't help but pry. It was lurid enough that my curiosity got the better of me. Like those reality TV show marathons.

He handed me the napkin, staring deeply into my eyes. "Dunno. After I talked with her, she seemed a little too wild for me. She was practically spitting blood when talking about Raina. I don't need that kind of negativity in my life. I'm trying to be more discerning, if you know what I mean. But I'm keeping my options open."

Was he flirting with me? I couldn't tell. It felt awkward, so my gaze dropped to the napkin, and I studied Cody's scrawled handwriting. "Thanks. I appreciate this. You did good."

Cody beamed and brushed his floppy, curly golden hair off his forehead. "Of course I did. I was in Baghdad for six months, you know. I even wrote some articles."

I took another pull from my beer. Cody wouldn't stop with that cocky grin. I considered leaving but wanted to know more about Molly. In my experience, a reporter needed to talk to a source as quickly as possible.

Also, if I showed up alone, she might not talk to me.

"How about we go pay Molly a visit now?" I asked.

"Guess we could."

He waved down the bartender to get the check. While we waited, he showed me photos of a model shoot he'd done on the beach.

"When do you find the time?" I asked. "You kayak, you work for the paper, you hang with your grandma. You're a busy guy."

"Oh, let me show you photos of Grammy. Here she is outside her trailer. That's where I'm living."

He scrolled to a photo of a thin woman with a tall beehive outside an aqua-hued mobile home. She looked like a caricature of an elderly lady from the fifties, with her black cat-eye sunglasses and a sassy smile. I pointed at the display on the back of the camera. "She looks like the kind of woman I'd get along with."

"She's a hoot." He fiddled with a few buttons on the camera. "And get a load of these."

He scrolled to another photo of a line of sunflowers against the aqua trailer. "Those are her pride and joy."

"Impressive. I've never been able to grow those well."

The bartender came, and Cody paid in cash. Once we got outside, I freed Stanley from the carrier and attached a leash to his collar so he could trot alongside us and mark some fresh territory. The night air was blissfully cool and not too humid. We strolled the short distance, passing small pink and white beach bungalows.

"These were once rental cabins for vacationers," I pointed out. "Now a lot of service workers on the island live here."

Cody pointed up ahead. "She lives in the third pink house on the right, with the VW Jetta out front."

The pathway to the front door was a carpet of crushed shells. It was a charming little place, with squat palm trees and deep-green foliage. There was even a small porch area with a white cast-iron love seat and a matching chair, and all sported navy-and-white-striped cushions. Cody knocked at the door, and it swung open immediately.

Tonight, Molly's hair was frizzier and bigger than it had been at the studio, and it practically glowed scarlet in the light coming from her house.

"Hey, you!" Her expression was bright and cheery until she spotted me. Her face fell and she wrinkled her nose, as if I were the personification of a dead fish. "Oh. Hi."

"Molly, do you remember Lana? She works at the local paper. She's looking into a story about that yoga teacher, and I was telling her about our conversation."

She crossed her arms over her chest. She wore a white T-shirt, black leggings, and pink fuzzy slippers. Her eyes drifted to Stanley, who was straining at his leash.

"He's a cutie," she rasped, kneeling down. I gave the leash some slack, and the puppy hurled himself toward her. Much tail wagging ensued, and Molly looked up. Stanley was becoming an excellent reporting tool. Maybe I needed to bring him along more often to get folks to open up.

"I'll talk with you. Let me grab my smokes and we can sit outside." She slipped back indoors. The porch light flickered on, bathing everything in a wan yellowish glow.

Cody sprawled on the love seat, and I nestled Stanley in the chair next to me. He stretched out on his belly and his eyes closed. Molly came back outside and sank next to Cody. I had to admit, they were a striking pair. Hipster chic.

"Mind if I record this on my phone?"

She shrugged. "What do you want to know? I'm not sure I want my name used. Can we keep this off the record?" I tried not to stare at the dolphin tattoos on her thighs and couldn't make out the pattern around her ankles.

"I guess I can keep you anonymous. I'm curious to know anything about Raina. How long have you known her? Is there anything weird or unusual about her?"

She lit her cigarette, took a long drag, then blew the smoke out the side of her mouth. In a voice that Janis Joplin would've envied, she recounted everything that Cody had told me at the bar. She gestured forcefully as she spoke, her voice growing louder by the second. I nodded along.

"She was relentless in trying to sell me on new classes, new seminars, one-on-one coaching. It got annoying after a while. Too bad, because I loved going to her class. She was a brilliant teacher. When you were in her class, it was like ninety minutes of bliss. I think that's why people endured the rest of Raina's toxic personality, because they loved those classes."

"Did she do that to everyone? Try to upsell her classes and seminars?" I asked.

"I think so. But it seemed like I was the only one who was annoyed. I barely could afford the yoga, much less anything else. A lot of the other students there seemed to be a lot richer, so they could afford it. Or maybe they were better at saying no than I was."

"But you still went to Costa Rica. That cost a lot, didn't it?"

She sighed. "Yeah, I put that entire trip on a credit card. Stupid of me. I have an issue with impulse control."

I studied at my phone for a second, making sure it was still recording, then focused on her. "Can you think of anyone who wanted her dead?"

She blew a few smoke rings. "Her boyfriend appeared real smooth and calm. But to hear those screaming matches they had was kinda scary. One time I was waiting for a massage and they were going at it. I don't think they knew I was there, waiting. It was in between classes. My money would be on him. They had some knock-down, drag-out fights in Costa Rica too."

"I'm hearing he has an alibi."

She raised a shoulder. "Maybe he had help."

"What about Shawn?"

She crushed the cigarette out. "He's kind of weird. Dunno where he gets all his money. It was clear he was in love with Raina, and she did nothing to discourage him. Which made for a real weird dynamic with Kai. He doesn't seem like a murderer, though. Sorry I can't be more helpful."

I nodded thoughtfully. The humid night air was still and thick, and in the distance, the sound of waves from the Gulf wafted in our direction. I pawed around in my purse and found a business card from Perkatory. "Call me if you can think of anything important. Or stop by the coffee shop."

She accepted the card. "Will do."

"One more question. Why did you seem so upset at the press conference the other day when you really disliked Raina?"

A sigh leaked from her lips. "I liked the actual yoga. And it's terrible to see someone our age die. She didn't deserve to be murdered. It's complicated. I try to project positivity, but it's hard to ignore the truth. Raina was a user. But she was also a great teacher. Ugh. You must think we're all two-faced."

I didn't want to agree, so I pursed my lips and gave a noncommittal, "Hmm, it does seem like she projected one image when people first met her, then a whole other image later on."

Molly extended her hand in my direction. "That's exactly it. You never knew which you were going to get, and you kept hoping for the good Raina, the one who gave an amazing performance during her classes. Because that's what it was when she taught: a performance."

I nodded thoughtfully, knowing people like that could be exhausting and wondering if this emotional manipulation and hot-and-cold personality had led to Raina's death. By now, Stanley was snoring. I gently picked him up and rested him on my shoulder. "Well, I'll let the two of you have a fun night." I stood up. "Cody, thanks a bunch. Molly, you too. Much appreciated."

Cody gave me a lopsided grin. "You still kinda got a boyfriend?" he asked with a drawl. Then he turned to Molly. "Lana's dating the police chief."

She flicked a Zippo lighter, firing up another smoke. Her eyes narrowed to slits, and she let out a raspy grunt. Her tone had all the charm of an inmate about to whip out a shiv. "I'm not a fan of coppers."

"Who is?" Cody chuckled.

"Thanks again, kids. Toodle-oo." I waved my hand in the air and took a few steps toward the walkway.

Cody piped up. "I'm gonna stay here and do a private photo shoot with Molly."

Okay then. "Sounds great! See y'all around."

I scurried off, wanting to put as much distance between me and them as possible. Something about both Cody and Molly felt off to me, and I didn't exhale until I was halfway home.

Back in the serenity of my house, I studied the Dante's Inferno website. All the photos of Raina looked as though they had been ripped from a glossy magazine. Many had been taken right here on the island.

My beautiful home of Devil's Beach, it read. She hadn't been here long and called the island home. As a native, it always shocked me when newcomers did this, embracing this place like it was their own. Part of me felt protective of my island. Sometimes I wanted to pull up the drawbridge leading to the mainland and never let another soul land here again. Silly, I know, since I made my living largely from tourists. But it annoyed me that people like Raina would come here to possibly take advantage of people.

I scrolled along, skimming each page of Raina's website. *Join me for beach yoga. All levels welcome.*

Fraud. Lies. Jealousy. Her reality had differed significantly from what she portrayed online.

Tomorrow was a beach yoga day, and as I studied the photo of Raina and a crowded class on the sand, an idea hit me. Barbara and Dad were working the morning rush at Perkatory. I grabbed my cell to text Erica.

Hey. Think you can tear yourself away from Joey tomorrow morning to go to beach yoga with me for some reporting at nine?
Do we have to wear clothes?
Sadly, yes
Joey wants to go.

I couldn't imagine the tatted-up, redheaded bar owner who was the son of a mafioso at beach yoga, but then again, I wasn't exactly the portrait of a perfect athlete either.

The more the merrier.

Chapter Twenty

The following morning, I dressed in a pair of teal capri leggings and a matching tank top with strappy accents. I'd unearthed it from the back of my closet, another old outfit from my Miami days. It made me feel a bit like a trussed ham, but I soldiered on by hoisting my mat so it rested on my shoulder and walked to Crystal Beach.

It was the closest beach to downtown and Perkatory. Since I didn't want Dad to know I was (a) going to yoga and (b) sleuthing around, I took the long way around to avoid walking past the coffee shop. If he knew, he might think I was suddenly into his New Age lifestyle, or worse, feel bad that he couldn't come to class with me. The last thing I wanted was to hurt his feelings.

I kicked off my flip-flops once I hit the fine sugar sand. The Gulf of Mexico glittered in the distance. The sight of it always put me in a good mood.

I lived where others vacationed.

Usually, though, I preferred a beach chair, an umbrella, and a tall cup of iced coffee when I visited the beach. Since it was about a quarter to nine, the sun was already well above the horizon and scorching every inch of my skin. Fortunately, I'd worn sunscreen, but it trickled into my eyes and made them burn.

Resisting the urge to itch, I trudged toward the coral-colored lifeguard stand. The class was supposed to be held near there, and I could already see a large group of people stretching their limbs while lying, standing, and sitting on mats. There had to be forty people here. Who knew these classes were so popular? I was usually working, or recovering from working. Obviously, I needed to get out more.

No one noticed when I approached, and I made my way to the back row.

Unrolling my mat should've been easy, but it was more fraught with problems than I'd expected. Sand sprayed at the top, and when I got on all fours to brush it off, more sand crept in from the sides and back.

I hated this already. It wasn't as though I were a stranger to yoga; Mom and Dad had done it off and on throughout my childhood. But it had been a gentle, hippie version of yoga, with lots of long stretches and lying around on mats in their hippie friends' living rooms. I'd loved it as a child, but in recent years, I'd noticed, yoga had become something of a competitive sport, and that irked me. It seemed wrong somehow.

Within seconds, sand clung to my arms, mixing with the sticky sunscreen. I swept the sand off the top, sending it smack into the blue mat in front of me. There was no one sitting there, and I leaned forward to brush it off. My knee sank into the sand, and now it too was coated like an ice cream with sprinkles.

"Next time bring a towel. It really helps," came a squeaky voice to my right.

I sat on my heels and looked over. It was a woman with short, dark hair. I recognized her immediately as Heidi, the woman who'd been sobbing uncontrollably at the news conference. She smiled kindly and peeled back a blue dolphin towel to reveal a black mat.

"That's a great idea." I took off my sunglasses and slipped them into my bag, which, like everything else, was coated in sand. You'd think I'd have been used to this, growing up on an island.

"I'm Heidi," she squeaked.

"I remember you. I'm Lana Lewis."

"The owner of Perkatory and the reporter! It's great you can take a morning class."

"I'm working later today." Thursdays were my late shift.

"Nice." She hesitated, her eyes blooming with tears. "That was a beautiful story you did about Raina the other day. So respectful. How do you find enough hours in the day to do it all?"

I shrugged. If I was going to continue with my freelance journalism career, it was a question I'd have to eventually figure out. Perkatory took a significant amount of time, and it was becoming increasingly wrong to take hours away from the store so I could play reporter. "I used to work full-time as a journalist in Miami."

Out of the corner of my eye, I saw Erica and Joey making their way toward us. Both were in black shorts and black T-shirts, and they carried purple mats in their tattooed arms. They were like the Goth brigade. I stifled a giggle.

"Hey, Lana. Long time no see." Joey reached down to squeeze my shoulder.

"You two can set up here." I waved to my left, where there was an expanse of unused sand.

While Erica and Joey rolled out their mats, I turned back to Heidi.

"How are you holding up, anyway? You seemed really upset at that news conference. I felt so bad for you," I offered sympathetically.

She shuddered in a breath. "I'm taking it day by day. I was close to Raina. I considered her a mentor, even though she was almost twenty years younger."

Finally. Someone who didn't hate the victim. I leaned in and lowered my voice. "Would you like to talk with me for a story? I'm planning on writing a follow-up."

"Sure." She wiped the corner of her eye.

Crap, I had to pitch that follow-up story. I made a mental note to call Mike after class. Although, given how fit he was, it wouldn't surprise me if he showed up. I knew he'd practiced at Raina's studio a few times. I scanned the people lounging on mats and didn't see him.

As I turned to Erica to ask her how her night had been, a pair of tan legs crossed my line of vision.

"Lana Lewis, fancy meeting you here." The voice was low and velvety and entirely familiar.

It was Noah, and he was apparently the owner of the blue yoga mat in front of me. I glanced up, sheepishly, as my skin prickled with awareness. A wry smile spread across his lips, and he lowered himself on all fours. Then crawled toward me, which made my already sweaty body feel like combusting.

He kissed my cheek and allowed his lips to linger against my ear. "Busted," he whispered.

"Maybe I wanted to do yoga." I pinched his side, and he laughed.

"Yeah, right." Noah crawled to his own mat.

The sound of clapping hands came from the front of the class, which was nearest the water. It was Jennis, the studio manager and yoga teacher. Today she wore a black bodysuit with small shoulder straps, and I immediately empathized. She was going to roast in this sun.

But it was good news for me. Between her and Heidi, I'd likely get some information today. Jennis welcomed us to class and mentioned something about studio announcements. I strained to listen, the sound of waves and a nearby music speaker on a tourist's beach blanket nearly drowning out her voice.

"I know that some of you attend only this class, so it's the first time we're seeing each other in a week. You probably all know by now that Raina Rose has passed." Jennis took a deep breath, and if I hadn't known her, I'd have sworn she was about to burst into tears. Where was all that righteous fire and brimstone from our interview?

I inched toward the top of my yoga mat, refolding my sweaty legs.

"Raina was brutally murdered"—Jennis paused, as if for dramatic effect—"and we're praying for justice."

Heidi next to me let out a whimper. I glanced her way with a kind smile. She reached her hand to me, and I clasped hers. It seemed she was someone who needed support, and my heart ached for her.

"We're all shocked by this news, and I'd like to dedicate today's practice to Raina, our fearless, brave, and beautiful spiritual warrior."

An elderly woman in the front, who was decked out in a hot-pink sports bra and matching hot-pink bike shorts, raised her hand. "Will there be a memorial service or funeral here on the island?"

Jennis shook her head, then swiped her fingers over her cheek, as if she was brushing away tears. Which was odd, since she'd been dry-eyed and rough as she talked about Raina last night. Was this all an act? Was she really that fake?

"I spoke with Kai, and with Raina's mother, last night. Raina's body's being cremated, and her ashes will be scattered at a later date in Bali. We're talking about plans for a communitywide class, so I'll keep you posted."

Another woman, one who sat in front of Noah, raised her hand. Jennis pointed to her. I spied a familiar shock of red hair, but today it was tied in a severe bun.

"Yes, Molly?"

She looked different in the light of day. Refreshed and younger. Today she was wearing a pale-blue sports bra that matched her tight Lycra shorts. She gracefully climbed to her feet.

"We can use this class as a memorial." Her voice sounded like it had been rubbed raw with sandpaper and whiskey after a long night.

Jennis pointed. "Yes. Yes! I love that. It's so authentic."

With the cadence of a zombie, Molly shuffled toward Jennis. It was awkward to watch the two of them embrace. I wasn't sure why, but this public display of grief left me uncomfortable. Odd, since I'd been a crime reporter for years. Also strange since Molly hadn't had a kind word to say about Raina last night. Were all these people hypocrites?

After wiping her nose with her hand, Molly untangled herself from Jennis and returned to her mat, lightly touching people's shoulders on the way. She spotted me and did a double take, then sat on her mat, her back to me.

"Okay, let's stand at the top of our mats," Jennis commanded. "We're going to begin with a vigorous sun salutation."

I winced. Sounded sweaty. All this sun and the toaster waffles I'd eaten earlier were making me sleepy. I sneaked a glance to my left at Erica, who was snapping her neck and rolling her shoulders like a prizefighter. Oh dear. What had I gotten myself into?

"Raise your arms above your head, then swan dive to fold," Jennis called out.

Okay, this was easy. I could do this. I stood so my big toes were in the sand but the rest of my feet were on the mat.

"Lift yourself halfway up to a flat back, then fold forward again. Jump or step back to plank; then we'll meet into downward-facing dog. Remember, this is the warm-up. We've got bigger potatoes to peel later in class."

The only thing I wanted to peel was my clothes, away from my sticky body. Already I was terribly lost, and I looked up. With a flat back. I gripped my knees and wobbled forward.

The only thing in my line of vision was Noah, who had taken off his shirt. He was hovering in a push-up position, his feet and legs only inches from my mat. Goodness, he was nicely built. Who knew a human back had all those muscles? I zoned out for a second, studying the peaks and valleys near his shoulder blades. Inadvertently, I stepped forward a few inches.

Then he inverted himself, banging into my face with his thigh.

"Oof," I said, toppling over and tumbling onto the sand. I landed in the sand between my mat and Erica's. Somehow my wrist got jammed in a wonky position, and pain shot through the joint.

"Yikes," Erica cried, dropping to her knees. Joey stared, owllike.

"I'm fine," I hissed, my wrist throbbing. "Hush."

"What happened? Did you get a cramp? I didn't see what happened."

"No. Noah hit me in the nose," I whispered.

Even in his upside-down V pose, Noah twisted around so he was looking at me under his armpit. "Lana? You okay?"

"Yes," I mouthed. "I'm fine."

I scrambled to get in position, desperately wanting to blend in. With my smarting wrist, I tried to emulate the rest of the class, hoping that no one—specifically Noah—hadn't seen my undignified roll onto the ground. Something was definitely amiss with my wrist. Probably not broken, but maybe sprained? I didn't dare take my hand from the ground to check, mostly because I was frozen in pain.

"Looking good. We're going to stay here to ground ourselves for several more breaths," Jennis called out. Somehow she'd materialized near our row, and I cricked my neck in time to see her bending down in front of Noah and placing her hands atop his.

A bubble of jealousy fizzed in my stomach, but it was soon overtaken by the burning sensation in the back of my thighs. How long were we going to stay in this pose, anyway?

I heard the soft crunch of sand and saw Jennis's red toes pass by my mat.

"I'm going to adjust you a little so you get a better stretch," she said.

I wasn't entirely sure she was talking to me until I detected her hands on my inner thighs, a move that seemed deeply personal. She pulled back, hard, and all the breath left my body. Well, at least I wasn't focused on the pain in my wrist now, probably because every muscle in my legs screamed in agony.

"How's that?" she asked me.

"Blergh," I responded, drooling a little. I definitely didn't recall Mom and Dad doing yoga like this. They'd spent most of their time breathing and chanting with their eyes closed.

"Excellent. Remember to keep breathing." She let go of my legs and walked away.

"Easy for you to say," I muttered. Breathing in this humid, sultry morning air was like inhaling the contents of an oven on broil.

I dropped to my knees and let out a breath while looking around. Erica was amazing, effortless. So was Noah. Joey? He was decent with the yoga poses but already getting pink around his neck. I wanted to run over and ask him if he'd used sunscreen today. Same for Molly. Redheads really shouldn't be out in this sun.

I mopped my brow with the hem of my shirt and noticed Noah staring at me through his legs. He winked. I snort-laughed.

We switched to a different pose: standing at the front of our mats. This I could do. Then we went into a dizzying array of postures, something Jennis called "vibrant vinyasa." They didn't resemble the gentle stretches my parents used to do. I tried valiantly to keep up while sweating buckets in the hot sunshine.

Meanwhile, Jennis had morphed from a gentle, encouraging woman to a Marine drill sergeant. One who didn't sweat.

"Are you working, or are you lurking?" She barked.

"Definitely lurking," I wheezed. Thank goodness everyone was in their zone and not paying attention to me. Noah moved with the grace of the offspring of a gazelle and a Cirque du Soleil performer. I made a mental note to ask him how he'd gotten so bendy, but the thought disappeared when my calf cramped up while we were in a lunge pose.

"Holy guacamole," I whispered, wondering if I should move to get rid of the cramp or allow myself to fall over. Pressing my hands into my hips, I shortened my stance and lifted myself a little higher. That was marginally better. My wrist throbbed.

"Lana, try to get that back knee a little lower. Don't be weak. Let's pulse it out and level up. Level up, people!"

Cold Brew Corpse

I wasn't sure what she meant by level up, but I was certain I didn't want any part of it. I was just fine with the level I'd been at prior to class. I ignored her and focused on not falling over. That was a success, right? A nearby group of guys unfolded beach chairs, and my eyes drifted in their direction. They were ogling Jennis, who was yelling to be heard over the music.

"Okay, now we're going to work on our triangle pose. Anyone who is feeling overwhelmed for any reason—emotionally, spiritually, physically—can take corpse pose. Lie down on your back and relax. That means you, Lana."

I didn't need to be told twice. Feeling a twinge of embarrassment, I dropped to my knees and flopped onto my back. This was exactly my kind of yoga. Corpse pose. I closed my eyes and rested my painful wrist on my stomach, drifting off to the barking orders of Jennis's voice and the soothing sounds of the Gulf of Mexico.

Chapter
Twenty-One

"Cupcake. Time to wake up."
A smile spread on my face. I was having the most delicious dream about snuggling with Noah.

"Yikes. Her nose looks burned. I wonder if she put enough sun block on."

Erica? Why was she in my dream? I unstuck my tongue from the roof of my mouth.

"Is she okay? Like, did she pass out?"

I peeled my eyes open, and my gaze landed on Heidi. She was peering at me, her brow etched with concern. Erica, Noah, and Joey also stared down.

They all backed away as I sat up. "Must've fallen asleep. Guess I was that relaxed."

Or that exhausted.

"Wow, it's bright out." I pawed around for my sunglasses and slipped them on. The skin on the bridge of my nose smarted. "Ow. I think I got a little sunburned."

My wrist also sported a faint throb, and my inglorious tumble came rushing back to me. Gah. I had so much to do, between my shift at the café this afternoon and doing more reporting. I glanced at Heidi, who was rolling up her mat, then searched for Molly and Jennis. They were already gone.

Well, at least I could talk with Heidi. I turned to her. "Hey, would you want to grab a coffee over at Perkatory? It's on me."

She tucked a wisp of hair behind her ear. Her wide-eyed doe look made her seem flustered. "Oh. Oh! I guess I have a little time. Sure. I have to call my husband and let him know. So I'll wait for you up there." She pointed a few yards away, toward the sidewalk.

"Awesome. Let me pack up and we can walk over." As I rolled my mat, I caught Noah's gaze. He arched an eyebrow, and I smiled coyly.

"What?" I asked.

"Nothing. I know you're doing your job as a reporter."

He stood, and I did too. "Do you have any tips for me? Any pending arrests?"

"Let's see. Arrests? Probably not this afternoon. Tips? Wear more sunscreen."

I rolled my eyes. "Will I see you tonight?"

He sighed. "Sadly, no. My family's going to be nearby, on the mainland. I'm planning to drive over and meet them for dinner."

Well. Apparently I was girlfriend material but not to the level of meet-the-parents. Although it made sense—heck, we hadn't even been out on a formal date yet—it still stung a bit.

"Oh! Well, have a great time." I tried to sound bubbly.

"I'll call you after."

"Okay. I mean, I'm pretty beat, as you can see. I still have a shift at the coffee shop and some reporting to do. I don't know how long I'll be up. But definitely, talk to you soon."

I gave him a little finger wave and turned to bounce away, attempting a carefree and casual strut.

"Lana." His voice beckoned me back, and I whirled.

"Noah?"

He took a few steps, then cupped my face in his hands and kissed me. Right there, in front of everyone. My face, which felt like I had exposed it to a heating coil, now flared as though I had pressed it to the surface of the sun.

"I'll bring you to meet my parents another time, okay?" He looked into my eyes. "We have some family stuff to discuss tonight, and I'm trying to spare you the drama."

"Okay," I murmured.

"Do you have aloe for that nose? And something for the wrist?"

"I doubt it. I'll pick some up. 'Bye."

He kissed my cheek, and a wave of happiness surged through me.

I bopped over to Heidi. It was impossible not to smile. "Hey. Thanks for waiting for me."

"You and the chief seem quite cozy. Are you dating?" From any other person, especially a stranger, a question like this might be too probing. But in her high-pitched voice, it was about as threatening as if it came from a baby bird. In fact, that's what she reminded me of—a skittish chick.

Still, I wasn't in the mood to discuss my love life with a source. I shifted the mat out of my right hand—my wrist hurt something fierce—and murmured, "Something like that."

We wandered down the street, and I changed the subject. "So I'm doing this article on Raina. It's like a follow-up. A profile."

At least I hoped I was.

"Okay," she agreed in a guarded tone.

"I was hoping you'd explain what kind of teacher Raina was, and about your relationship."

By now we'd reached Perkatory, and I opened the door for Heidi. She walked through and let out a sigh. "I'd love to. I really feel like there are many people who are misrepresenting her memory."

Just then, Dad rushed up. He was in his usual jeans, T-shirt, and black apron. "How was yoga? Did you love it? The lifeguard called and told me you were there."

Of course he did. "Well, then you should already know that I fell asleep, got a sunburn, and maybe sprained my wrist."

"How'd you do that?" Dad stroked his goatee. "Were you trying to do crow pose or something?"

"I was staring at Noah's naked back, and I fell onto my face and wrist."

Next to me, Heidi giggled.

"But what pose were you in?"

I motioned as if I were going to fold my body in half. "I was bent over."

Dad shook his head as if to say, *I raised you with more flexibility than that.* I ignored him and rested my hand on Heidi's arm, then introduced them.

"We're going to do an interview here for the next few minutes; then I'll start my shift. Can you get us a coffee and a . . ." I turned to her. "What would you like?"

She waved her hand. "I'd love one of those . . . what do you call it?"

Oh boy. She was going to choose either a froufrou coffee drink or a tea. I could tell. She probably didn't eat sugar either. Dad and I looked at her expectantly.

"Triple espresso, black, extra sugar," she finally decided.

"Whoa. Didn't expect that."

She laughed in response. I was beginning to like her.

I gestured toward a table in the corner, past a young couple in beach attire who were sitting on one of the robin's-egg-blue sofas and smooching.

We sank into the cool, wooden seats. More than anything I appreciated how Perkatory was crisply air-conditioned today. I reached into my bag for my notebook, and pain shot up my arm.

"Ow," I whispered.

"You okay?" she squeaked. "I saw you take a fall during class."

I winced at the memory. "I'm okay. Jammed my wrist a little."

Ugh. How was I going to make coffee today? Did I need a brace? I wondered if anyone here had a brace. Maybe Dad would go buy me one. I extracted the notebook and a pen from my bag, then tapped at my cell.

"Do you mind if I record this?"

She shook her head.

"Perfect. Tell me all about Raina." I flipped open the notebook.

A beatific smile spread on her face. "Gosh. She was so special. Almost like a little sister, except she was wiser than I was."

I nodded, urging her to go on.

"When she opened her studio, I started taking her class. When I first moved here, I attended class at another studio, one in a geodesic dome." She wrinkled her nose. "It was okay there but didn't fit with what I wanted out of a practice."

"Which was what?"

"Something spiritual. Something uplifting. Something . . ." She got a faraway look in her eye. "Empowering."

"And Raina's classes fit that bill?"

"Oh, absolutely. Yes. She became more than a yoga teacher. She became a genuine friend. Helped me through a lot of difficult moments and challenges."

A sob escaped her throat, and this was the moment Dad came over with a tray holding our coffee and two glasses of water. I shot him a warning stare.

He ignored me and turned to Heidi. "You seem so familiar."

"Dad," I said between gritted teeth. "I'm doing an interview over here."

Heidi shuddered in a breath. "I recognize you too. I think from Wolf Yoga?"

He snapped his fingers and grinned. "That's it!"

"Dad," I chided again in a low tone. "I think there's a customer at the counter."

Finally he got the hint, whirling around to check. "Oh. Of course. Here's your coffee and your water. Enjoy."

He scurried off, and I smiled at Heidi tightly. "Dad knows everyone around the island."

"That's what I remember. He was so kind in class." She took a sip and glanced at the door.

I needed to get her back on track, but first, it was essential to make her feel comfortable. "How long have you been on Devil's Beach, anyway?"

I casually sipped my coffee and didn't write anything down. All I wanted was for her to talk freely again, to loosen up so I could ask more questions about Raina.

"My husband and I moved here two years ago, right around the time our son graduated from college. We'd spent a lifetime in the military. Well, my husband was in the military. I was a military wife. My husband retired from the Air Force. He's a doctor and ended up taking a civilian job running the walk-in clinic here. We figured this would be a great place to spend our golden years."

The look on her face was anything but jubilant. Odd, since most people who had moved here from anywhere else gushed and raved about the place. "How are you liking it?"

She swallowed grimly. "Love it."

Then why did she seem so miserable? I nodded slowly. She was hiding something. I could feel it in my bones.

"Sorry. I'm still thinking about Raina. I miss her a lot. That retreat in Costa Rica was life changing." She took a long sip of her espresso.

My eyebrows shot up. "Yeah? In what way?"

"We had a lot of private conversations, and she helped me through some stuff that I'd rather not discuss. Personal stuff. About my marriage."

I nodded. Had Raina used any personal details against Heidi? I needed to find out. "Listen, I heard from a lot of people that Raina was one way when you met her, then changed once you got to know her. That she might have been a little emotionally manipulative. Is that true?"

Heidi made a *tsk* sound with her tongue. "No. That was just some silly stuff some of the other students said because they were jealous. They'd talk about Good Raina and Bad Raina. People said she had a split personality, when in reality she was nothing but sweet. At least to me."

Interesting. "Did you ever invest in her studio or business?"

Heidi's eyes dropped to the table. "I fought with my husband about it, and I was going to after the retreat."

There certainly was a story with Heidi and her husband, but one I didn't want to delve into. And had Raina abstained from any emotional abuse with Heidi because she was hoping for some cash?

"Gotcha. One more question. Did you know if anyone else on the trip had problems with Raina? Did she get into a fight with anyone? Any of the teachers? Her boyfriend, Kai? And what about Shawn Sims?"

She waved her hand in the air. "Shawn's a good guy. He and I and a few others adored Raina. There were others who have had issues with her off and on, but nothing out of the ordinary in Costa Rica. There's always yoga drama, anyway. So much yoga drama."

"Yoga drama?"

"Yeah. That's what Raina used to call all the gossip and infighting between teachers and studios. There's always someone who is jealous or angry. I try to ignore it."

"Do you think yoga drama led to Raina's murder?"

Tears welled in her eyes. "I doubt it."

"Then what did?"

She leaned forward. "I think it might have been a stalker."

Oh ho. I hesitated with my pen in midair. "Shawn?"

She shook her head. "No. He wouldn't hurt any living creature. Raina had a lot of online admirers. Men who followed her on Instagram. I always told her to be careful, but she maintained that any of the negatives from the creeps online were outweighed by the positives of spreading the word of yoga and building her brand."

Spreading the word of yoga. The more I learned about Raina, the more she sounded like a cult leader. I scribbled in my notebook. "So you think it might be someone online?"

Heidi nodded. "Totally. Look at her Insta. You'll see all the creeps commenting on her photos. Asking her out. I think someone knew she was recently back from Costa Rica, came to the island, stalked her, and killed her. Then dumped her body."

I winced. "That's awful."

A fat tear rolled down her cheek. "I'm so sorry. This conversation is too triggering for me. I need to go. Plus, I'm supposed to meet my husband for lunch. I'm going to be late. It's going to take me a while to get home."

"Don't you live on Devil's Beach?"

"Yes, but I'm on my bike. My husband took my car because his is in the shop." She stood up hurriedly, knocking the water onto the table. Soaking my notebook.

I yelped and stood, waving my notebook in the air, trying to salvage my notes. Were they ruined?

"Oh, gosh, I'm so sorry, Lana," she squealed.

I dabbed at the notebook with a wad of paper napkins. "I think most of it can be saved. I hope it can, anyway."

She chirped several more apologies and squeezed my shoulder. "I really should be going. Sorry."

"No worries." I fanned my notebook in the air. "Thanks again."

She fluttered out and I sank into the seat, going over my notebook to see how much was ruined. I had the cell phone recordings as a backup, but I hated relying on technology. I'd seen it go wrong for too many reporters.

I drank my coffee slowly, savoring it, while airing out my notebook. I tore out a dry page and started making a to-do list—it was something I was obsessed with, planners and lists—when the biggest item of all hit me.

"Crap," I whispered, writing the item down carefully in big, blocky letters. My wrist pulsed with pain.

CALL MIKE

I found my phone and dialed. He answered on the second ring.

"Speak of the devil," he said.

"What?"

"I was thinking about you. Well, your coffee."

"I'm at Perkatory. About to start my shift. Come on over."

"I'll be there in five."

Mike's paper, the *Devil's Beach Beacon*, was located on the other end of Main Street, about a ten-minute walk. Even less if you were Mike, who at sixty had a long gait and was a trained ultramarathoner.

I'd no sooner taken another sip of my coffee than he materialized in the shop.

"Hey, kiddo." He slid across from me.

"You need a coffee? I'll grab it for you."

He shook his head. "I'll get it to go. Don't have a ton of time."

I perked up. "Is there breaking news? Something happen?"

He shrugged. "The monkeys are acting up again. We got a great video from a tourist of the monkeys dive-bombing someone in a kayak."

"Impressive." Those primates were a never-ending source of news on the island. "Listen, Mike. I wanted to bring you up to speed on the Raina story." I rattled off everything I had, including the interviews with Shawn, Heidi, Jennis, and the Wolfman. "I really think we could do an interesting and full portrait of who she was. I could knock that out for you in a day or two."

Mike shifted from one foot to the other. "Er, Lana? I might have to get a staff writer to work on the story."

I shrugged. "Okay. I don't mind sharing a byline."

He shook his head. "I don't have the freelance budget for another story from you. I'm sorry. Not this month. We've had too much news lately."

My jaw hung open. Was he turning down my idea? "But I've gathered some really great stuff. Let me tell you about this one interview—"

"I know," He cut me off. "And I'm sure it's amazing. I can't pay you, though."

"Well, what about if you pay me next month? I'll still write it now."

He blew out a sigh while running a hand through his short, curly gray hair. "I guess we could do that. I've sliced and diced that darn budget so much, I don't even know if that will help." His voice was low, almost as if he were speaking to himself. It made me wonder about the long-term health of the paper, and that chilled me to the bone. What if Devil's Beach was without a newspaper?

It was unfathomable. But then again, small papers all over the United States had closed. I twisted my fingers together. "I'd really hate for this material to go to waste."

"I know. Me too. Let me mull it over, okay, Lana? I'll try to make it work."

I paused. It wasn't like I could offer the material to any other newspaper. The *Beacon* was the only one on the island. Would the papers on the mainland be interested? Probably not. My old paper in Miami, four hours away? Definitely not. They didn't have enough money to buy their remaining reporters notebooks and pencils, much less a freelance budget.

What would I do if Mike didn't want my story? Writing was the thing I loved more than, well, almost anything.

Still, I tried to call Mike's bluff. "Don't think too long, okay? Time is of the essence, and I have all this great stuff. I don't want someone else to get the scoop."

He nodded slowly. "Get an outline down and we'll talk in a day or two, okay?"

"Sure," I muttered, suddenly deflated.

He rose, and I did too. "It's not you, Lana. If I could, I'd hire you for six figures and let you write anything you wanted."

We gave each other a quick hug and he left, grabbing a coffee from Dad on his way out. I dropped into my seat. Why was I doing all this reporting if it wouldn't be published? I had a café to run. A business to build. Perhaps my fantasies of going back to reporting, even in a part-time capacity, were too absurd. I'd had my hopes dashed by newspapers once. Why did I keep setting myself up for further heartbreak?

I should let this story about Raina go. That would be the smart thing to do. Run the coffee shop and be a recovering journalist.

Murder investigations and news stories would have to wait, because I had coffee to serve.

With a sigh, I hauled myself to my feet and donned my apron. My wrist smarted, and I rubbed it with my left hand. I went to check on the cold brew. I'd tried a slightly different mix of water and coffee in hopes of eliminating the bitter taste. For the next half hour, I tasted and stirred, wondering what had gone wrong with my previously foolproof recipe.

When I emerged, Dad zoomed up to me with a brown paper bag in his hands. "Noah stopped by and left you this."

My heart plummeted. "You could've told me."

"He was in a rush and double-parked."

I pulled open the bag to find a tube of aloe and a bottle of Tylenol.

"Chocolates?" Dad asked.

"Nope." Noah's thoughtful gifts, and the fact that he'd taken the time to buy them, were more romantic than any box of chocolates. Better than roses, even.

Maybe things weren't so bad after all.

Chapter Twenty-Two

As the sun inched toward the edge of the Gulf in a blaze of pink and orange on Friday evening, I drove to the marina to meet up with Erica. She'd invited Joey, me, Stanley, Dad, and Barbara over for drinks.

I wore a casual tank top dress in my favorite shade of pale blue, and Stanley in the tie-dye pooch carrier on my front. The sparkly flip-flops from the other night made purposeful thwacks as I walked down the dock, looking for Erica's sailboat. It was difficult to tell one boat from the other, because to me they all looked like sleek white vessels.

Finally, I found it: the *Mutiny*. The ship's name was painted in a blood-red hue that stood out against the white hull. She'd also affixed an icon of a lady pirate with a knife in her mouth near the letters. So Goth. So Erica.

"Hey," I called out, stepping onto the boat.

Erica poked her head out from the cabin and stepped onto the deck. "Hey you! Welcome aboard!"

I'd made a charcuterie plate with cheese, crackers, sliced meats, and tiny pickles and brought a tub of vegan cheese for Dad. I'd put everything in a cooler on wheels because my wrist still hurt. Erica took the cooler handle from me, kneeling to look inside.

"Sweet! Can't wait to dig in." She rubbed her hands together.

Joey popped out from the cabin. "Lana, how's it going? How's your wrist?"

I sank onto a fiberglass bench. "Took two Tylenol and it feels better."

"Want a beer? We've got some Cigar City Maduro." Joey pointed at a cooler, and I nodded.

Erica sat next to me, munching on a piece of cheese. "You could've brought Noah, you know."

I sighed. "He's with his family tonight, having dinner on the mainland."

"Aha. It's a little soon for dinner with the parents."

"Probably so. He said he had to discuss some things with his mom and dad, and I wanted to give him space."

Joey handed me an open beer, and one to Erica. We drank and talked about the boat, and I freed Stanley from his harness.

"Want to see the cabin?" Erica asked.

"Sure. I don't want Stanley to jump in the water, though." He didn't seem interested in checking out anything but the charcuterie plate, but I needed to be extra careful.

"I'll watch him." Joey reached for the puppy.

We went down below. Erica showed me the impressively large cabin, which included a full kitchen, a bedroom with a soft, fuzzy black blanket and matching black pillows, and a bathroom with a shower.

"This really is livable." I inspected the kitchen, which sported sleek stainless-steel mini appliances. I noted that a stovetop espresso maker was the only visible culinary tool. Erica was a coffee purist, through and through.

"You could make a full meal here." I skimmed my hand over the white counter top edged with shiny teakwood.

"And the best part is, I'm not tied down to one place."

I glanced at her, alarmed. Was she planning on leaving Devil's Beach, and Perkatory, so soon? She'd just started, and customers loved her. I loved her. Erica was the best barista we'd ever had.

She dismissed me with a wave. "Don't worry, I'm not going anywhere. I'm digging it here. I'm planning on staying a while. I like to get out on the water when I want to clear my head. You know, day sailing. So this is a perfect setup for me."

I clutched my chest. I didn't let a lot of people into my inner circle, and Erica had made her way there quickly. "Thank goodness. I've gotten attached to you in a short period of time."

New voices and Stanley's bark wafted from above deck. "Must be my dad."

We emerged to find Dad and Barbara sitting side by side on one of the fiberglass benches. I greeted him with a kiss on the cheek. Stanley was already clamoring to get in his lap, and he hoisted the puppy up.

We all settled in, snacking on crackers and cheese and drinking beers. The sunlight faded, and Erica lit a couple of citronella candles, sending out a pungent grassy aroma that mixed with the salt air.

"So, any news on Raina?" Barbara asked.

All eyes swung to me. "There's lots of smoke but no actual fire. So many people disliked her, it's hard to say what really happened to her."

"What did Wolfie say?" Dad asked.

Erica and I glanced at each other. "He wasn't a fan," she said.

"That reminds me." I snapped my fingers, which sent a jolt of pain to my injured wrist. "I need to check his alibi with his wife."

"You think Wolfie is a suspect?" Dad yelped, his fingers going to the crystal around his neck. "Wolfie's got way too much Buddha-nature for that. Don't you think?"

Barbara nodded in agreement.

"No. Yes. I don't know." I threw my hands in the air. "Raina stole his yoga client newsletter list. She spread rumors about him. He was understandably upset."

"But upset enough to kill? That's the million-dollar question," Erica piped up.

I tilted the neck of my beer bottle in her direction. "No more upset than Kai, who seemed to be jealous of Raina's relationship with Shawn. And Shawn was also jealous of Kai and thought he was holding Raina back."

"Sounds complicated." Barbara took a swig of her beer. "Could anyone else have done it?"

I lifted my shoulders. "Jennis claimed Raina humiliated her during the retreat. Molly alleged Raina stiffed her out of money. And get this: Raina was charged with fraud some years ago in Jacksonville. I'm still trying to get the details on that case. But who knows what else she's done in the past. Or who she upset on her spiritual journey to fame. She was clearly an emotional manipulator who got others to do her bidding with a bit of coercion and a lot of drama. But others said she was giving and kind and really helped them find clarity in their lives. She was complicated, that's for sure."

My words hung in the air. We were all silent, except for the sound of the line clanging against the steel mast.

Dad set his beer on the table. "Well, you'll get to the bottom of it. Or Noah will. Just keep digging." He stood, and I was glad that he didn't ask where Noah was.

"You headed out, Dad?" I asked, also standing.

He handed Stanley to me. "Yeah, we're taking off."

Barbara, who was wearing a peach-colored peasant dress with her Birkenstocks and chunky silver bracelets on each arm, rose and gave me a half hug. "It'll all work out," she whispered in my ear.

Soon after they left, I yawned. "I think this is my cue to head on out too."

I hugged Joey and Erica good-bye, trying to keep a smile pasted on my face until I left. But in the car, a feeling of melancholy washed over me.

Erica and Joey were clearly pairing up and getting cozy in their own quirky way. I was happy for them.

Somehow Noah and I couldn't sync our schedules to spend more than fifteen minutes together. When would life slow down so we could spend time with each other like normal people? Oddly, there had been a time in my life when I thrived on the chaos of breaking news. Now all I wanted was a boring week or two to get to know Noah better.

It didn't seem like that was happening anytime soon.

I glanced at my dog in the back. He was strapped into his plush car seat, but that didn't stop him from wagging his fluffy tail.

"It's me and you against the world, pupper."

He yawned.

"Want to listen to some Fleetwood Mac?"

I took his silence as a yes. At a stop sign, I scrolled to the song "Landslide" on my phone and turned up the volume.

Chapter
Twenty-Three

The next day started brutally early, with a call from Mike.

"It's five in the morning," I groaned.

"Don't you have to be at the café at six?"

"Yeah, but that means I don't usually get up until five thirty." Next to me, Stanley heaved a dissatisfied puppy sigh. I was interrupting his beauty sleep. "What's up? It's gotta be important for you to call this early."

"A friend from the fire department called. A homeless guy found Raina's bike yesterday."

I sat up, suddenly wide awake. "No way. Where?"

"You know that unofficial dump by the bridge?"

What unofficial dump? I'd been back on the island for only a little over three months. "Can't say I remember that."

"There's an empty lot on the road leading to that old fishing pier. It's right next to the Journey's End Mobile Home Park. People use the lot as a dumping ground. There's all kinds of rusted junk and garbage there."

"How'd they figure out it was Raina's bike?" I scratched Stanley's side, and he rolled over onto his back, exposing his belly.

"The homeless guy tried to sell the bike at the pawn shop. It was too mangled, and the shop owner saw a splotch of blood on it. Well, on a sticker. Apparently Raina had a white-and-purple peace sign sticker, and the blood was on that. It really stood out. Oh, and it was missing a pedal."

"Whoa. So was the homeless guy arrested? Is he the killer?"

"He was detained. But he had an alibi. He was volunteering at a shelter on the mainland the day she disappeared. It was a community event, a walk for the homeless. The organizers had photos of him and everything. He stayed at the shelter that night."

"Well, that rules him out. And it means whoever killed Raina dumped her bike there, right?"

"Yep. Probably."

"Do you need me to write a story?" I gnawed on my cheek, worried. I couldn't shirk my café duties today. How would I fit everything in?

"No, it's okay. I've already written the story, actually. I wanted to call you first thing because I knew you'd be interested."

"Thanks, Mike." I knew he sometimes pitched in with writing articles at the paper when they were short-staffed, so I couldn't feel too bad that he hadn't asked me to handle the story.

"Anytime, kiddo. I'm still thinking about whether I can afford a longer piece from you. I'll get back to you soon."

At least it wasn't a no. Money was always appreciated, but I craved the byline. "I appreciate it."

We hung up, and I rushed through my morning routine so I could make it to Perkatory in time. At least my wrist felt a little better, but it was probably because of the Tylenol.

Still, I couldn't get Raina's case out of my head for hours, and I told Erica every new detail when she came in.

"Creepy," she whispered when I recounted what Mike had told me about the bike. "So there's a killer in our midst."

"Seems like it." I eyed the customers warily. "It could literally be anyone."

But more likely it was someone who'd had a problem with Raina. That didn't narrow the suspect list down, unfortunately. Between customers, Erica and I huddled around my phone as she read Mike's story aloud.

The badly mangled, aqua-colored beach cruiser was found atop a heap of junk on the east side of the island. The front wheel was twisted and that was one reason Devil's Pawn didn't buy it, said Anthony Mello, the owner of the pawn shop.

"Not only would I not buy something that was obviously damaged, but I spotted a dried, rust-colored substance on the tire," said Mello. "I had to call authorities right away. I've watched enough CSI to know my blood spatter."

"Everybody's a forensic investigator," I muttered.

Officials matched the bike with photos provided by the victim's boyfriend. Lab tests will be performed to officially determine if the rust-colored substance is blood and if it is a match with the slain yoga teacher.

"Could someone have hit her while she was riding?" Erica asked.

"A possibility. I wonder if that's how she died." The alternative—that she'd still been alive when she was dumped in the swamp—was too disturbing to consider.

I had to cut my investigative thoughts short because it was a crazy-busy morning at the café, and that took all my available energy. A customer slipped and fell near the bathroom. We ran out of hazelnut syrup. There was another complaint about the cold brew. Once again, it tasted like dishwater. And my failure was all on me. I was the only one to have made the concoction.

"This is unreal," I whispered into the cold brew vat at the end of the day. Why was this continuing to give me trouble? What could cause it to be delicious one day and terrible the next? I'd thought I could solve the problem by cleaning the vats and the buckets. But no.

"Maybe I should let you make it," I groaned to Erica as we were closing up.

She shook her head. "I know nothing about cold brew. I'm strictly a hot kinda chick."

I let out a heavy sigh and locked the door behind us.

"Someone's Ms. Crankypants today," she observed as we strolled down the sidewalk. Her scooter was parked in the alley, and I was walking the two blocks home.

"I'm uneasy." We stopped at the entrance to the alley, where her little red Vespa stood against the back brick wall of Perkatory.

"About Raina's murder? Why? Do you feel unsafe?"

I shrugged. "It seems weird that cops haven't made an arrest. But I'm also anxious about the article and whether I'm writing it. Or not writing it."

Erica side-eyed me. "You're not great with uncertainty, are you?"

"How'd you guess?"

"I think I was tipped off when I saw you making weekly lists of the amount of food waste generated at the shop." She grinned.

I knew she was teasing me about my control-freak qualities, but gently. "Seriously. Sometimes stuff is out of your control. You need to let it go."

"I thought you were going to tell me to double down on my investigation into Raina's murder. I'm surprised."

She let out a *pfft* sound. "I meant the article. Let that go. You don't need the money. Or the headache of a deadline. But if you enjoy sleuthing around about the murder, why not continue doing it?"

I frowned. "It's not that I love it, exactly. Well, I do. I enjoy the puzzle of putting a story together, how the pieces and interviews all fit. And I'm insanely curious to know what happened to her. Doesn't seem right that she'd be living, breathing, doing her yoga business and then she'd turn up dead."

"So continue to investigate."

A laugh erupted from my lips. "Investigating murders isn't a hobby. What are you proposing? That I act like a quasi police official, going around the island and interviewing people for clues? Order a citizen's arrest?"

"Well, yeah. Actually."

"That seems inadvisable for so many reasons." Noah's handsome face, with a reproachful stare, popped into my mind.

Erica leaned against the brick wall, bending her knee so one foot was flat on the side of the building. She looked effortlessly cool in her skinny black jeans, black T-shirt, and black sneakers. "Why does everything have to have a purpose?"

I rolled my eyes. "Is this some wacky existential philosophy? Have you been talking with my dad?"

"No. Hear me out. Why not report for the joy of it? And then decide what to do with the material? Maybe you freelance the story if Mike doesn't ultimately want it."

"Freelancing's a hustle. Don't have time."

"Sounds like an excuse. So write a book. Or a magazine article. Or go on a podcast. A blog. Goodness, Lana. You have so many options. Do something for the fun of it."

"Fun?" I snorted.

"Well, maybe not fun. But a sense of purpose. That's what life's about, you know."

I growled. "I'll think about it, Ms. Punk Rock Kierkegaard. Listen, I need to get home to Stanley."

"Okay. Don't worry so much. Things are usually not that important in the long run." She cocked her finger and thumb like a pistol and made a clicking noise with her tongue. "Put that in your skillet and sauté it."

Laughing, I watched as she donned her red helmet and drove off.

Our conversation put me in a weird frame of mind as I walked. I ran through my interviews, wondering if I even had enough to put together a story on the off chance Mike said it was a go. I had Shawn, with some great quotes. I had Heidi, Jennis, and Kai. The Wolfman. And surely there were more people who had come into Raina's complicated orbit and been either attracted to or repelled by her. And what of Molly, who had spoken with Cody in the bar but seemed to cry crocodile tears publicly?

I might be the only person who hadn't had an especially strong feeling about Raina one way or the other.

It took me five minutes to get home, and when I turned up the walkway of my house, I was struck with an intense nostalgia, tinged with happiness. In Portuguese the word was *saudade*, I'd learned from a Brazilian friend in Miami, and it meant intense, bittersweet longing. That's what I felt every time I saw the landscaping in our front yard in the right light.

Tonight was a perfect example. Despite the late-summer heat, my coral-colored wax begonia hedge was blooming, and in the soft sunset hue of the early evening, it was ablaze with color. Mom had planted these years ago, and they were still going strong.

This was why I'd returned home to Devil's Beach after a layoff from my old paper, after my divorce. Moments of stillness and beauty. Connection with Dad and Mom.

The mood boost of the flowers put a little pep in my step, and I bounded up the three stairs to my front door. I could already hear Stanley's short, sharp bark, the one that signaled how excited he was to see me. Another blessing.

Why was I overthinking this story about Raina? Why couldn't I just forget about it?

I pulled open the screen door, and a flyer stuck in the doorjamb fluttered to my feet. Probably another menu for Beach Pizza or Flying Lotus, the island's Chinese food restaurant. Mmm. Chinese. I stooped to grab the paper, thinking about ordering lo mein.

Instead, it was a paper menu from Bay-Bays, the restaurant near Perkatory. Eh. I wasn't in the mood for grouper, as much as I loved it. I was about to crumple the flyer when I noticed handwritten words scrawled on the blank back side of the menu.

You're on the right track. Why don't you ask Shawn about his car?

I burst inside, my heart pounding. As I scooped homemade dog food into Stanley's ceramic bowl, the words on the note circled my mind like a mantra.

"What's up with his car?" I murmured to the puppy, who looked up at me and licked his chops. I plopped another dollop of pâté-like chicken and rice in his dish.

No longer hungry because adrenaline was coursing through my veins, I went over my interview with Shawn, even getting out my notebook and reviewing his words. There was no mention of a car, only Jet Skis.

Hmm. I poured myself a glass of wine, then got an idea. Someone wouldn't have written this clue and left it on my porch if it were insignificant. It was my experience as a newspaper reporter that the people who sent tips fell into two categories: those who were crazy, and those who wanted to get the truth out.

While I had to be mindful of the former—it was Devil's Beach, after all—I was strongly leaning toward the latter when it came to this note left between my screen and front doors. It didn't have the hallmarks of a conspiracy theorist or crackpot, mostly due to its brevity and readability.

You're on the right track. Why don't you ask Shawn about his car?

Determined, I changed out of my work clothes and took a shower. Thoughts began to gel. As unsettling as it was that someone had come to my home to give me a tip, I wasn't scared. Whoever left the note had wanted me to have information. Wanted to lead me down a path.

They were on my side. The side of the truth. Whoever had come by knew I was working on an article.

That I might not be working on an article wasn't an issue at the moment. I was certain Mike would want the piece now. How could he not?

I sipped a second glass of wine and hoisted Stanley onto the sofa next to me, petting his golden puppy fur. He responded by showing me his belly.

Why Shawn's car? There was one possibility: it was the murder weapon. The autopsy report hadn't yet been released, so how Raina was killed hadn't been released to the public.

My brain kicked into high gear. It had been days since Raina's body was found. Surely the autopsy was finished by now, and Noah had chosen not to release it. Or the state officials had made that decision. However, autopsy reports were public record . . .

Once I was clean and in my sweat pants and oversized T-shirt, I dialed Noah.

"Lana?" he answered in a drowsy tone.

"Are you sleeping?"

"Mmph. I kind of drifted off. I've been up since four AM."

I sipped my wine. "Oh yeah? How come?"

He yawned. "Working on Raina's case. I was reviewing it here on my sofa when you called. What's going on with you?"

I paused, wondering if I should tell him about the note. "Oh, not much. Just got home from work. Drinking a glass of wine. I was wondering about something and thought you'd know."

He chuckled softly. "Something tells me this isn't a social call."

"Well, it is. I was thinking about you, of course," I purred. "But I got to thinking about Raina too. Did you ever get the autopsy report on her?" Noah was friends with the county's medical examiner on the mainland.

"Not yet. Hoping for that on Monday. It's taking a long time because they're being extra thorough."

"Ah, because of Kai's father."

"Exactly."

"Hmm."

"That *hmm* sounds ominous."

"No, no," I added hastily. If I told him about the note, he'd probably worry unnecessarily. And I wanted to do a bit of sleuthing first. "Just curious."

He made another soft groan. "I'll be sure to let you know what I find out. So tell me about your day. How's your wrist? Your sunburn?"

I smiled into the phone. It felt like my chest could burst from happiness. "Both are better, thanks to the aloe and Tylenol. You're a sweetheart for bringing that to me."

As I chattered on, I jotted a few notes in my trusty journal. The first order of business Monday morning was to visit the medical examiner's office and get that autopsy report before anyone else. Noah probably wouldn't like that, but that wasn't my concern.

An hour after we hung up, I climbed into bed with my dog. My phone vibrated with a text from Noah.

Sweet dreams, cupcake

I tried not to think about Raina's murder, Noah's reaction to my snooping, or Mike's freelance budget. But I knew that in the next few days, I'd have to face the truth—possibly about everything.

Chapter
Twenty-Four

On Monday, after successfully talking Dad into coming to the café and covering for a few hours, I poured a generous amount of our house blend into my favorite travel mug. On the side of the plastic cup was a Stevie Nicks quote: DON'T BE A LADY, BE A LEGEND.

Then I hopped in my car and drove over the bridge that separated Devil's Beach from the mainland, counting the number of dolphins in the blue water of Devil's Bay. (I spotted three.)

It took me nearly forty-five minutes in heavy tourist traffic to reach my destination: the county medical examiner's office. It was in a low-slung, beige stucco building close to Interstate 75, adjacent to the county's mosquito control office and the wastewater treatment plant.

Feeling purposeful, I parked and marched into the lobby. It was air-conditioned to a subzero level, but from experience, I knew that was for reasons other than the hot weather outside.

A fiftysomething woman behind a Plexiglas barrier was playing Candy Crush on her phone. She looked up and flipped her cell facedown. "How can I help you?"

"I'm Lana Lewis with the *Devil's Beach Beacon*. I'm here to get a copy of an autopsy report. The name of the victim is Raina Romero. Has the medical examiner finished the report? It should be a public record by now."

The woman tapped with long, purple fingernails on her keyboard. "Looks like it is. Let me run this by the records department. I'll be right back. You can have a seat over there."

She pointed to a gray leather-covered bench. I sank down, taking in the lobby. It had the smell of sawdust and looked like it was a new building. There was also the faint tinge of earthiness, and only someone who had been in an ME's office before would detect the unmistakable odor: corpse.

Pretending I was unbothered, I focused on the magazines on a small side table. Something about the fact that the ME had *People* magazine in the lobby, like a doctor's office, struck me as humorous, and I fought back a grin. My phone in my purse buzzed, and I took it out.

It was Noah. I pondered whether to answer it, but since I was here waiting for an indeterminate amount of time, I figured I would, in case some news was breaking in Raina's case.

"Hey," I said brightly.

"How's the medical examiner's office? You like their new digs? They opened that office about six months ago."

My jaw dropped. "How do you know where I am?"

"Because I'm friends with the ME and he just called. He knows you're there to pick up a copy of Raina's autopsy. That's what you're doing, right?"

"You're not the boss of me."

He chuckled. "I know I'm not. Why didn't you have them email it? It would've saved you the drive. Or you could've asked me, since I got it two hours ago. All you would've had to do is bring me one of those Nutella brownies of yours."

"I'm trying to keep my business and personal life separate. Didn't we agree to that?"

"I guess we did."

"I don't like giving people the opportunity to say no or not return calls or be evasive. Showing up in person's always better if possible. It's harder to say no to me in person."

"Don't I know it," he murmured.

I fanned my face with my notebook. "Are you trying to prevent me from getting this report?"

I mashed my molars together. It didn't matter how sexy Noah was; I didn't like him interfering with my reporting.

He sighed. "No. I can't do that. The report is a public record. But I'm going to make a request."

"Okay. I'm not sure I'll agree, but shoot."

"Before you print anything, can you please call me for comment? We've got some things happening right now that might interest you."

"Like what?"

"Can't tell you yet. Let's say things are unfolding as we speak. The situation is fluid."

"You're speaking in cop clichés."

He laughed.

I paused, declining to tell him that Mike might not even want an article from me. "You promise to speak on the record?"

"I promise."

"Okay. Deal."

"Thanks. I appreciate it. Talk soon."

He hung up before I could ask him if he wanted me to bring over a few extra chocolate-chip cookies from Perkatory. My gaze went to the Plexiglas window, where the secretary was sinking into her chair. I jumped up, eager to get the report and scram.

"That'll be five dollars," she said. "One dollar per page."

"Erm. Right." Crud. I'd thought I had more cash on me. I dug around in my purse and found four dollar bills and some change. As I was counting out pennies, a man came into the lobby from the inside of the office and stood behind me.

"I only have four dollars and seventy-two cents." I slid the money and coins onto the stainless steel beneath the opening. "Lemme go out to my car and raid the center console."

The man, who had the fireplug build of a body builder, chuckled, and I turned. "No need to worry about the rest. We've got you covered."

"Uh, okay. You sure? Thanks a bunch."

The woman scowled as she took the money and slid the report under the glass.

"Sorry, I'm Vern Black, the medical examiner. You must be Lana." He held out his hand.

So this was Noah's college friend. He'd mentioned that they met for breakfast often. "It's nice to meet you."

"Noah's told me a lot about you."

A smile spread on my face. "He has, has he?"

Vern nodded. "Mentioned you were pretty nosy. Well, he actually said pretty and nosy."

Not exactly the ringing endorsement one would want from a boyfriend, but it wasn't wrong. "I am a little curious, in fact, about this report." I held up the sheaf of papers.

"Yeah, Noah and I go way back, to college. He's a great friend." The guy eyed me up and down. "Glad you could stop by and pick up the copy in person. I think you're going to find it interesting. Pay close attention to page four." He winked. "Well, gotta get back to work. Had a terrible car crash in East County and have to run tox reports on two people. See you around. Say hi to our mutual friend for me."

I waved good-bye and walked in the opposite direction, out the glass door. *Pay close attention to page four.*

I'd intended to wait until I returned to Devil's Beach to read the report, but between Noah's call and Vern's reading suggestion, my curiosity was piqued. I fired up my Honda and cranked the air all the way to four. It blew mildly cool air and made an ominous rattling sound. I'd definitely need to get the car looked at soon.

But first, I wanted to scan the report from the very top.

DECEDENT: RAINA ROMERO
MANNER OF DEATH: HOMICIDE

A chill of awareness flowed down my spine as I took in the basic details: the date, the time, and the listing of doctors who had performed the exam.

CAUSE OF DEATH: CEREBRAL INJURIES, CRANIAL FRACTURES

I winced. Someone had hit her in the skull? How had she gotten into the swamp? Was she killed before or after?

I read on, making notes in the margins and shuffling the papers until I got to page four. That's where Vern had written several meaty paragraphs about the exam.

History of being reported missing and subsequently being found unresponsive in an obvious state of death in a mangrove swamp on Devil's Beach. The decedent is a 29-year-old Caucasian female who has a largely unknown medical history at the time of this autopsy.

I'd almost forgotten how dry these reports could be. I skimmed the paragraphs, looking for the juicy details.

The body exhibits mild to moderate decomposition comprising generalized discoloration, bloating and skin slippage . . . At autopsy, there were numerous abrasions on the legs, and a fractured left tibia . . .

There was extensive evidence of internal injury to the spleen, kidneys, gallbladder and stomach . . . Evidence of subarachnoid hemorrhage, along with contusions and lacerations to the head indicate blunt force trauma.

There was no water or other debris in the stomach that matched the flora or fauna of where the deceased was located; therefore, we are of the opinion that the decedent was killed elsewhere.

And then, on page four, the detail that tied everything together.

The victim had tire marks on her skin.

"Holy crap," I whispered. "So she was hit by a car."

But who would run her over, then dump her in a swamp?

Why don't you ask Shawn about his car?

I swallowed hard. This was huge. Before I called Mike, I wanted to give the report another once-over. My mind reeled with all that I needed to accomplish over the next few hours. Namely, talk with Shawn again and ask him about his car. How would I do that? I also wanted to find Molly again. Hopefully she was working at Bay-Bays today.

Oh, and I had a mountain of work back at the café. I cranked the car's engine and roared off.

* * *

On the way back to Devil's Beach, I sketched out the article in my mind.

> A popular Devil's Beach yoga studio owner died from head injuries sustained in a hit-and-run crash, according to a county medical examiner's report.
>
> Raina Rose Romero was found dead Tuesday in a watery grave in Angelwing Park. Police have made no arrests in the case, which has been officially classified as a homicide. An autopsy report made public by the medical examiner revealed that Romero died when she was hit by a vehicle. The killer then moved her body to the swamp in the nature preserve.
>
> Devil's Beach police chief Noah Garcia said . . .

What would Noah say? I had to call him. But not yet.

Driving five miles over the speed limit, I reached the island in record time and made a beeline to the spot where Shawn had his Jet Ski booth. I circled the block, looking for a parking space, and eventually found one.

This week was busy on the island because of a shell collector convention, and there were tourists everywhere, drinking from Perkatory cups (yay) and lapping up ice cream from Give Me Chills, a popular food truck on Devil's Island.

Cold Brew Corpse

Since I had to be back at Perkatory to relieve Dad, I did a slow jog to the booth. As I approached, I realized Shawn wasn't there, but a young woman was. She was a redhead with typical ginger coloring: freckles, pale skin. She wore an olive-green fisherman's hat and a khaki romper getup, which made her look like one of those safari tour guides at animal theme parks.

"Hi," I huffed.

"Hello there! Would you like to rent a Jet Ski today? We have two- and four-person watercraft, and we have a special on parasailing. We also have paddleboards to rent by the hour. You look like a paddleboard person."

I held up my hand. "I'm definitely not a paddleboard person. I'm looking for Shawn."

Her chipper expression didn't budge. "Oh, he's not here. Had to go to Fort Lauderdale today."

My face fell. "I see. When will he be back?"

Her eyes rolled upward, and she appeared to study the sky. "I'm not sure. He went to the port to drop something off."

The port? Weird. I only knew of cruise ships that left from the Fort Lauderdale port. I stepped closer and pretended to inspect a brochure. "Oh yeah? Is he going on a cruise?"

She shook her head. "No, he's dropping his SUV off. He sold it to a friend who's moving to Brazil, and they're putting it on a container ship. I was like, whatever, why couldn't his friend buy a ride in South America? It would be a lot simpler, don't you think?"

I blinked. What? He was sending his vehicle out of the country? "His SUV?"

"Yeah, isn't that the craziest thing ever? Who does that?"

"W-what kind of car?"

The way she rolled her hazel eyes told me that she was almost done answering my questions. "I dunno. One of those big SUVs.

249

Like a fancy Mercedes or something. It looks like something you'd see in the desert. He had it fixed up. I had to admit, it had swagger."

"Fixed up," I yelped. "How?"

"Yeah. Fixed up. Painted. It used to be silver, and he had it painted black. Why are you so interested?"

"Uh, like you said Who fixes up a Mercedes SUV and then sends it to South America?" I mumbled. "Well, thanks. I'll catch up with him later."

I started to walk away when she called after me. "Can I tell him your name?"

I waved her off and kept walking. This was an enormous scoop. Massive. It would rock the *Devil's Beach Beacon* front page like no other story had. I reached for my phone and dialed Mike at the paper.

"Holy crap, you're not going to believe what I've found," I said, breathless. By now I'd reached my car, and I unlocked it.

"Oh jeez, Lana. I've been meaning to call you, but I've been so busy. We're not going to have the budget for your story after all."

"What? No, Mike, you don't understand. I drove to the mainland and paid for the autopsy report. Raina died because she was hit by a car. I have the report here. And I have proof of who probably killed her." I recounted my conversation with the woman in the kiosk, but Mike interrupted me.

"Hey, Cody, call over to the ME's office and get the autopsy report on Raina," Mike called out. "I'm so sorry, Lana. We'll take it from here. I wish I could pay you for the article. Can I have Cody call you? I'll get him down to the kiosk. I'm a little busy. Trying to put out a fire with an advertiser."

My mouth hung open. "Cody? But isn't he a photographer?"

"He is, but he's also a decent writer. And since I've brought him on board full-time, I might as well put him to work as a multimedia reporter—I'm paying him a salary anyway. I'm really sorry, kiddo. We've got a strict budget, and I overspent last month with all the news."

"But, but . . ." my voice trailed off and I was met with silence. There was nothing I could do—I was only a freelancer. "Have Cody call me." Disappointment made my heart plummet to my knees. Writing a story gave me a sense of purpose, and now that feeling had imploded.

"Good. Good. I hope you understand. Times are really tight. There's been some massive budget shortfalls; finance briefed me on them today. Advertisers have pulled out because of the economy. You know how it goes at papers, kiddo."

"I do know how it goes." A flashback to my layoff in Miami made me feel even more like a loser.

"Let's talk soon, okay?"

"Yeah, yeah. Talk soon." We hung up and I scrunched my eyes shut, willing away the tears. Reporting on Raina's death felt so natural. I loved the research, the interviews, and the connection between the two. Not following it up to the logical conclusion—writing an article—felt like having a phantom limb. Not only did I have a potentially explosive story that could crack Raina's murder wide open, but I had to give it to an arrogant photographer who knew nothing about local news and probably couldn't write his way out of a paper bag.

Great. Just great. Why was I even bothering? There was no point in talking with Molly at Bay Bays now, despite that strange note left on my doorstep.

And crap, I had to get back to Perkatory, because the coffee supplier was coming in an hour. And yet, I wasn't ready to let the story go. Even though I knew I should. I massaged my forehead with my fingers. What to do?

I dialed Noah, wanting to talk about it with someone. Now that I wasn't writing an article, I figured I could unload the contents of my notebook for him. As much as I adored him, it still seemed wrong for me to provide information to the authorities before printing it in a newspaper. With a sigh, I dialed his number.

"Hey cupcake, how was Vern?"

"He says hi."

"Good guy, that Vern. Remind me to tell you about the time we were on a fishing trip in the Glades together."

"Sorry, Noah. I'm not calling to hear about your memories with Vern the medical examiner."

"You're not?" He chuckled. Goodness, that man knew how to push my buttons.

"No. Listen, I read the autopsy report. Twice. And I got a potentially explosive piece of information during an interview. Since I'm not doing a story, I think it's my duty to share everything with you."

"Whatcha got?"

Why did he sound so amused? He should really take this murder far more seriously. I spoke for about five minutes nonstop, telling him about the note on my porch, and then my conversation with the woman at the Jet Ski kiosk. He mm-hmmed and uh-huhed.

"Sounds like you dug up some great stuff."

"I did! Shawn's employee said his SUV had been recently painted. She didn't say where, but I'm sure it's easy to find out.

Isn't there a way to determine if a car's repainted after it hit a person? I recall reading a news story about that. Anyway. I think Shawn has something to do with this. No, I know he does," I said breathlessly. "He seemed nice, but also sketchy. Too effusive when he talked about Raina. He's putting his luxury SUV in a container right now, and I'll bet you anything it's damaged."

There was a pause, and silence, and I barreled on. "It's all so creepy. I wonder why he became so obsessed with her."

I heard the shuffling of papers in the background. "You know, Lana, you're not a half-bad investigator. If you ever want a job as an officer, maybe we could talk about sponsoring you to go to the police academy."

This wasn't the response I'd expected, and I bit my lip. "Gah," I said out loud. "I'm not looking for another career. I've got two going right now, but the journalism one isn't going so well. So what do you think of my theory? My information? Seems big, right?"

"Why aren't you putting all this in the paper?"

"Because Mike doesn't have the budget and he's asked a staffer to write it." I tried to hide the disappointment in my voice.

"Bummer."

"Whatever. I'm over it. Why aren't you more interested in what I told you? It's huge. You seem less than interested."

"I'm actually very enthused about this information."

"Then what gives?"

"It's not new."

"What?" I shifted the phone to my other ear. How could that be?

Noah sighed. "I'm going to tell you this off the record, okay?"

"Okay."

"I'm serious. I don't want to see this in the paper yet. Don't share this with anyone."

"I'm officially not a reporter right now." Even saying those words was like a swift jab to the solar plexus. "I won't be breaking any news."

"State agents are about to arrest Shawn at the port in Fort Lauderdale any minute."

Chapter
Twenty-Five

Later that day, Erica and I walked through downtown Devil's Beach to the bank. I had a deposit to make, and she was tagging along.

"Would you stop looking at your phone?" she admonished.

"Sorry. I can't help it. Every time it buzzes, I think it's a headline alert from the paper, with the news of Shawn's arrest."

"You think he's guilty?"

We were a block from the bank, passing Beach Books. I slowed to check out the new offerings in the window. "It's hard for me to say. He was so effusive about Raina. I didn't get an overwhelming vibe that he was a killer, though. But maybe I'm not the best judge of that."

"I'd think you would be, given your background in crime reporting and all."

I lifted my shoulders. "Being a reporter means you have to be unbiased. I try not to judge people when I'm interviewing."

"Oh, come on. You don't judge people in your mind as you talk with them?"

I shook my head. "I've learned that seemingly good people can do evil things. And folks who appear like they're awful can have hearts of gold."

"Hmph. Interesting. I assume everyone's sketchy until proven otherwise."

By now we were at the bank. I pulled open the door and locked eyes with none other than Heidi.

"Oh, hey there," I said, surprised. I itched to tell her about Shawn's arrest. Probably not the best idea to bring it up here in public, given how upset she was over Raina. And Noah had asked me not to say anything, and I'd abided by his request—except when it came to Erica, of course. She could keep a secret. It wasn't like I'd told Dad, who would broadcast the news to the entire island.

Heidi's gaze flitted to me, then back to the man she was with. They were standing next to a small counter where people signed checks and did other paperwork. It was at the entrance to the roped-off queue area, and Erica and I had to step around them.

"Who's that?" the man hissed loudly.

Heidi looked flustered. "No one. I mean, she's the owner of Perkatory."

"That place next to the yoga studio?" His lips pressed together in a thin, angry line.

"Yes," she replied in a small voice.

The man, who was silver haired and held himself with military-like precision, eyed me warily.

"Hi, Lana." Heidi fidgeted with her short hair, repeatedly trying to tuck a lock behind her ear.

Weird. What was this all about? I opened my mouth to say something, but the man snapped his fingers in front of her face.

"Hey. Stay focused. What did you do with the check? Did you lose it? I swear to God, I married an imbecile."

I visibly cringed. Erica and I exchanged horrified glances, and we slipped past them. At the far end of the room, sitting in a waiting area, was Mickey Dotson, the owner of Island Brewnette, my competition. We made eye contact, and I waved.

He lowered his head to his phone, and Erica, who saw the whole exchange, snorted. "My word, he is such a jerk," she whispered. "Just ignore him."

It took only a few minutes to make the deposit. When we turned around, Heidi and her husband were gone.

"That was strange," I muttered as we left.

"What?"

"Heidi. The way her husband talked to her like that."

Erica smirked. "It's par for the course with a lot of men, unfortunately. My ex up north used to act like that."

"So true," I murmured, once again thanking all the gods and goddesses in the universe I wasn't in a terrible or abusive relationship. "My ex was a jerk, but not that kind of jerk. He was sickeningly sweet to my face but couldn't resist other women."

Erica rolled her eyes. "Men."

We'd no sooner left the bank when my phone buzzed. With sweaty palms, I pulled it out of my pocket. "Here it is," I nearly shouted.

Erica and I huddled under the bank awning in the shade, out of the strong Florida sun, as I read aloud.

"Cody's byline, of course. Look at that," I muttered bitterly.

WATER SPORTS COMPANY OWNER ARRESTED IN MURDER OF POPULAR YOGA TEACHER

Devil's Beach police chief Noah Garcia said Monday that an island man was arrested and charged with first-degree murder in connection with the death of Raina Rose Romero, the owner of an island yoga studio.

"Boring first sentence."

"Keep reading." Erica flapped her hands.

Shawn Sims was arrested in Fort Lauderdale. Garcia said Sims struck Romero with his car, then deposited her body in Angelwing Park.

I grimaced. "Deposited? What a terrible verb."

Sims placed the car on a container ship to Brazil. Officials were unable to obtain the vehicle because the ship had already left by the time detectives arrived. But Garcia said the SUV will be impounded in Brazil when it docks. There was enough other evidence to justify an arrest, said Garcia. "The suspect could not provide his whereabouts on the day Ms. Romero died and did not have an alibi. We do have other evidence that connects him to the crime," Garcia said.

"Other evidence? I wonder what," Erica said.

"I wonder as well." I read the rest of the article aloud in a fast and buzzy tone. It was about Raina's studio, her popularity, her Instagram prowess, and her beauty. Several paragraphs about her beauty, with quotes.

Erica leaned back against the brick wall of the bank. "Dang. Even in death, women are judged for their looks."

I snorted. "Ain't that the truth. Not surprised, given the writer."

"That article really didn't tell us much, did it?"

"No. And I'm shocked there weren't more details about the autopsy. Very little from the report is in that article. I wonder if he even got the report."

Erica's eyes widened. "You going to go talk with Kai? Or Molly? Or anyone else?"

"For an article? No. I'm not. As far as I'm concerned, I'm done with this story."

"Then why do you look so skeptical?"

"Dunno. Something doesn't sit right with me about it. That police weren't able to impound the car. There's a lot of unanswered questions. Something doesn't add up with what Shawn told me and the arrest."

"He's probably lying. Criminals do that, you know."

"I wish I could ask him more questions, you know?"

Erica snatched the phone out of my hand and tapped on the screen. She squinted and tilted her head downward. "Shawn's enjoying three hots and a cot at the county jail. If you have questions, it's not like he's going anywhere."

"A jailhouse interview," I said, suddenly perking up. If I snagged that, surely Mike would want an article. And Cody, for all his foreign correspondent experience, probably didn't know one could march over to the jail and boldly ask for a sit-down during regular visiting hours. It was a tactic I'd used in Miami often. "That's not a bad idea at all."

Erica handed me the phone back. "Who's got your back?"

We grinned and walked down the street, changing the subject to the cold brew problem. But my mind was already turning and thinking about how I was going to interview Shawn in jail without Noah—or Cody—immediately finding out.

The last thing I wanted was either of them ruining a potential scoop. One I desperately needed if I wanted to write another newspaper article.

Chapter Twenty-Six

As it turned out, visiting hours at the jail weren't until the next day, so I had to cool my heels for the rest of Monday. Which was probably good, because I still hadn't gotten a handle on the cold brew problem. We'd been serving iced coffee only in recent days, and customers were clamoring for the smoother cold brew.

"I don't get it." I turned to Erica, sipping my latest concoction. "What kind of water do you use?"

"I use filtered. Even bought some from the store. And I tweaked the amount of coffee I used too. I can't figure it out."

"Maybe we need to get a filtering system for the entire shop."

I rubbed my lips together. Did we have the money for that? I'd hoped to use any extra for hiring a new person. We'd been busier ever since winning the barista championship, and I knew our small team would get burned out if I didn't give them some relief. But delicious cold brew was a must on the menu, since it was such a popular and lucrative drink. "It's hard to know what to focus on sometimes."

Erica wiped down the counter with a rag. "In my humble opinion, the product is top priority."

"Yeah, but I feel like I'm working you and Barbara and Dad too hard. Barbara's already taken on an extra day. Dad didn't want to work full-time, but he's being kind about it. And I . . ." My voice faded.

"You want time off to sleuth," Erica said.

"Yeah. I do."

"Were okay. We can handle the customers. Make sure the cold brew's great, and everything will work out." Erica squeezed my arm as she passed by me. "You can do it. I believe in you."

I tapped out a quick email to my coffee supplier, telling him about the issue I'd been having with the cold brew. He answered right away, asking me to send an overnight FedEx sample of my grind to him because he wanted to do an emergency cupping.

Yikes. This was serious. Suppliers did emergency cuppings only if they thought the batch was bad.

My attention was ripped away from my phone when two people entered the café, arguing.

Heidi and her silver-haired husband.

"Will you stop nagging me about what I'm eating and drinking?" The two of them paused near the front door. They hissed at each other in hushed tones and finally moved when a mother and her daughter tried to leave.

Heidi and her husband approached the counter.

"I'm trying to help, dear," she replied in her squeaky voice.

"It's not helping, it's nagging. I hate it when you do that, so shut up. Please." The husband seemed oblivious to the fact that nearly everyone in the café was staring at him in horror. He held his head high and marched up to me.

Erica came up behind me and stood close. "That guy's a real piece of work."

"Yep," I agreed, noticing our customers turning back to their conversations and laptops. I'd seen more than a few marital arguments in my time here at Perkatory, but this guy's attitude was among the worst.

"Welcome to Perkatory." I tried to sound cheery. "Long time no see, Heidi."

"Black coffee," he barked.

"How are you, Lana?" She smiled softly.

"I'm well, thanks. You? How are you holding up?"

She sighed, blowing a lock of hair out of her face. "I'm okay. Still reeling from the news of Raina. It would help to have closure if we had a memorial or a funeral. I heard Kai's going to Bali, by the way."

"Oh yeah?"

"Excuse me, did you hear me? I'd like a cup of black coffee. We're in a hurry here," the man interrupted.

Yikes. "Of course." I held up my hand in Heidi's direction, indicating that I'd be back to chat more. I scurried away to pour a to-go cup.

Erica sidled up to me. "So Kai's able to leave the county, I guess," she whispered.

"There's been an arrest, so he's cleared of any suspicion."

I returned to the counter with the nasty guy's coffee. That's when I noticed there was a long, fresh scratch on his neck. And another that disappeared into his polo shirt, along his collarbone. Whoa. What was that about?

"Here's your coffee, sir." My heart was beating fast as I speculated on how he'd received those scratches. I was less worried about him than I was about Heidi, who had to be ninety-eight pounds soaking wet. I started to speculate about their life. Did they have money, with him being a doctor and all. What if he'd hooked up with Raina and Heidi was jealous? My mind reeled with possibilities, and I released a long breath. "Heidi, what would you like?"

"Um, let's see. I'd like a tea. Not chamomile, but mint sounds good. So does the rooibos," she murmured. "Oh, and this is my husband, Charles."

I waved.

"Let's get this show on the road," he said harshly.

My stomach tightened just hearing that tone. Erica slipped past me.

"The mint is excellent," she told Heidi in a gentle voice.

"I'll take that."

Erica touched my arm. "I've got this."

"Thanks." Heidi glanced at me. "How's your article coming along? You must be writing your fingers off now that there's been an arrest. I can't imagine that Shawn could have done such a thing. What a shock, to know he ran her over with his car. While she was bicycling. Who could have—"

"Would you stop talking about that? It's all we freaking discuss. Raina, Raina's murder. Raina's killer. I get it, Heidi. You're sad. But you need to get over this and put it behind you. Remember what I told you?"

I reared back. What kind of man would talk to his own wife like this? When she was obviously so upset?

"Losing someone affects everyone differently," I asserted. "We all grieve in different ways, and Heidi was close to Raina. She's entitled to feel any way she wants, for as long as she wants."

Charles glared at me, and he opened his mouth to speak. Erica chose that moment to return with the tea.

"It's hot, and I put it in two cups, so be extra careful. Heidi, when it's ready to drink, be sure to remove the outer cup. But be careful, okay?"

"Thanks," she squeaked. "Nice seeing you both."

"Come on." Charles drummed his fingers on the counter. He glared at me one last time, then turned and stalked toward the door.

Erica and I watched as they left the café. I let out a breath.

"Holy pupperoni. That guy's a piece of work."

Erica snorted. "No kidding. I know his type exactly."

I turned to her. "Why did you tell her to remove the outer cup when it was ready to drink? You never do that when you serve tea."

A devious smile danced on her lips. "Because I wrote a special message on the cup for her. In Sharpie."

"A message? What did it say?"

She lifted her shoulders. "That if she ever needs help, she can call us here at Perkatory and we'll get her to safety."

"Impressive." I high fived her. "Listen, I need to call Noah to see if he can fill me in on any details of Shawn's arrest. I want to be armed with all possible info before I go to the jail."

"Go for it. Looks like we're in a lull here."

I grabbed the phone out of my pocket and slipped into the back room, where I kept the cold brew.

Hey. Can you talk?

Noah called almost immediately. "Hi, I'm in between conference calls. Don't have much time. I take it you saw the news?"

"I did. Wish I was writing a story. I have so many questions."

Noah sighed heavily. "Me too, Lana. Me too."

"What do you mean?"

"The FDLE made the case. They made the arrest. Oh, my officers were there and we're technically the arresting agency. But they bigfooted this, took over the investigation. I had nothing to do with any of it. That's what I couldn't tell you earlier."

"All because of Kai's dad?"

"Mm-hmm. Listen, gotta go. I'll try to call you tonight, but it'll be iffy. I have a police chiefs meeting in Tampa and will probably be staying at my folks' house."

I squelched my disappointment. As much as I wanted to hear about the case, I also wanted a few hours of uninterrupted time with Noah.

Was that asking too much?

Sighing, I poured a scoop of the ground coffee into a plastic bag. I had just enough time to get to the shipping store on the island to send the grounds to the supplier. Perhaps this was one mystery that could be solved.

* * *

The sign in the visitors' waiting room of the county jail announced in bold type: NO FOOD—NO DRINKS—NO INAPPROPRIATE ATTIRE.

I glanced down at my polka dot blouse and jeans as I waited at the window. It was early the next morning, and I'd come to the jail during morning visiting hours.

I'd shuffled in with a small crowd of about twenty-five people. Mostly women who were there to visit husbands or sons or brothers.

"How long's your man in for?" one woman with thick, long hair asked me.

Probably wouldn't be the best idea if I launched into my real reason for visiting—how I was trying to do a news story but might get shot down and how I had an unnatural interest in a murder case. So I shrugged. "Dunno yet. He was arrested yesterday."

"Your first time here?" She regarded me sympathetically.

I nodded. It was my first time at this jail; I'd visited the jails in Miami during my previous job as a reporter several times.

"Make sure you don't wear no skirts. Like, ever. Wear pants like the ones you've got on. They're worried you're going to flash your guy."

I winced. "Thanks for the tip," I replied.

After an interminable, hour-long wait, we were ushered into another room. It was the decor equivalent of a bowl of oatmeal, with light beige everywhere. Beige walls, beige tile floor, beige seats facing thick glass windows partitioned from each other by more beige walls. My eyes ached for the bright blue of the sky and the vibrant green of the palm trees outside.

The guard directed us to sit in individual cubbies, and I eased down on the beige round stool. Everything here seemed filthy and institutional all at once. Gah. How long would we have to wait in here?

I realized the inmates were coming out when some of the women began to sob. I didn't want to peer around my partitions to stare, so I faced straight ahead.

Shawn sat across from me, separated by a thick pane of glass. He wore an orange jumpsuit with black letters that said COUNTY JAIL on the chest.

I picked up the phone on my side of the window, and he did the same on his. The phone, which was beige, had a layer of scuzz on the part of the receiver closest to my mouth. I waved, which made me feel ridiculous.

"Hi, can you hear me?" I yelled.

"No need to speak that loud. I can hear you just fine. My lawyer said I shouldn't talk to the press. When I heard you were here for visiting hour, I almost didn't come out."

I waved my hand in the air. "Thanks for meeting with me. I appreciate it. Truly. But please, don't worry. I'm not doing a story for the paper. Not right now, anyway. I want to talk first. I have a lot of questions, and I don't think you killed Raina."

"I didn't," he cried.

"Keep it down," I hissed. Shawn and I glanced around, but I couldn't see where the guard was standing.

We both leaned in.

"It's awful here," he whispered, his face crumpling.

I nodded. "I can't even imagine. I saw that the judge set bail at five hundred thousand. That means, what? You have to come up with fifty thousand to be released?"

"Yeah. Like I've got that. Not with business being the way it is. My mom's trying to get the money together, but she's out of state and elderly, so . . ." He swallowed hard, and for a second I thought he was going to bawl. No, Shawn didn't seem like a hardened killer, but I'd interviewed people who had massacred entire groups of people and they hadn't seemed evil either.

Still, with his sun-kissed hair, deep tan, and frat-boy tribal tattoos, I imagined that Shawn wasn't exactly familiar with the inside of a county jail. I made a mental note to check his criminal record as soon as I returned to Devil's Beach. You never knew in Florida.

"So," I offered.

His frown deepened. "Why are you here?"

"Something doesn't add up for me. A lot doesn't add up, honestly. Do you have an alibi for the day Raina disappeared?"

"Sort of. I tried to tell them, but my lawyer told me to shut up and said we'd fight it in court."

"You don't sound like you have a rock-solid alibi." His guilt was looking more certain now.

He sighed, and his shoulders rounded into a slump. "I'd been intimate with Raina," he said quietly. "Recently. As in, that Saturday."

"Oh. Oh! What?"

"That morning, she and Kai got into a fight and he went to the studio. She called me right away. I drove to her house, and we were together. Like, together, together. That's why they have, um, some incriminating DNA evidence."

Aha. I nodded slowly. "Go on."

"And then I left. It was the last time I saw her. I went home, and I live alone. I don't have an alibi for that afternoon."

"Okay, that doesn't sound good. What about your car? And the paint job?"

He shook his head. "It's a Mercedes G-Class."

"Means nothing to me."

He sniffed. "It's a luxury off-road SUV. Looks like a safari vehicle. It's five years old, and when I bought it new, I paid six figures for it."

I wrinkled my nose. Why would anyone do such a thing? Did Jet Ski rentals pay that well? Apparently so. Obviously I'd chosen not one, but two, low-paying careers. "And did you get some body work done on it recently?"

"I sold it to my buddy who's moving to Brazil. He wanted it painted from silver to black, and I knew a guy who does that kind of work on the island. Nothing more than that. There was no damage. It was pristine."

"What's the name of the body shop? Haven't police talked to the people there?"

He shook his head. "My lawyer thinks I was arrested on the DNA evidence alone. He says we'll introduce the SUV details in a motion soon."

"Can you tell me the name of the body shop so I can confirm it? Please?"

He paused. "I don't think I should."

Because I wasn't taking notes, I tried to mentally burn all these details into my brain. "What about the other stuff? That you loaned Raina money and you asked for it back?"

"That's all true. I loaned her ten grand to upgrade her website to some fancy online booking service. And gave her cash for some other things. But I asked for it back because business has been down this summer."

"Were you mad at her?"

"No. No way. I loved her. All I wanted was for her to leave Kai."

"Were you angry that she hadn't?"

"Of course. Not angry enough to kill her, though."

"Why did she stay with Kai, I wonder?"

"Because he was rich." He heaved a sigh. "She liked rich guys."

"Not very yogi-like," I mumbled. "Anyway. Who do you think killed her? And why would someone slip a note under the door at my home, asking me to look into your car?"

"What?" His eyes widened in shock.

"A couple of days ago. It said, *You're on the right track. Why don't you ask Shawn about his car?*"

He snorted. "Someone's trying to frame me."

"But who? Another yoga student? A teacher? Someone else? Kai?"

He shook his head. "I actually don't think it's Kai. From what I hear, he was at the yoga studio all day and there's surveillance video to prove it. Plus, there were security cameras in the yoga studio that confirmed he was there all day."

"But he's the one who probably got state agents to arrest you."

"I know," he said miserably. "But I meditated on it and realized that Kai wouldn't kill Raina."

"Then why'd you tell me otherwise that day I came to interview you?"

He threw his hands in the air. "Ego. Pure and simple. Jealousy. Kai and I have been at each other's throats for months now. Which is stupid. It was Raina who pitted us against each other. I see that clearly now."

"Look, I appreciate your self-awareness, but you've got to give me something," I implored, scooting to the edge of my seat. "Think back to the retreat. Who had weird interactions with her? If you were, ah, intimate with Raina, surely she talked about her students."

"Heidi," he said firmly.

A pang shot through me at the memory of the blond and her husband arguing in Perkatory.

"The way she talks, she and Raina were close. I've interviewed her. She never had a bad word about Raina. I can't imagine she'd murder her."

Shawn shook his head. "I don't know. They had a real weird relationship. It was almost codependent. Unhealthy. When we were in Costa Rica, Heidi got emotional one night on the beach. We were all around a bonfire, and she started crying, saying that Raina had helped her make an important decision. Something about leaving her husband. It was super emotional, even for a yoga retreat. Heidi claimed her husband was controlling and that she needed to leave."

"How did Raina respond?"

"She stayed with Heidi for hours on the beach, talking."

"And what happened after that?"

"No one mentioned it. Heidi was back to her happy, sunny self. Raina seemed really pleased, talking about how she'd facilitated a spiritual breakthrough. But she always talked like that, so I didn't pay much attention. She always worked miracles like that, helping people find inner truth."

"But if Raina helped Heidi come to some important epiphany, then why would Heidi kill her with her car? Doesn't make sense."

"I don't think Heidi killed her, Lana. I think Heidi went home and told her husband about her feelings, said she was leaving him, and he blamed Raina."

"And maybe killed her?" I whispered into the phone.

Shawn nodded. "Bingo."

Seemed a bit farfetched, and like a scenario that an accused man would dream up. Still, it was worth checking out. Heidi's husband did seem to have anger issues. I drummed my fingers on the stainless-steel counter. "Do you know what kind of car he drives? Or his wife?"

"They both drive Beemers. BMWs. His is black, hers is white. Both are SUVs."

All these luxury cars. I shot him an appreciative smile. "Thanks, Shawn. That gives me something to go on. I could ask around to see if anyone's worked on a BMW." And try to confirm his story about his expensive SUV.

"There aren't that many body shops on Devil's Beach. Trust me, I know, because I researched them all when I needed to get my car painted. You might even check with the shops on the mainland."

We were about to say our good-byes when I paused. "Why'd you run away from us that day in the swamp?" I blurted.

He let out a sigh, and his whole body seemed to deflate. "I didn't feel like answering questions. I was too drained and was there having my own personal moment with the place where Raina was found."

A tear rolled down his cheek, and for the first time, I felt genuinely terrible for him. "I'm sorry," I whispered.

"And you came on really strong that day you walked up to the kiosk."

I nodded slowly. Now I didn't know what to think. It was difficult to believe that anyone saw me as intimidating.

"Do you think you can help me?"

"I'll see what I can do. The last thing I want to see is an innocent man sitting behind bars."

"Can you please try? Please? I'm not sure about my lawyer. He's a kid, and I know he's trying hard. But I need all the assistance I can get. Write something and put it in the paper. Anything." His expression was wild and unfocused.

"I'll try," I said.

For the first time he smiled, despite his watery eyes. I felt guilty for possibly getting Shawn's hopes up. There was no guarantee I'd even be able to write a news article, much less free him from jail.

Chapter Twenty-Seven

When I got back into my car, the first thing I did was check my email. Sure enough, my friend Sheila had sent me a note about Raina's court case in Jacksonville.

> Here's what I found: Raina Romero was arrested seven years ago on fraud charges. She was an orderly at a nursing home. Family of an elderly woman said she ripped off a three-carat diamond ring. She denied it, but the ring was never found. Pleaded the case to a misdemeanor and fine. Documents attached.

"Whoa," I whispered. So Raina hadn't always been a seeker of light and truth. She'd been a garden-variety fraudster.

But what did it all mean? Anything? Was Shawn lying? After all, he had a lawyer working on his behalf. Did any of it matter now that I wasn't writing an article? A heavy feeling settled in my stomach, and I made my way back to Devil's Beach.

I parked at home, intending to walk to Perkatory. When I pulled into the driveway, I saw Dad coming out the front door. He waved and loped over as I climbed out of the car. He reeked of marijuana, as if he were a living, breathing Cheech and Chong movie.

"What happened to Sober September?" I asked, sniffing the air.

He shrugged and giggled. "I just fed Stanley, and then I'm taking a stroll to meet Barbara. I'm going to help comb the beach for driftwood. What did you find out?" he asked, his voice tinged with excitement.

I told him everything, including about the note and Raina's fraud conviction.

Dad's expression was similar to Stanley's when I cooked bacon. "I can't wait to see all this in the paper, munchkin. You're going to blow the lid off this story."

I brushed off his hug. "Well, that's a problem. Mike doesn't have the money for a freelance article."

Dad let out a long breath. "Want me to talk with him?"

"No," I cried. Here I was, thirty years old, and my father was about to intervene in my work. It was the last thing I wanted. "It's nothing personal. It's the way it is in journalism."

"So you're going to let all that significant information go to waste?"

I emitted a frustrated groan. "I'll talk with Noah, but it seems like the state has additional evidence against Shawn. And they're in charge of the investigation. Or Shawn's lying to me. I'm stumped, unfortunately."

He stroked his silver beard. "Let me think. Let me think . . ."

"Listen, while you think, I've got to get to Perkatory."

"Okay, dear. But I think you should, at the very least, try to stop in at Bay-Bays and talk to Molly. She might have an important clue. That note for you was on a menu from there. Don't forget that."

"We'll see," I grumbled while giving him a quick hug.

Slinging my laptop bag over my shoulder, I set off for downtown. When I approached, I spied Bay-Bays. It was diagonal to my coffee shop. There were no cars in sight, and I dashed across the street and into the restaurant. Like many of the joints on Devil's Beach, its specialties were seafood and stiff drinks. They made my favorite grouper chowder, and my stomach growled a little when I stepped inside.

Today, a cluster of people sat at the bar, watching some sportsball game. Janey, a woman who'd been a friend of my mom's, stood at the hostess station. Since I saw her all the time at Perkatory, I gave her a wave.

"Table for one? Your favorite chowder is the special today."

I shook my head. "I was hoping you could help me with something."

"Sure, anything."

"When does Molly Wayne work? She's a server here. Gorgeous redhead, tall. Do you know her?"

"Oh yeah. Awesome person." Janey beamed. "I was so sad when she gave notice and left."

"What?" My eyes peeled open.

"What day is today? Tuesday? Yeah, she told us on Saturday that she was leaving, after her final shift. I guess she left Sunday, so two days ago."

Whoa. This was potentially huge. Molly had been at yoga Thursday morning. "Leaving to where? Did she say?"

Janey shook her head. "Said something about a yoga teacher training course. Up north somewhere. Massachusetts?"

"Did she leave a forwarding address? A phone number?"

Her mouth twisted back and forth. "Not with me, no. Maybe with the manager? I'll check around when she comes in tonight."

I gnawed on my cheek for a second. "Do you know everyone's schedule here? If I told you a date, would you know if Molly worked that day?"

"I could find out pretty easily."

I rattled off the date Raina went missing.

Janey held up a hand. "One second. Going to the break room where all the schedules are posted. Be back in a flash."

I stood there for several long minutes, thinking of all the people who had sketchy ties to Raina. Shawn. Kai. Jennis. Heidi and her mean husband Charles. The Wolfman. And now Molly.

An older, red-faced man at the bar caught my eye and pointed at me, then pointed at his drink. "Want to join me?" he hollered.

I shook my head and averted my eyes to stare at the floor, not wanting to deal with drunk dudes.

"Lana?" Janey touched my shoulder. She held a paper bag in her hands. "First, here's a bowl of chowder, on the house."

I beamed and thanked her. My hometown rocked. "Did you find anything about Molly?"

"She worked that Saturday, the day Raina went missing. Molly did a double. Eleven AM to ten PM. I wasn't here that day, but the bartender over there was. He remembers seeing her." She pointed toward the bar, where a cute young guy was polishing a glass. He waved.

"Okay, thanks. I'll come back if I need to know more."

"Is this about that yoga instructor who was found murdered? Are you doing another article? I saw your name in the paper the other day."

"Possibly. I'll keep you posted. Thanks again for the chowder." I squeezed her shoulder and swept out.

So Molly had been working the day Raina disappeared. And a week later, she'd gone to yoga, then skipped town not long after. Why?

Was it because she was trying to hide something—like a murder? Now I was really confused. I was also running out of time and had to get into the coffee shop. Sleuthing would have to wait.

*   *   *

Early the next morning, Erica poked her head in the back room as I was reading an urgent email from the coffee supplier in Miami.

"You're not gonna believe this." I pointed at my phone.

"What? More on Raina and Shawn?"

"No. The supplier did a cupping and discovered that the beans they sent to us were the last of that batch. They were stored improperly. They're sending replacements today." I threw my head back and let out a long groan. "All that for an issue that wasn't even my fault."

"What a relief. At least you got to the bottom of it. Listen." She tapped her foot while beaming crookedly. "You ready to do some detective work?"

I swear, Erica loved this stuff almost as much as me. When I'd returned to Perkatory from the jail, I'd told her all about my exchange with Shawn. She'd volunteered to return after her shift and scope out the auto body shops with me.

"Definitely. I couldn't sleep last night, thinking Shawn might be innocent."

"Good deal. Hey, I did some research. Made a list of all the body shops on Devil's Beach. There are only five, including Larry's. I plotted them out on a map on my phone."

I wiped my hands on my apron. "Impressive organizational skills. Now we just have to figure out how to approach these guys at the body shops. We can't walk in with guns blazing, demanding to know if they fixed the mangled bumper of a BMW or a Range Rover. And I'm a little concerned about how I'll identify myself. I'm not really a reporter, but I think if I got the right information, Mike would let me write a story—"

"*Lana*," Erica interrupted. "Lana, stop."

"What? I like to be ethical." I untied my apron and tugged it over my head. It snagged on my ponytail, and I grunted.

"Lana. You're not doing this for an article. You're sleuthing. We're sleuthing."

I tossed the apron on the counter. "But why are we sleuthing? What's the point of sleuthing if I'm not writing about it?"

Erica rolled her eyes. "You didn't take my joy lecture to heart."

"Not really, no. I like to have a purpose."

She hopped off the stool. "Okay, here's the purpose. Do you think Shawn's innocent?"

I moved my head back and forth and twisted my mouth before I spoke. "Possibly. The way the state agents made an arrest so soon was sketchy."

"How do you feel about the state accusing an innocent man?" She folded her arms and stared at me with unblinking, dark eyes.

"Terrible. Obviously. If he's innocent."

"Then it's our duty to find the truth. Because clearly no one else is doing it."

"Well, I'm sure Noah's working on it," I protested. "But is he, since the state agents made the actual arrest?"

She cocked her thumb and forefinger like a gun and made a clicking noise with her tongue. "Exactamundo. How much control does Noah really have over this investigation?"

"Probably more than us," I grumbled. "And what if we come up with evidence that exonerates Shawn?"

Erica ran her hand through her jet-black-and-electric-blue hair. "We'll deal with that when the time comes. Flexibility: that's your word of the day. Hang loose, Lana. This afternoon, we're going to talk to some mechanics and try to get some answers."

* * *

We struck out at Island Auto, our first stop. We didn't even ask questions the fiftysomething guy told us straightaway that he didn't do extensive body work, only glass replacement.

"But I can do a mean oil change." He eyed my Honda. "How you doin' with the maintenance on that thing?"

I squinted at my twelve-year-old car. It hadn't seen a wash in months, and I'd last had an oil change in . . . well, I couldn't remember. "Doing good, thanks," I replied briskly.

Erica and I walked back to my car, and she tapped on her cell phone screen. "The next location on the map is Larry's. It's on Elm and Beach."

"I know where it is. Larry's been on the island for as long as I remember. He's kind of a character."

Erica snorted. "Isn't everyone on Devil's Beach a character?"

"Yeah, well, Larry's a piece of work. He's into wildlife."

"As in animals? Or is that slang for something kinky?"

Erica could always make me laugh. "His side hustle is as a wildlife trapper."

"Oh, so like if there's a rabid raccoon in your yard, he's the one to call?"

I made a clicking noise with my mouth and turned onto Beach Drive. "Well, sort of. But he doesn't deal with fur, only reptiles. If there's a ten-foot-long python under your porch, he's the one to call. I remember my folks called him about an iguana family that took up residence in my mom's vegetable garden. He came out and hauled them all away."

Her face froze in a grimace. "How much business does he do, if he only handles reptiles?"

"Now, I don't think that much. Back when I was in high school, there was a real problem here with some nonnative giant lizards. Someone had let a few loose, and they reproduced all over the island. So he was busy back then."

"Like snakes? I despise snakes."

"I'm not a fan either. Yeah, he sometimes traps snakes. And those stupid lizards, the ones that terrorized me when I was a teenager. Lived in fear of them coming into the house. They weren't those little tiny ones, either. They were like four-foot-long things."

Erica clutched at her heart, and I turned into Larry's Body Shop. "See the little painted gecko on the sign?" I pointed.

"There better not be any snakes in there," she muttered.

As we marched in, I imagined that we were in a buddy movie. A badly executed one, because I still wasn't sure how I'd introduce myself. A reporter? A friend of Shawn's? A concerned citizen? I repeated the word *flexibility* in my mind.

Hang loose, Lana.

I went first into the shop's office. There was an oddly pungent smell, musky even, with an undercurrent of paint. That, I understood—Larry and his employees were probably spraying a car. But the other smell? Odd.

That's when I saw it: a giant fish tank with a large, yellow-and-white snake inside. Ick. I averted my gaze and looked at the desk instead.

Ring Bell for Service, a placard read, next to a red buzzer. I was about to push it when Erica let out a guttural groan.

"What is that?" Erica shrieked.

"In the tank?" I turned and noticed she was huffing. "That looks to be a Burmese python. But I'm no snake expert. I only know that because I did a story about pythons once when I was in Miami."

She swallowed, or tried to, but instead looked like she was gasping for air. Now, I hadn't known Erica long, but she was as cool as the other side of the pillow. Collected. Unflappable in the face of adversity. Heck, I'd seen her politely and rationally go toe-to-toe with some of Perkatory's most difficult customers.

Now, however, she was a mess. "You okay?"

She shook her head. "I'm gonna have to sit in the car."

"Okay, no worries. You look greenish. Like you might throw up."

She pressed her lips together and nodded, then turned and ran out of the office. Guess I'd be doing this one alone. I jabbed at the button and took a seat on a worn, green leather chair. Instead of staring at the snake in the tank, I focused on my cell, rereading that email from the coffee supplier and marveling that something as simple as improper coffee bean storage could yield crappy-tasting cold brew.

That was life, I guess. One tiny mistake could affect everything.

Five minutes passed, and I shifted in my seat. I was about to text Erica when the door to the garage area swung open. It was Larry, in all his white-haired, crazy-eyed glory.

"Sorry to keep you waiting. How can I help you?"

I jumped to my feet. "I don't know if you remember me, but I'm Peter Lewis' daughter, Lana."

Larry wiped his dirty hands on an equally dingy cloth. "That's why you looked familiar. You're running Perkatory now, aren't you?"

"Sure am."

He pointed at me. "You having problems with lizards at your place? I heard around town that someone saw a teju."

I wasn't sure what a teju was, nor did I want to ask. "No. Nothing like that. I'm here for another reason." I paused, took a breath, and hoped the gods of journalism would forgive me for what I was about to say. "I'm working on a news article. I'm a journalist, you know."

He scratched his jaw with a pen. "Your dad told me all about it. He's so proud of you. I dunno about answering questions, though."

Ugh. I'd have to cajole him into answering.

"I'm writing about the murder of Raina Rose Romero, the yoga studio owner. I did an interview with the man accused of her murder. Shawn Sims. He said he had his SUV painted. I wondered if you were the one who did the work."

Larry sniffed and sat in the chair behind the desk, sliding a pair of reading glasses onto his face from where they hung around his neck. "We've done a lot of business recently. What's the name and make of car?"

I repeated Shawn's full name. "He said it was an expensive Mercedes SUV."

"Sims, Sims, Sims," Larry muttered as he riffled through a stack of paper. "Ah. Got it right here. Yep. Full-body paint job. Real sweet ride. Very unique. Never painted one of those before."

He held the paper out, and I stepped forward to scrutinize it. Shawn had paid ten grand for the work—two days after the murder. There was no notation of any other kind of body work on the invoice.

"Did you notice any damage to the bumper?"

Larry frowned. "The bumper? I don't think so. I recall that car because it was unusual. It was in perfect shape, too. We don't get a lot of those. But I appreciate you being thorough, so let's do a little investigation." He opened a laptop. "I keep photos of all the before-and-afters here."

"Oh, excellent. Thanks."

He tapped on the computer, then turned it to my direction. "There. Here's what it looked like before."

I leaned down and peered at the screen. There were four square photos, all of the car, from different angles.

"The bumpers look pristine. The whole car does," I said.

"Sure do. That was a beautiful car. It's all coming back to me. He sold it to a friend, who was bringing it to South America."

"That's right. Have police been by to look at these?"

"Nope." He turned the laptop away from me. "Shawn didn't strike me as the type of guy who would kill someone, though. Seemed pretty harmless. You can put that in your article. Hey, why aren't you taking notes?"

"Oh." I dug around in my bag, flustered. I needed to tell Noah about this. "You were way too quick with the info. Hang on."

I made a show of taking notes with my reporter's notebook. "Did Shawn happen to say anything about Raina while he was here?"

"Nope. Not a thing."

"Hmph. Okay."

"That all?"

I tapped my pen on my chin. "I have one more question. Did you fix any bumpers of any cars in the past, oh, ten days?"

Larry let out an explosive laugh. "Kid, we fix bumpers all the time. You'll have to be more specific."

"A BMW? Did you work on a BMW? It would have been black or white. Maybe an SUV."

"A BMW?" He scratched his chin. "Can't say I remember one of those."

I paused for a beat, expecting him to flip through the stack of papers once again. When he didn't, I pointed. "Could you check?"

He stood up and walked around the desk. "I said I don't remember a BMW. Sorry, but I don't like all these questions. I've helped you plenty, and I'm in a hurry." His tone was curt. "I hope I satisfied your curiosity, but I need to get back to work. Say hi to your dad."

He advanced on me, and I backed up toward the exit. Something made me feel vaguely uneasy, and I pulled on the doorknob.

"Will do, Larry. Thanks again."

I'd no sooner stepped out of the shop than the door slammed behind me, the lock snicking into place. I power walked to my car with a heavy feeling in my stomach. Erica was leaning against it, her eyes closed and face tilted to the sun. She opened one eye.

"How'd it go?"

"Bizarre. Get in the car," I said.

We both climbed in. I twisted the ignition and backed out of the driveway a little faster than I should have, barely missing a garbage can.

"Hey, watch out! What happened? Ew, you smell like that snake. So gross." Erica twisted the knob on the air conditioner, but it let out a faint wheeze of cool air. I rolled down all the windows as we pulled onto Beach Drive.

"I think Shawn's telling the truth."

She stopped fiddling with the air vent. "Oh yeah?"

"Yeah. I saw photos of his SUV before it was painted. No bumper damage."

"So that worked out! Awesome. I felt bad I couldn't be there for the interview. I couldn't do it without barfing."

I chewed on my lip and drove, deep in thought.

"Okay, the next place we're going is Beach Auto Body. It's on Industrial Drive. Hopefully it'll be snake-free. What's wrong? You don't want to go? That smell on your clothes getting to you? Can't blame you. Makes me want to hurl." Erica's expression was pinched.

"No. Something else happened with Larry. It was odd."

"Worse than the snake?"

I nodded. "I think he might have worked on Charles's car."

While we drove to the next body shop, I explained my conversation with Larry. Erica listened, her brow furrowing deeper by the second. We pulled into the third body shop on our list.

"It could be significant, but it might not. Maybe he was sick of your questions," she said.

"Maybe I'm hypersensitive. Or maybe he knows more than he's letting on."

"Let's evaluate once we've visited all the shops. C'mon."

We discovered nothing at the third body shop. Or at the next, or at the final one. I drove Erica back to the marina where her sailboat was docked and parked in a space near Shawn's water sports kiosk. I glanced over and saw that no one was behind the counter, a stark reminder that he was in jail and probably worried about the future of his business, among other things.

I heaved a sigh. "I think we've hit a dead end."

Erica unbuckled her seat belt. "Don't say that. Nothing is over until it's over."

"But I'm worried that Shawn really is innocent, like he says. And he's sitting in jail." I squeezed the worn steering wheel as if the motion could somehow ward off all the uncomfortable feelings welling inside me.

She held up a hand. "Perhaps there are more people we can talk with. We just need to think a little harder. What are our other options?"

"I'll tell Noah. Although it sounds like the state agents have taken investigation out of his hands. Sometimes those state officers can be pretty territorial and freeze out the local cops."

"Telling Noah is a start. If that doesn't work, let's sleep on it, and maybe we'll come up with some new angles for tomorrow."

I gave her a quick hug. "Thanks."

"For what?"

"For being there for me. For indulging my curiosity and listening to my theories and worries."

She made a *pfft* sound, then broke into a wide smile. "You kidding? I love this. Remember: stay flexible. Except when it comes to snakes."

Chapter
Twenty-Eight

I texted Noah when I got home, and he immediately replied, saying he was in a meeting and that we'd talk later in the evening.

Good, I typed. ***I have something super important to tell you.***

Over the next couple of hours I tried to occupy my brain by doing paperwork, but I was jittery and anxious. I'd not only failed miserably at writing a story about Raina, but I hadn't helped Shawn at all. The fact that the alleged murder weapon—his luxury SUV—didn't have body damage when it was repainted and that it was on a ship to South America left the entire case up in the air, in my opinion.

And I was certain that no one had looked into Charles.

Then again, maybe Shawn *was* guilty. Chances were good I didn't have all the evidence, and he could be concealing crucial details. That's what criminals did. He'd admitted to being intimate with Raina on the day she disappeared; authorities surely considered that important and incriminating evidence.

What more did they have on him? State agents couldn't keep an innocent man in jail, could they?

Sadly, I knew from experience that they could and sometimes did. In my years at a newspaper, I'd covered more than one story about innocent men being released from prison after decades behind bars.

I didn't want Shawn to be one of those men who stepped out of prison looking wan and haunted.

What about his lawyer? Why was he waiting to introduce the key evidence? I tapped Shawn's case into the county court records website and found his lawyer's name. Maybe if I spoke with the attorney, he'd be able to shed some light on the situation. I called the law firm's after-hours number and left my name and contact info with an answering service.

A half hour passed, and the lawyer didn't call back. Blergh.

The more I thought about the murder, the more uneasy I became. Back when I worked at a newspaper, I'd always felt as though I had the ability—the privilege, even—to right wrongs. Now I was powerless. It dawned on me that this had been my biggest fear about leaving journalism. Lacking the power to change the world.

Tears of frustration welled in my eyes. I had to tell someone about the evidence I'd found. But how? Who?

Since Noah wasn't available, I dialed Mike at the paper. It went straight to voice mail, and I left a long, rambling message. *Drat.*

Using my old newspaper's public records log-in, I looked up Shawn's criminal record. Other than the recent arrest for the first-degree murder of Raina, he had no prior charges. My stomach sank.

What if he really was innocent?

While playing fetch with Stanley, I thought about all the interviews I'd done so far. Nothing seemed to add up, and yet Shawn was in jail. The pupper and I romped so hard in the backyard that he shuffled inside, lapped up some water, and then flung himself on his sheepskin dog bed in the corner of the living room.

It was only seven PM, and my little energizer Shih Tzu was out like a light. I, on the other hand, was wide awake and eager to stave off the looming feeling of dread in my brain. And I was starving. That grouper chowder I'd eaten earlier was a distant memory for my stomach. Food would be a temporary distraction from Raina's murder and Shawn's situation.

I wandered into the kitchen and pulled open the fridge. I hadn't had time to go to the store lately and was greeted by the pathetic sight of wilted celery, a half-open pack of dry deli turkey, and a half-full bottle of Chardonnay. I shut the door with a sigh. It was another night of delivery or takeout.

Or . . .

I grabbed my phone and texted Noah, too impatient to wait for him to get in touch with me.

Hey there. You back from Tampa?
I am and was about to call you. Finishing up at the station soon.
Want to grab dinner? It would be better if I told him about Shawn's SUV in person.
You read my mind.
I bit my lip. **Square Grouper?**
See you around seven thirty or eight. Sorry I can't be more punctual, cupcake.

I tapped a heart emoji on the screen but wondered if that was too much, so I erased it and replaced it with a more mature **Sounds good, I'll get there early and have a drink.**

I quickly threw on a sexy, low-cut black jumpsuit from my Miami days. Since the Square Grouper was probably the nicest restaurant on the island, I wore the Louboutin heels. So what if it was Tuesday? Maybe getting dressed up would improve my mood. I piled my hair into a messy updo, emphasis on messy, and swiped on some red lipstick.

Before I left, I approached Stanley, who was flopped on his dog bed, snoring. I kneeled down gingerly, not wanting to topple over in my tall shoes. "Be good, little man." When I stroked his golden fur, he let out a satisfied puppy sigh.

As I drove to the Grouper in a cloud of jasmine-scented perfume, I tried not to give in to my ruminations about Raina's death. Tried to forget that at this very moment, poor Shawn was probably stretched out on his cot in jail. The more I thought about how state agents hadn't interviewed Larry or seen his photos of Shawn's car, the angrier I became.

What was the state's other evidence against Shawn? Had they talked to any of Raina's students or teachers? And what had happened to Molly? So many questions loomed in my mind as I parked at the Grouper and picked my way over the gravel parking lot. I wasn't used to wearing heels anymore, and these things really slowed me down.

Still, I knew I looked good. If this didn't inspire Noah into spilling some details on Shawn's case, nothing would. The hostess, a woman who couldn't be more than eighteen, glanced up when I walked in.

"Welcome to the Square Grouper," she said. "Are you meeting someone?"

I craned my neck around the restaurant, then into the bar. "I don't see him. I think I'm early. Is Joey working tonight?" The restaurant was owned by Erica's new squeeze.

"It's his night off."

Too bad. I wanted to pry and see how he and Erica were getting along. I'd played matchmaker with the two of them, and when I'd last seen them at yoga, they'd seemed to have hit it off. "I'll wait at the bar."

I tottered to a stool and hopped up. The bartender, an older woman sporting gray hair with magenta highlights, approached.

"You're Peter Lewis' daughter, right?"

"Sure am."

She introduced herself and chattered on about seeing my dad at yoga class, saying how hilarious and adorable he was. "I'm new here and getting settled on the island. Is he single?"

My mouth opened in surprise, and I laughed nervously. The idea of Dad going on a date was too weird.

She giggled. "Sorry. Probably not the thing to ask his daughter. What will you have?"

"Whatever she's having, I'll pay for it." I recognized the voice.

I turned in my seat and saw a handsome yet slightly unwelcome face. "Cody?"

"Fancy running into you here. Hey, you look great." His gaze roamed from my eyes to my chest. I crossed my arms, thinking about how he'd written what was supposed to be my article. Written it poorly, actually. Journalistic jealousy flared in me. Irrational, yes. It wasn't Cody's fault that his editor had frozen me out of the story for budgetary reasons.

"I'm waiting for my date." I pressed my lips together in a polite smile. "How about you?"

He slipped into the seat next to me, setting his expensive Nikon and his phone on the bar. "I just finished up an assignment. Thought I'd stop here for a cold one and some fish and chips."

I turned to the bartender. "I'll have a Merlot."

Cody ordered a beer, and the bartender left.

"So what was your assignment?" I didn't want to give him the satisfaction of knowing it upset me to have lost the story on Raina. He seemed like the type of man who would gloat, and I was in no mood for that.

"Ah, let me show you." He picked up his camera and pressed the on button. Cody sure did like to show off his photos.

The bartender came over and set our drinks down. Since Cody was still scrolling, absorbed in his camera, I grabbed my wine and took a sip. The rich Merlot slid down my throat, warming my insides. I couldn't wait for Noah to get here—I didn't want to be around a hefty pour of wine and this arrogant guy for long. No telling what might come out of my mouth.

"Here." He tilted the back of the camera so I could see the display, then thumbed the dial to scroll to a photo. "I was out at the nature preserve today to shoot a feature on the monkeys. Took my kayak. It was a perfect day. Bit hot, but perfect."

"Nice," I responded, wondering if I should share the story about my grandfather, who'd once owned a roadside zoo and the ancestors of the current crop of wild monkeys. I decided against it. Sometimes I didn't feel like explaining my quirky family history here on the island. And I didn't feel like sharing anything with Cody anyway.

I sneaked a glance at my phone. It was five after eight. Where was Noah?

He scrolled through several photos, all of the rhesus macaque monkeys. I oohed and aahed at appropriate times. There were only so many impressive monkey photos, and I'd seen my fair share over the years. To newcomers like him, the primates were a novelty. To me, the monkeys were as common as squirrels.

He scrolled on to a few other photos of his kayak and the mangroves. I stifled a yawn. This guy sure loved to brag about his work. My eyes drifted to the corner of the display, where the date appeared in red digital numbers. The photo on the screen wasn't from today—it was taken the day Raina went missing.

He shut the camera off and set it on the bar. "I think I'm really going to like it here on Devil's Beach. Great kayaking spots, killer beaches, great bars." He winked at me. "Friendly people."

"Yeah." I slowly sipped my wine. Had I seen that date correctly?

The sound of a phone vibrating jolted me out of my thoughts, and I lunged for my cell. "It's not me," I said, disappointed.

"It's my grandmother. Gotta take this. Watch my stuff for me?"

"Sure."

He barked a hello into the phone.

"Gram, let me step into the hall where I can hear you. It's kind of loud." He winked at me, walking out of the bar area and down the hall to where the bathrooms were located. He was out of eyesight. Impulsively, I grabbed his camera and powered it on.

I'd worked with enough photojournalists to know my way around an expensive DSLR. Using the wheel on the back of the camera, I scrolled through the photos, past the dozens of monkey pictures. There.

It was a photo of the tip of his kayak and the tea-colored water of the swamp. And it was dated the afternoon Raina disappeared. I scrolled further back. There were several similar photos, all nature shots. An alligator. An ibis. A turtle. All with the same date and in the same two-hour time frame.

I licked my lips and continued to scroll back. When I reached the next set of photos, I gasped.

It was a picture of a woman outside a mobile home. It was his grandmother, the same lady he'd showed me the photo of days ago. To anyone else, it would've looked like a sweet picture of an old lady. But the shot revealed something else: the home was right next to the dumping area where Raina's bike had been found.

I set the camera down as if it were a hot iron ingot. This had to mean something, didn't it? Or was it all a weird coincidence? At the very least, shouldn't he have talked with cops about being at the Swamp on the day she disappeared? Surely Noah would have told me if Cody was a suspect, or if he'd offered any information at all.

I flashed back to the day Raina's body was discovered at the Swamp and how I'd peeked into Cody's messy SUV. All those vehicle parts.

A mangled bicycle pedal on the passenger seat.

My stomach soured. Was that from Raina's bike? Was it still in his car?

I had to tell Noah. Had to show Noah this evidence. I glanced around, looking for Cody, feeling a little crazed. He was still somewhere near the bathroom, which was down a long hallway. I spied the bartender at the far end of the bar, talking with a couple.

I grabbed my phone, feeling a little crazed.

Hey there, you close?
Be there soon, cupcake.
Hurry up. I've found something important.

On an impulse, I threw the phone in my purse and snatched up the camera. I hopped off the stool and walked as fast as I could out of the restaurant.

I heaved a sigh of relief as I reached the door. First, I'd peer into Cody's SUV to see if the bike pedal was still there, then wait for Noah in my car with the evidence. Surely it would take Cody a few minutes to figure out what was going on.

I'd no sooner stepped through the front door than I felt a large hand clamp around my elbow.

"Seems like you left with something that's not yours, little Lana." Cody's normally easygoing dude-bro voice was menacing. "I didn't take you for a petty thief."

I tried to wrench my arm out of his grip while pulling the camera toward my chest with my other hand. "I think the police will be very interested in these photos."

He chuckled, a low, nasty sound. That's when I tried to make a break for it, but I stumbled and nearly fell. Stupid heels.

Before I knew what was happening, he'd picked me up like a sack of potatoes and hoisted me over his shoulder. Goodness, he was strong. I protested by thumping on his back with the lens part of his camera. With every ounce of energy in my body, I struggled against his grip and hollered into the night air. Hopefully someone inside would hear me. But since it was a weeknight, there weren't many cars in the parking lot. There was no one around.

"Put me down, jerkface." I got in a few more blows to his kidneys.

Where was Noah?

Cody dumped me on my feet next to his SUV, slamming my back into the passenger door. I wobbled because of the heels and let out a grunt, lunging forward into a run. Which was impossible in these hellacious, impractical shoes. He laughed and yanked me back by my arm while unlocking the passenger door with his key fob.

"You killed her," I yelled. "You killed Raina, didn't you?"

I swung and missed. It wasn't easy to land a punch while holding tight to the camera and staying upright in designer heels. I was no match for Cody's strength. He wrenched the camera away and deposited it in the back seat, then pushed me into the messy passenger seat. My butt struck something sharp, and I pulled it out from under me.

The mangled pedal.

"This is from Raina's bike, isn't it?" I hollered, while trying to kick my way out.

He slammed the door and locked it, and I hurled the pedal at him. It bounced off the window, and he grinned. Uh-oh.

I tried the handle, but it wouldn't budge, and by the time he came around to the driver's side, I'd resorted to pounding on the window with the heel of my hand.

"I'm afraid your *sort of* cop boyfriend won't be much help now." He shut the driver's side door, and I stilled. Holy crap. This guy was pure danger. In the wan glow of the parking lot light, his eyes were wild and manic.

"Where are you taking me?" My heart raced.

He grinned. "How about the Swamp? It's quite nice in the evening. You and I can take a moonlight kayak trip. You're not really dressed for it, though. You'll have to take off those sexy heels."

My stilettos. I squirmed my body to look at him, bending slightly to touch the back of the shoe with my hand. "Is that what you did with Raina? Took her on a kayak ride and killed her? What made you want to kill her, anyway? Did she reject you or something?"

He chuckled and shook his head, cranking the ignition. "Oh, Lana. You're so dramatic. It wasn't planned. It was an accident. I'm not a murderer."

He accelerated and pulled out of the parking space. My mouth went dry. I needed to do something. Couldn't stay in here with him. I slipped my heel out of my shoe.

"An accident?"

He slowly wound his way around a few parked cars. "I was coming back from kayaking that day and accidentally hit her. It was a mistake. Honest. I was coming around that curve, and she was in the road. I was fiddling with my phone and didn't see her. I was being stupid and careless, but I also wasn't about to turn myself in."

"So why didn't you call the police?"

He accelerated through the parking lot, then slowed to a stop at the sign. He looked toward me, to his right, for oncoming traffic. There was none. The muscles in his jaw bunched. "I'd had a little incident in Baghdad. But I'm trying to get my life back on track here."

"You're doing an outstanding job of that," I muttered. "Listen. I'll give your camera back and you can let me go. Deal?"

He glanced in my direction to check traffic and stopped for a few oncoming cars. Oh, now he was law-abiding. Great.

"No way, Lana. You're dating the police chief. The first thing you'll do is tell him. There's no way you can keep a secret."

Well, he had that part of me pegged. "So you're going to kill me too? You won't get away with this. People will know I'm gone."

He cracked a smile. "I can see the headline now: *Local Barista Missing.*"

"You suck at writing headlines," I spat. "It'll read *Troubled Ex-Journalist Indicted in Two Murders, Faces Death Penalty*."

He laughed. "It'll never make the paper because they'll never suspect me. Why would they?"

Ooh, nothing made me angrier than arrogant men who felt entitled when it came to escaping the consequences of their actions. I stared at him so hard my eyes hurt.

"They might not even find your body, Lana. Just like your little high school friend Gisela."

I gasped. "What do you know about Gisela?"

"Your pretty head doesn't need to overanalyze. I had nothing to do with her disappearance. Mike showed me your stories from years ago at the paper. That was so quaint, you playing newspaper girl when you were a kid."

Fury and bile mixed in my stomach and rose in my throat. I had to do something. He glanced to his left to check for cars.

This was my chance. I pulled my heel all the way off and whacked him in the temple. Hard. One blow to that soft spot would incapacitate him, if not kill him. I was a pacifist, but one who didn't have time to consider the morals of the situation. This was self-defense.

"Let me go," I screamed, striking him a second and a third time and letting out some choice swear words in the process. The heel connected with his head and his cheek, and within a few seconds, my knuckles were covered in blood.

Anger welled in my chest. How dare he kill Raina, hoodwink Mike at the paper, and then kidnap me? I might have taken him by surprise with my shoe, but he recovered quickly. Crap.

Apparently that strike to the temple wasn't the lethal blow I'd assumed it was, and he put the car in park and slapped me in the face.

Right as he lunged for me again, a police cruiser roared up beside us.

I screamed Noah's name, then let out a guttural wail. Cody grabbed my wrist, the one I'd injured during yoga. I writhed as pain shot up my arm.

"You couldn't leave Raina's death alone, could you?" he snarled.

By the time Cody's hands were around my neck, Noah was out of his cruiser with his gun drawn.

Epilogue

It took longer than usual to walk the two blocks from my house to Perkatory. It was partially due to the fact that I hadn't been outside in ten days and I wanted to savor every flower, every palm frond, every bit of Erica's laughter. Also, my muscles were stiffer than a mannequin's.

I'd suffered a bruised windpipe and a fractured wrist and spent forty-eight hours in the hospital. The rest of the time, I'd been at home with Stanley.

I'd been lucky that those were my only injuries. Now, after days of sleeping, eating Dad's vegan lasagna, and watching bad reality TV, I almost felt back to normal. The bruises on my neck where Cody had tried to strangle me had faded to a sickening jaundice hue.

I'd be lying if I said I didn't still have nightmares about the attack.

But I was safe. And thrilled to be strolling down the street next to Erica on this unusually mild fall night in Florida. I was under the impression we were headed to Perkatory, but for some reason, she checked her phone, then steered me toward the beach.

"Let's check out the sunset," she said.

"Sunset's not for another half hour."

"I know. But it's still gorgeous outside. You need some fresh air."

"Sounds fine by me." I shrugged.

We hit Crystal Beach, and I slipped off my sparkly flip-flops. Although the stilettos had saved my life, I wanted only comfort these days. Maybe I'd don the heels for a date with Noah, if we ever had one. He'd stopped by nearly every day while I was recovering, but the visits were all too brief, because he'd had a ton of work to do in the wake of Cody's arrest.

I inhaled deep, the salt air invigorating, and stretched my bandage-clad wrist in the air. "Wow, this feels awesome."

We sauntered to the Gulf of Mexico, then waded up to our ankles. It was seven PM, and an earlier rain had given way to cool temperatures and fluffy clouds that framed the setting sun. Erica squatted to look through a pile of shells.

"I need to get to the beach more. I live here, and I don't come often enough." I squinted at the horizon. "You know, I came to some conclusions while lying on my sofa."

"Oh yeah?" She looked up at me, then rose to standing.

"I'm going to take yoga once my wrist heals. Maybe not hot yoga, though. Definitely not naked yoga."

"Wolfie's studio might be a good place to start."

"Yeah. That's what I was thinking. But maybe I'll work up to Dante's Inferno someday. And it would make Dad happy."

Erica smiled. "He'd love it if you went to yoga with him."

I skimmed the water gently with my toe. "I realize I need to get out more. Be more flexible, like you said. I've got to build a life here."

Tonight the Gulf was still and beautiful, like a sheet of blue sea glass. A memory came to mind, of walking on this very beach with Gisela all those years ago. Part of me still hoped she'd be found someday. And that she hadn't met the same fate Raina had.

I turned to Erica and swallowed the lump in my throat. "I missed Perkatory a lot these past ten days. Missed you and the customers and everything. It's hard saying that out loud."

"I'm glad you did," she replied in a tender voice. We stared at the water for a bit, then she did a little dance. "You will not believe the new nitro tap. I can't wait for you to taste the coffee tonight."

"Nothing gets me out of the house like the promise of excellent coffee." In my absence, Dad had made the executive decision to order a nitrous tap for the cold brew, which would allow us to pour chilled coffee similar in consistency to beer. "Seriously, I'm just glad to be outdoors. I'm ready to get back in action. Maybe not with daily journalism, though."

"No?"

"I was thinking about possibly working on a true crime book."

"Ooh. Really? About what?"

I shrugged. "Maybe that serial killer I wrote about in Miami when I was at the paper. Maybe about Raina. Or about Gisela. I dunno. I'm open to all possibilities. This has made me realize how much of an effect Gisela's disappearance had on my life, and maybe I need to explore that more. In the meantime, I'm coming back to work tomorrow."

"I think you should take it easy." Erica shot me a worried look. "Is your wrist okay to make drinks? Since tomorrow's Saturday, maybe you should come back on Monday, or even Tuesday. Start the week fresh. We're cool for the weekend."

"I'm getting antsy. I need to do something productive. I'm fine." I moved my hand slowly in a circle, mimicking the exercises the physical therapist had given me while in hospital. "Hey, did you read the paper today?"

She winced. "Sorry. I didn't. I know I should. I'm bad." Her gaze dropped to her phone. "Hey, we need to get to Perkatory now."

"Are you guys planning a surprise?"

"No. No," she said, flustered. Which meant they were.

I bit back a grin. "Anyway, I'm going to turn you into a newspaper reader yet."

"What happened? Was there an interesting article?"

"There was another bail hearing for Cody. The judge revoked it because he attacked a guard while in jail."

"Whoa. No way." Her eyes grew wide with alarm.

"Yeah. He's unhinged. Turned out that he assaulted a woman in Baghdad, another journalist. That's why his freelance career over there dried up. Let's just say I'm relieved he's in jail until trial." We trudged up the sand.

Cody had been charged with manslaughter in Raina's death and aggravated assault because of me. As it turned out, he was telling the truth: he had been coming back from kayaking when he accidentally struck Raina as she rode her bike. He panicked and put her body in his SUV.

Later that night under the cover of darkness, he rolled the corpse into his kayak and paddled into the Swamp, where he shoved Raina into the water. Evidence—including her blood and her bike pedal—was found throughout his vehicle. He'd stupidly dumped the bike near his grandmother's trailer. His arrogance did him in; he told detectives he hadn't thought anyone would catch him. Cops found Raina's ID and her phone in his bureau at his grandma's house.

For a few tense days, officials also wondered if Molly the yoga student was somehow involved. But they'd caught up with her in Massachusetts and realized she had a rock-solid alibi. She'd told Cody all about Shawn and his luxury SUV paint job. And since Cody knew she was leaving town, he'd swiped a menu from Bay-Bays, scrawling a note to me in an attempt to steer cops'—and my—attention to Shawn.

I was trying not to think about all that, though. Tonight, I focused on the pretty, soft light that made the palm trees glow green and the red hibiscus hedges that clung to life in the early-fall Florida heat. The island was quiet this time of the year, without many tourists, and its stillness soothed my soul.

Erica and I approached Perkatory, and she skipped ahead.

"I sense a surprise." I picked up my pace, eager to get inside.

She pulled the door open for me, beaming.

I walked in, then immediately stopped in my tracks. A cheer went up from the dozens of people inside. It was an actual party, with seemingly half the island in attendance. "Welcome back," several people called out. "Woot! Lana's finally here!"

There was Barbara, and Janey from Bay-Bays. Kai and Jennis from Dante's Inferno. Bernadette with her parrot perched on her shoulder. So many people, some whom I'd known since I was born.

I pressed my hands to my mouth, then burst out laughing. "This isn't a coffee tasting."

"Yes it is," Erica cried. "And it's a party."

I waved at the Wolfman and his wife. Then at Shawn. Oh, and there was Mike, the editor. On one long table sat a display of delicious-looking sweet treats. I spied mini key lime pies, and my mouth watered.

"Lana!" Dad cried, emerging from the crowd. He had Stanley in the dog carrier on his chest. "Welcome home. The snacks are catered from Sugar Rush down the street, that new bakery. So delicious."

We gently embraced, careful not to squash Stanley in the middle. Tears welled in my eyes. How I'd missed this place and its white-and-pale blue decor. And its stacks of games and oversized coffee table books. And the rich coffee aroma. This was every bit my home, maybe more so than the bungalow two blocks away.

"Thanks, Dad."

"We wanted to do something special for you when you felt well enough. I'm so glad you're alive." He sniffled, then pulled back. "Your neck's still bruised. I still think you need some Reiki healing."

"I'm perfectly fine," I said, trying to downplay the emotion welling in both of us. I didn't want to bawl in front of all these people. "Why don't you show me the nitro tap."

Dad and I walked behind the counter. "Here it is," he said, his chest puffing with pride.

It looked exactly like a beer tap. "Wow! May I?"

"Only if your wrist is strong enough."

"I believe it is."

Dad handed me a tall glass, and I set it under the spout. There was a faint twinge of pain when I pulled down on the handle, but the dark, cool espresso and the creamy foam of the coffee made me forget all about any discomfort.

"Incredible," I said, taking a whiff of the coffee. I took a sip and shut my eyes. "It's like heaven in a glass." It was rich and creamy, not too bitter, with notes of citrus and vanilla. It was going to be a hit with customers. I wandered back out into the crowd, smiling and hugging everyone. More than a few of our best customers were there, and I stopped to chat.

Bernadette's parrot even swore at me, and I laughed until tears leaked out of my eyes.

The only one who wasn't here to greet me was the one person I wanted to see: Noah. Where was he? Surely he'd been invited. He was probably still at the station. I was beginning to wonder if he was a workaholic and if our relationship would ever go anywhere. Disappointment gnawed at my stomach.

Mike approached as I was taking a sip of coffee. He dug his hands into the pockets of his jeans. He looked as awkward as I felt; I hadn't talked with him since the day he gave the article to Cody. "Hey, kiddo."

"Hey." I couldn't be mad at him. Too much had happened since, and it all seemed insignificant now.

"I owe you an apology."

I waved my good hand. "No, you don't."

"I feel responsible somehow."

"Well, you're not. Cody was a talented photographer. You had no idea that he'd run someone over and then try to cover up the crime."

"You were in danger. I'd have never forgiven myself if something happened to you." He swallowed hard. "And I feel awful that I didn't give you the story because of the budget."

"Don't. Really. It all worked out in the end. Who knows? If you'd given me that story, I might have never discovered Cody was the killer."

"Fate works in mysterious ways," he murmured as he gave me a quick hug. Gah, I was going to cry again.

Dad, probably sensing my discomfort, whisked him away to try a glass of the nitro coffee.

I turned to find Kai, Shawn, and Jennis standing there. They were all drinking tea. My eyebrows shot up, because they were all smiling. "Hey. Wow. Didn't expect to see you all here. Together."

"I wanted to say thanks for all that you did," Shawn said, gently folding me into a hug. "You're a really special person."

"Aw, it was nothing. Just wanted to get to the truth. I'm a fan of justice." I eyed Jennis and Kai, who both wore those similar, blue-veined rings. What did it all mean? Maybe nothing. Maybe something slightly scandalous. Regardless, I had to let it go. I didn't need to know every detail of their lives. The reason for those rings was personal and had nothing to do with Raina's death.

I held up my glass in a toast. "How are you two doing?"

Kai ran a hand over his bald head and glanced at Jennis, who smiled serenely. "It's hard, I won't lie. I got back from Bali and Raina's funeral a couple of days ago. It was beautiful and cathartic. But I'm trying to forgive and forget. Forgive Raina for all that she did, and forgive others too." He looked uneasily over at Shawn. "We need to put everything aside for the good of the studio. We can all agree on that."

Shawn nodded. "Exactly. We're trying to get along in honor of Raina, who we both loved. She created something amazing, and we're carrying on her legacy."

I had to admit, I was impressed. "That seems very mature of both of you."

Jennis reached out and squeezed my good arm. She wore a jade-green unitard. Did she only wear tight jumpsuits? Her unwavering commitment to that fashion choice was impressive. "We'd love to have you at yoga, when you're feeling better. Free classes whenever you want."

"I might take you up on that. But not the nude candlelight class," I deadpanned.

Shawn wasn't aware of my nude candlelight yoga faux pas, so I regaled him with the story. As I finished, Heidi approached. She wore a cute pink sundress and had on makeup that brightened her face.

"Hey," she squeaked.

We embraced. "You look beautiful," I said. *And happier than when I last saw you.* But I didn't say that, because I wasn't sure if her creepy husband was lurking around.

"I feel beautiful." She rubbed my upper arms. "Empowered, just like Raina said I would. I took her advice and left my husband, you know."

"Oh. Oh! I didn't know." I recalled how he'd been so nasty that day here at Perkatory. "Well, good for you. He seemed . . . difficult."

"Raina helped me get to a place where I could leave him. She got me to understand that I needed to separate because he was emotionally abusive. I had so many breakthroughs with her. I'm glad I'm finally carrying through with what we talked about."

I pressed my lips together in a sad smile. Raina, for all her faults, hadn't been all bad. "You'll always have that memory of her."

Heidi nodded. "So I moved out, and I'm in a condo. And now I'm looking for a job! The first time in years. I've been only a mom."

"There's no *only* a mom," I said. "That's a career in itself. What kind of work are you looking for?"

"Anything. Retail, restaurant. I used to work in a diner when I was in college."

An idea bloomed, and I tilted my head. "Hmm. You seemed to like the coffee when you came here before and ordered a triple espresso. Would you want to work here? We could give it a try."

"I would love that!" She clapped her hands together.

"Come see me on Monday or Tuesday. We'll get you trained." I looked around for Erica and motioned for her to come over.

She made a beeline for us, and I told her what I had planned. "That sounds awesome," Erica said, high fiving Heidi. "Hey, it looks like there's another surprise for you. Check this out."

She pointed at the front door. Dad was holding it open for Noah, who swept in with an armful of red roses.

I pressed my hand to my chest and gasped. Noah walked over, a huge smile on his face.

"Hey, cupcake," he said, then kissed me full on the lips. The entire room made a unanimous *aw* noise, and I felt my face grow hot from all the attention.

He handed the flowers to me. "For you."

"Thanks," I whispered. "Um, come into the back with me to find a vase?" I wanted a few minutes of alone time with him, away from the scrutiny of what felt like the entire town.

As we walked through the crowd, Noah kept his hand on the small of my back, which made my stomach do little somersaults of happiness. Once in the prep room, I set the flowers on the table and turned to him.

"When I arrived and didn't see you, I got concerned."

He slipped his hands around my hips and gently pulled me close. "Wouldn't miss this for the world."

I wrapped my arms around his neck, and we hugged in silence for several seconds. I broke away and stared into his dark eyes, framed by black lashes. He was so gorgeous, I felt myself blushing.

"You feeling better?" he murmured. His gaze traveled to my neck.

"I am. My wrist barely hurts. I'm going back to Perkatory tomorrow, so I can work some weekend shifts and relieve Dad, Barbara, and Erica."

"About that." He kissed my forehead, and a little ripple of joy went through me. "It just so happens that it's the first full three days that I have free since coming to Devil's Beach."

"Oh, really?" The corners of my mouth turned upward.

"Really. And I thought that maybe we could go away. Together. We could get a two-bedroom suite somewhere, or two rooms. Or one room. Whatever you want. I'm flexible. Totally up to you and your comfort level. I ran the idea by your dad and Erica, and they said they'd handle the café this weekend."

Oh, so that was why Erica was cagey about me returning to work. I laughed. "Only us? What about Stanley?"

"He can come. We'll find a dog-friendly place. No work, no newspapers, no news. No crime. Only us. If you're feeling up to it, that is."

I leaned in and gave him a soft kiss. "I'm feeling more than up to it. Where do you have in mind?"

"Anywhere you want, cupcake. Anywhere you want."

Acknowledgments

M y gratitude goes to the Crooked Lane team for their help. Also to Amanda Leuck, my agent, who has been an unwavering cheerleader for my work. A special thanks to Kat Faitour, Janice Peacock and Stacy Stewart. And last but not least, I owe all of my love and appreciation to my family—Peter, Nanci, and Marco—who have supported me in this journey.